A Harlequin
JANET
DAILEY
Collector's Edition

Harlequin

JANET DAILEY

Collector's Editions

A Harlequin

JANET DAILEY

Collector's Edition

Harlequin Books

TORONTO • NEW YORK • LONDON
AMSTERDAM • PARIS • SYDNEY • HAMBURG
STOCKHOLM • ATHENS • TOKYO • MILAN

These books by Janet Dailey were originally published as
follows:

STRANGE BEDFELLOW
Copyright © 1979 by Janet Dailey
First published by Mills & Boon Limited in 1979
Harlequin Presents edition (#296) published
July 1979

WILD AND WONDERFUL
Copyright © 1980 by Janet Dailey
First published by Mills & Boon Limited in 1980
Harlequin Presents edition (#416) published
March 1981

ISBN 0-373-80609-4
First edition May 1984
The Harlequin trademark, consisting of the word
HARLEQUIN and the portrayal of a Harlequin,
is registered in the United States Patent and Trademark
Office and in the Canada Trade Marks Office.

PRINTED IN U.S.A.

CONTENTS

STRANGE BEDFELLOW

"I'VE COME THROUGH HELL
TO GET BACK TO YOU."

Dina sensed the accusation in his low tone. "I'm glad you came back safely," were the only welcoming words she could offer that had a ring of truth.

The muscles in her stomach contracted sharply at the realization that Blake was waiting... for her kiss. She forced herself to bring her lips against his. His arms became a vise, fingers forcing her slender curves against the hard contours of his body. His touch was almost alien. The hungry demand of his bruising mouth asked more than Dina could give to a man who seemed more like a stranger than her husband.

Blake released her in a gesture of disgust. "You're my wife, not my widow."

It sounded like a life sentence the way he said it.

CHAPTER ONE

THE AIR WAS CLEAR and the moon over Rhode Island was new, but there was a tangle of cobwebs in her mind. Dina Chandler couldn't seem to think her way out of the confusion. She shut her ears to the voices quietly celebrating in other parts of the house and stared out the window.

A shudder passed through her. It couldn't have been from the night's chill, since the house was comfortably heated. Her blue eyes slid to her arms, crossed in front of her, hugging her middle. Perhaps it was the cold weight of the precious metal around her finger.

Dina turned from the window. Her restless gaze swept the library, noting all that was familiar. Interrupting the dark, richly paneled sides of the room was a wall of bookshelves, floor to ceiling. A myriad of deeply toned bindings formed rows of muted rainbows. A sofa covered in antique velvet faced the fireplace, flanked by two chairs upholstered in a complementing patterned fabric. In a corner of the room stood a mahogany desk, its top neat and orderly.

The door to the library opened and Dina turned. Her hair shimmered in the dim light, a paler gold than the ring on her finger. A pang of regret raced through her that her solitude had been broken, followed by a twinge of remorse that she had felt the need to be alone at this time.

Closing the door, Chet Stanton walked toward her, smiling despite the faintly puzzled gleam in his eyes.

"So this is where you've got to," he murmured, an unspoken question behind the indulgent tone.

"Yes," Dina nodded, unaware of the sigh in her voice, or how forced her smile looked.

As he came closer, her gaze made a detached inspection of him. Like hers, his coloring was fair, sandy blond hair falling rakishly across his forehead, always seeming to invite fingers to push it back in place. His eyes were a smoke blue as opposed to the brilliant shade of hers.

At thirty-six, he was twelve years her senior, a contemporary of Blake's, but there was a boyish air about him that was an integral part of his charm. In fact, it was with Blake that Dina had first met Chet. The cobwebs spun around that thought to block it out. Slim and supple, Chet was only a few inches taller than she was in her heels.

He stopped in front of her, his intent gaze studying her expressionless face. Dina was unconscious of how totally she masked her inner turmoil. As his hands settled lightly on her shoulders, she was passive under his touch.

"What are you doing in here?" Chet cocked his head slightly to the side, his gaze still probing.

"I was thinking."

"That's forbidden." His hands slid around her and Dina yielded to his undemanding embrace, uncrossing her arms to spread them across his chest.

10

Why not? His shoulder had become a familiar resting place for her head, used often in the last two and a half years. Her eyes closed at the feathery caress of his lips over her temple and cheek.

"You should be in the living room noisily celebrating with the others," he told her in mock reproof.

Dina laughed softly in her throat. "They're not 'noisily' celebrating. They don't 'noisily' do anything, whether it's rejoice or grieve."

"Perhaps not," he conceded. "But even a restrained celebration should have the engaged couple in attendance, namely you and me. Not just me alone."

"I know," she sighed.

His shoulder wasn't as comfortable as it had seemed. Dina turned out of his unresisting embrace, nerves stretching taut again as the niggling sense of unease and confusion wouldn't leave. Her troubled gaze searched the night's darkness beyond the windowpanes as if expecting to find the answer there.

With her back turned to him, she felt Chet resting his hands on either side of her neck, where the contracted cords were hard bands of tension.

"Relax, honey. You've let yourself get all strung up again." His supple fingers began working their magic, gently kneading the coiled muscles in her neck and shoulders.

"I can't help it." A frown puckered her forehead despite the pleasant manipulations of his hands. "I simply don't know if I'm doing the right thing."

"Of course you are."

"Am I?" A corner of her mouth lifted in a half

11

smile, self-mocking and skeptical. "I don't know how I let you talk me into this engagement."

"Me? Talk *you* into it?" Chet laughed, his warm breath fanning the silver blond strands of her hair. "You make it sound as if I twisted your arm, and I'd never do that. You're much too beautiful to risk damaging."

"Flatterer!" But Dina felt old, old beyond her years.

"It got me you."

"And I know I agreed willingly to this engagement," she admitted.

"Willingly but hesitantly," added Chet, continuing the slow and relaxing massage of her shoulders and neck.

"I wasn't sure. And I still don't know if I'm sure."

"I didn't rush you into a decision. I gave you all the time you wanted because I understand why you felt you needed it," he reasoned. "And there won't be any marriage until you set the date. Our agreement is a little more than a trial engagement."

"I know." Her voice was flat. Dina didn't find the necessary reassurance in his words.

"Look—" Chet turned her to face him "—I was Blake's best friend."

Yes, Dina thought. He had been Blake's right arm; now he was hers. Always there, ready to support her decision, coaxing a smile when her spirits were low and the will to go on had faded.

"So I know what kind of man your husband was," he continued. "I'm not trying to take his place. As a matter of fact, I don't want to take his place any more than I want you to take his ring from your finger."

His remark drew her gaze to the intertwining gold band and diamond solitaire on the third finger of her left hand. The interlocking rings had been joined by a third, a diamond floret designed to complement the first pair. It was Chet's engagement ring to her.

He curved a finger under her chin to lift it. "All that I'm hoping is that with a little more patience and persistence I can carve some room in your heart to care for me."

"I do, Chet," Dina stated. "Without you, I don't know how I would have made it through those months when Blake was missing—when we didn't know if he was alive or dead. And when we were notified that he'd been kil—"

The rest of her words were silenced by his firm kiss. Then he gathered her into his arms to hold her close, molding her slenderly curved shape to his lean, muscular body.

His mouth was near her temple, moving against her silken hair as he spoke. "That's in the past. You have to forget it."

"I can't." There was a negative movement of her head against his. "I keep remembering the way I argued with Blake before he left on that South American trip," she sighed. "He wanted me to go to the airport with him, but I refused." Another sigh came from her lips, tinged with anger and regret. "Our quarrels were always over such petty things, things that seem so stupid now."

"The strong vying with the strong." Chet lifted his head to gaze at the rueful light in her eyes. "I'm partial to strong-minded women."

His teasing words provoked the smile he sought. "I suppose I have to admit to being that, don't I?"

A fire smoldered in his look, burning away the teasing light. "And I love you for being strong, Dina." His hand slid to the small of her back. "And I love you for being all woman."

Then his mouth was seeking hers again in a kiss that was warm and passionate. She submitted to his ardor, gradually responding in kind, reveling in the gentle caress of his hands that remained short of intimate. Chet never demanded more from her than she was willing to give. His understanding restraint endeared him to her, making her heart swell with quiet happiness.

When he lifted his head, Dina nestled into the crook of his arm, resting her cheek against his shoulder, smiling with tender pleasure. That lock of hair, the color of sun-bleached sand, was across his forehead. She gave in to the impulse to brush it back with the rest, knowing it would spring forward the instant it was done. Which it did.

"Feel better?" His fingers returned the caress by tracing the curve of her cheekbone.

"Mmm."

"What were you thinking about when I came in?"

Her hand slid to his shirt, smoothing the collar.

"I don't know. I guess I was wishing."

"Wishing what?"

Dina paused. She didn't know what she had been wishing. Finally she said, "That we hadn't told the others about our engagement, that we'd kept it to ourselves for a while. I wish we weren't having this engagement party."

"It's just family and friends. There's been no official announcement made," Chet reminded her.

"I know." She usually had no difficulty in expressing herself, but the uncertainty of her own thoughts made it impossible.

Something was bothering her, but she didn't know what it was. It wasn't as if she hadn't waited a proper time before deciding to marry again. It had been two and a half years since Blake had disappeared and a little more than a year since the South American authorities had notified her that they had found the plane wreckage and there had been no survivors.

And it wasn't as if she didn't love Chet, although not in the same tumultuous way she had loved Blake. This was a quieter and gentler emotion, and probably deeper.

"Darling—" his smile was infinitely patient "—we couldn't keep our engagement from our family and friends. They need time, too, to get adjusted to the idea that you soon won't be Mrs. Blake Chandler."

"That's true," Dina acknowledged. It was not an idea that could be implanted overnight.

The door to the library opened, and an older woman dressed in black was framed in its jamb. An indulgent smile curved her mouth as she spied the embracing pair. Dina stiffened for an instant in Chet's arms, then forced herself to relax.

"We've been wondering where the two of you had gone," the woman chided them. "It's time you came back to the party and received some of the toasts being made."

"We'll be there in a minute, Mother Chandler," Dina replied to the woman who was Blake's mother, her mother-in-law.

Norma Chandler was the epitome of a society matron, belonging to all the right garden clubs and fund-raising organizations for charity. Her role in life had always been the traditional one, centered around her home and family. With both husband and son dead, she clung to Dina as her family and to her home as security.

"If you don't, I'm afraid the party will move in here, and there's hardly enough room for them all." A hand touched the strands of pearls at her throat, the gesture indicating such a thing could never dare happen at one of her parties. The pearl-gray shade of her elegantly coiffed hair blended with the jewelry she wore.

"We'll be there in a minute, Mother Chandler," Chet added his promise to Dina's. With a nod the woman closed the door, and Chet glanced at Dina. "Do you suppose you'll be able to persuade her to wear something other than black to our wedding?"

"I doubt it." She moved out of his arms, a faintly cynical smile curving her lips. "Norma Chandler likes portraying the image of a tragic figure."

Within a few weeks after Dina's marriage to Blake, Kyle Chandler, his father, had died unexpectedly of a heart attack, and Norma Chandler had purchased an entire wardrobe of black. She had barely been out of mourning when they received news that Blake's plane was missing. Instantly Mrs. Chandler began dressing in black, not waiting for the notification that came a year ago declaring her son to be considered officially dead.

16

"She approves of our marriage. You know that, don't you?" Chet asked.

"Yes, she approves," Dina agreed, "for the sake of the company." And for the fact that there would only be one 'widow' Chandler instead of two—but Dina didn't say that, knowing it would sound small and unkind when her mother-in-law had been almost smothering in her love toward her.

"Mother Chandler still doesn't believe you're capable of running the company after all this time," Chet concluded from her response. He shook his head wryly.

"I couldn't do it without you." Dina stated it as a fact, not an expression of gratitude.

"I'm with you." He curved an arm around her waist as she started for the door to leave the room. "So you won't have to worry about that."

As Chet reached forward to open the door for her, Dina was reminded of that frozen instant when Norma Chandler had opened the door seconds ago. She wondered if the same thought had crossed her mother-in-law's mind as it had her own. She had recalled the numerous times Mrs. Chandler had opened the library door to find Dina sitting on Blake's lap locked in one of his crushing and possessive embraces. This time it had been Chet's arms that held her instead of Blake's. She wondered if her mother-in-law was as aware of the vast differences between the two men as she was.

In the last months, after the uncertainty of Blake's fate had been settled and there had been time to reflect, Dina had tried to imagine what the last two and a half years might have been like if

Blake had lived. Theirs had been such a brief, stormy marriage, carrying the portent of more years of the same, always with the possibility that one battle could have ended the union permanently.

Chet, on the other hand, was always predictable, and the time Dina spent with him was always pleasant. Under his supportive influence she had discovered skills and potentials she hadn't known she possessed. Her intelligence had been channeled into constructive fields and expanded to encompass more knowledge instead of being sharpened for warring exchanges with Blake.

Her personality had matured in a hurry, owing to the circumstances of Blake's disappearance. She had become a very confident and self-assured woman, and she gave all the credit for the change to Chet.

Some of her misgivings vanished as she walked out with Chet to rejoin the party in the main area of the house. There was no earthly reason not to enjoy the engagement party, none whatsoever.

The instant they returned to the spacious living room, they were engulfed by the sedate gathering of well-wishers. Each seemed to display a reverence for the antique furniture that abounded in the room, beautiful Victorian pieces enhanced by paintings and art objects. The atmosphere decreed formality and civil behavior.

"I see you found the two of them, Norma," Sam Lavecek announced belatedly. His voice had a tendency to boom, an abrasive sound that drew unnecessary attention to their absence from the party. "Off in some secluded corner, no doubt." He winked with faint suggestiveness at Dina. "Reminds me of the times you and Blake were always slipping away to cuddle in some corner." He glanced down at the brandy in his hand. "I miss that boy." It was an absent comment, his thoughts spoken aloud.

An awkward tension charged the moment. Chet, with his usual diplomacy, smoothed it over. "We all miss him, Sam," he asserted quietly, his arm curving protectively around Dina's shoulders.

"What?" Sam Lavecek's initial reaction was blankness, as if unaware that he said out loud what was on his mind. He flushed uncomfortably at the newly engaged pair. "Of course, we do, but it doesn't stop any of us from wishing you much happiness together," he insisted and lifted his glass, calling the others to a toast. "To Dina and Chet, and their future together."

Dina maintained her facade of smiling happiness, but it was an odd feeling to have the celebrants of their engagement party consist of Blake's family and friends. Without family herself, her parents having been killed in an automobile crash the year before she had met Blake, there had been no close relatives of her own to invite. What friends she had in Newport, she had met through Blake. Chet's family lived in Florida.

When Norma Chandler had asked to give them an engagement party, it had been a difficult offer to reject. Dina had chosen not to, finding it the easiest and quickest means to inform all of the Chandler relatives and friends of her decision to accept Chet's proposal. She wasn't blind to her mother-in-law's motives. Norma Chandler wished to remain close to her. All her instincts were maternal, and Dina was the only one left to mother.

But the engagement party had proved to be more of a trial than Dina had thought. The announcement had raised too much inner restlessness and vague doubts. None of the celebrants could see that. She was too well schooled in concealing her feelings. When the party ended at a suitable hour, no one was the wiser. Not even Chet suspected that she was still plagued by apprehensions when he kissed her good night. It was something Dina knew she would have to work out alone.

OVER THE WEEKEND, the news of their engagement had filtered into the main office of the Chandler hotel chain in Newport. Dina felt certain she had spent the bulk of the morning confirming the rumors that she was engaged to Chet.

She sincerely doubted that there was anyone in the building who had not stopped at her office to extend congratulations and questioning looks.

A mountain of work covered the massive walnut desk top—letters to be answered, reports to be read and memos to be issued. With her elbows on the desk top, Dina rested her forehead on her hands, rubbing the dull throb in its center. Her pale blond hair had grown to the point where it could be pulled to the nape of her neck in a neat bun, the style adding a few years to her relatively youthful appearance.

The clothing she wore to the office was chosen, too, with an eye to detracting from her youth. Today, it was a long-sleeved blouse of cream yellow with a wine-colored vest and skirt, attractive and stylish yet professional-looking.

The intercom buzzed and Dina lifted her head, reaching over to press the button. "Yes?"

"Harry Landers is here to see you, Mrs. Chandler," was the reply from her secretary, Amy Wentworth—about the only one of the executive staff younger than Dina was.

"Send him in."

Dina picked up her reading glasses, which were lying on a stack of papers she had been reading, and put them on. She could see to read without them, but invariably after hours of reading the eye strain became too much. Lately she had taken to wearing them almost constantly at the office to avoid the headaches that accompanied the strain, and subconsciously because they added a business-like air to her appearance. There was a wry twist of her mouth as the doorknob to her office turned, an inner acknowledgement that she had been wrong in thinking everyone had been in to offer congratulations. Harry Landers hadn't, and the omission was about to be corrected. As the door opened, her mouth finished its curve into a polite smile of greeting.

"Good morning, Harry."

The tall and brawny white-haired man who entered smiled and returned the greeting. "Good morning, Mrs. Chandler." Only Chet used her Christian name at the office, and then only when they were alone. "I just heard the news that you and Chet are getting married. Congratulations," he offered predictably.

21

"Thank you," she nodded for what seemed like the hundredth time that morning.

There was no silent, unasked question in the look he gave her. "I'm truly glad for you, Mrs. Chandler. I know there are some people here who think you're somehow being unfaithful to Blake's memory by marrying again. Personally, I think it speaks well of your marriage to him."

"You do?" Her voice was briskly cool; she did not care for discussions about her private life, although her curiosity was rising by degrees as she tried to follow his logic.

"Yes—I mean, obviously your marriage to Blake was very satisfactory or you wouldn't want to enter the wedded state again," he reasoned.

"I see." Her smile was tight, lacking warmth. "Blake and I did have a good marriage." Whether they did, she couldn't say. It had been too brief. "And I know Chet and I will, too."

"When is the wedding?"

"We haven't set the date yet."

"Be sure to send me an invitation."

"We will." Dina's hopes for a quiet wedding and no reception were fast dissipating under the rush of requests to attend. An elopement was beginning to look inviting.

"At least you won't have to concern yourself with the company after you're married," Harry Landers observed with a benign smile.

"I beg your pardon?" Dina was instantly alert and on the defensive, no longer mouthing the polite words she had repeated all morning.

"After you're married, you can go back to being

a simple housewife. Chet will make a good president," he replied.

Why the accent on "simple," Dina wondered bitterly. "My marriage to Chet will have no effect on the company. It will continue to be run jointly by both of us with myself as president," she stated, not wanting to remember that the work had been done by Blake alone. Rigid with anger, she turned to the papers on her desk. "I don't see the monthly report from the Florida hotel. Has it come in?"

"I don't believe so." Her abrupt change of subject warned the man he was treading on forbidden ground. His previous open expression became closed and officious.

"Frank Miller is the manager there, isn't he?"

"Yes."

"Call him and find out where the report is. I want it on my desk by four this afternoon even if he has to telex it," she ordered.

"I'll see to it right away, Mrs. Chandler."

When the door closed behind him, Dina rose from the overstuffed cushion on her swivel office chair and walked to the window. Afterquakes of resentment were still trembling through her. Almost since Blake's disappearance, she had run the company with Chet's help; but her competence to fill the position still wasn't recognized by some of the executive officers.

It hadn't been by design but through necessity that she had taken over. When Blake disappeared over South America, the company had been like a ship without a rudder, without guidance or direction. It had operated smoothly for a while, then it began to flounder helplessly.

The key members of the executive staff, those who might have been competent enough to take over, had resigned to take positions with more solid companies, like rats deserting a sinking ship. That was when Dina had been forced to step in, by virtue of the Chandler name.

It hadn't been easy. The odds were stacked against her because she was young and a woman and totally ignorant of the machinations of the company, not to say limited in experience. Exerting her authority had been the most difficult part. Most of the staff were old enough to be her parents; and some, like Harry Landers, were old enough to be her grandparents.

Dina had learned the hard way, by trial and many errors. The worries, the fears that she had about Blake, she had to keep to herself. Very early she discovered that the men who offered her a shoulder to cry on were also insistently offering their beds.

More and more in those early days, she began turning to Chet for his unselfish and undemanding support. Not once did he make a single overture toward her, not until several months after Blake's death had been confirmed. She trusted him implicitly and he had never given her a reason to doubt him.

But Harry Landers had just put a question in her mind—one Dina didn't like facing, but there seemed to be no eluding it.

Shaking her head, Dina walked back to her desk. She picked up the telephone receiver and hesitated, staring at the numbers on the dial. There was a

24

quick knock on her office door, followed by the click of the latch as it was opened without waiting for her permission to enter. Replacing the receiver, Dina turned to the door as Chet appeared.

"You'll never guess what I just heard," he whispered with exaggerated secrecy.

"What is it?" Dina grew tense.

"Chet Stanton is going to marry Mrs. Chandler."

What she expected him to say, Dina had no idea. But at his answer she laughed with a mixture of amusement and relief, some of her tension fleeing.

"You've heard that rumor, too, have you?" she retorted.

"Are you kidding?" He grimaced in a boyish fashion that made her heart warm to him all the more. "I've been trying to get to my office since nine o'clock this morning and haven't made it yet. I keep getting stopped along the way."

"As bad as that?" Dina smiled.

"The hallway is a veritable gauntlet."

She knew the feeling. "We should have called everybody together this morning, made the announcement, then gone to work. It would have made a more productive morning."

"Hindsight, my love," he chided, walking over to kiss her lightly on the cheek.

"Yes," Dina agreed. She removed her glasses and made a show of concentrating on them as she placed them on the desk top. "Now that everyone knows, they're all waiting for me to hand in my resignation and name you as the successor to the Chandler throne." Without seeming to, she watched Chet's reaction closely.

25

"I hope you set them straight about that," he replied without hesitation. "We make an excellent team. And there certainly isn't any reason to break up a winning combination in the company just because we're getting married."

"That's what I thought," she agreed.

Taking her by the shoulders, Chet turned her to face him, tipping his head to one side in an inquiring manner. "Have I told you this morning how beautiful you are?"

"No." The edges of her mouth dimpled slightly as she answered him in the same serious tone that he had used. "But you can tell me now."

"You're very beautiful, darling."

With the slightest pressure, he drew her yielding shape to him. As his mouth lightly took possession of hers, the intercom buzzed. Dina moved out of his arms with a rueful smile of apology.

She pressed the button. "Yes, Amy?"

"Jacob Stone is on line one," came the reply.

"Thank you." Dina broke the connection and glanced at Chet with a resigned shrug of her shoulders.

"Jake Stone," he repeated. "That's the Chandler family attorney, isn't it?"

"Yes," she nodded, reaching for the telephone. "Probably some business to do with Blake's estate."

"That's my cue for an exit." And Chet started for the door.

"Dinner tonight at eight?" Dina questioned.

"Perfect," he agreed with a wink.

"Call Mother Chandler and tell her I've invited you." She picked up the telephone receiver, her finger hovering above the blinking button on line one.

"Consider it done."

Dina watched him leave. Just for a few minutes, Harry Landers had made her suspect that Chet might be marrying her to elevate his position in the company. But his instant and casual rejection of the suggestion of becoming president had erased that. Her trust in him was once again complete.

She pushed the button. "Hello, Mr. Stone. Dina Chandler speaking."

"Ah, Mrs. Chandler. How are you?" came the gravelly voice in answer.

"Just fine, thank you."

CHAPTER TWO

BY THE END of the week, the excitement generated by the news of their engagement had died down and work was able to settle into a routine again. The invisible pressure the news had evoked eased as well.

Yet on Saturday morning Dina wakened with the sun, unable to go back to sleep. Finally she stopped trying, arose and dressed in slacks and white blouse with a pullover sweater. The other members of the household, Blake's mother and their housekeeper, Deirdre, were still asleep.

Dina hurriedly tidied the room, unfolding the blue satin coverlet from the foot of the four-poster bed and smoothing it over the mattress. Deirdre was such a perfectionist that she would probably do it over again. Fluffing the satin pillow shams, Dina placed them at the head of the bed.

The clothes she had worn last night were lying on the blue and gold brocade cushion of the love seat. Dina hung them up in the large closet. The neckscarf she folded and carried to its drawer.

Inside, the gilt edge of a picture frame gleamed amidst the lingerie and fashion accessories. It lay face down, concealing the photograph of Blake. Until Chet had given her an engagement ring, the picture had been on the bedside table, Now it was relegated to a dresser drawer, a photograph of the past that had nothing to do with the present. Dina closed the drawer and glanced around the room. Everything seemed to be in order.

After Blake's disappearance two and a half years ago, it had seemed senseless for both Dina and his mother to keep separate households, especially when the days began to stretch into weeks and months. In the end Dina had sublet the apartment she and Blake had in town to move to the suburbs with his mother.

She had thought it would ease her loneliness and provide an outlet for her inner fears, but it hadn't proved to be so. Dina had spent the bulk of her private time consoling Mother Chandler, as she called her mother-in-law, and had received little if any consolation in return.

Still, it was a suitable arrangement, a place to sleep and eat, with all the housekeeping and meals done by others. With most of her time and energy spent in keeping the company going, the arrangement had become a definite asset.

Now, as she tiptoed out of the house into the dawn, Dina wished for the privacy of her own home, where she could steal into the kitchen and fix an early morning breakfast without feeling she was invading someone else's turf. And Deirdre was jealously possessive about her kitchen.

Closing the door, she listened for the click of the lock. When she heard it, she turned to the steps leading to the driveway and the white Porsche parked there. Inside the house the telephone rang, loud in the silence of the pink morning.

Dina stopped and began rummaging through her oversize purse for the house key. It was seldom used since there was always someone to let her in. Before she found it, the phone had stopped ringing. She waited several seconds to see if it would start ringing again. Someone in the house must have answered it, Dina decided, or else the party must have decided to call later in the morning.

Skimming down the steps, she hurried to the Porsche, folding the top down before climbing in and starting the engine. With doughnuts and coffee in a Styrofoam container from a pastry shop, she drove through the quiet business streets.

There was a salty tang to the breeze ruffling her hair. Dina shook her head to let its cool fingers rake through the silken gold strands. Her blue eyes narrowed in decision as she turned the sports car away from the street that would take her to the office building and headed toward the solitude of an early morning ocean beach.

Sitting on a piece of driftwood, Dina watched the sun finish rising on Rhode Island Sound, the water shimmering and sparkling as the waves lapped the long strand of ocean beach. The city of Newport was located on the island of Rhode Island, from which the state derived its name.

The doughnut crumbs had been tossed to the seagulls, still swooping and soaring nearby in case she had missed one. It was peaceful and quiet. The nearest person was a surf fisherman, a stick figure distantly visible. It was one of those times when she thought of many things as she sat, but couldn't remember a single one when she rose to leave.

It was nine o'clock, the time she usually arrived at the office for a half-day's work, minimum. But Dina couldn't think of a single item that was pressing, except the one the family attorney had called about the first of the week.

Returning to her Porsche parked off the road near the beach, she drove to the nearest telephone booth and stopped. She rummaged through her purse for change and dialed the office number. It was answered on the second ring.

"Amy? This is Mrs. Chandler." She shut the door of the phone booth to close out the whine of the semitrailer going by. "I won't be in this morning, but there's some correspondence on the dictaphone I would like typed this morning."

"I've already started it," her young secretary answered.

"Good. When you have it done, leave it on my desk. Then you can call it a day. All right?"

"Yes, thank you, Mrs. Chandler." Amy Wentworth was obviously delighted.

"See you Monday," Dina said, and hung up.

Back in the white sports car, she headed for the boat marina where Blake's sailboat was docked. She parked the car by the small shed that served as an office. A man sat in a chair out front.

Balanced was the better word, as the chair was tilted back, allowing only the two rear legs to support it. The man's arms were folded in front of him and a faded captain's hat was pulled over his face, permitting only a glimpse of his double chin and the graying stubble of beard.

Dina hopped out of the sports car, smiling at the

man who hadn't changed in almost three years. "Good morning, Cap'n Tate."

She waited for his slow, drawling New England voice to return the greeting. He was a character and he enjoyed being one.

The chair came down with a thump as a large hand pushed the hat back on top of his head. Gray eyes stared at her blankly for a minute before recognition flickered in them.

"How do, Miz Chandler." He rose lumberingly to his feet, pulling his faded trousers up to cover his paunch. The end result was to accentuate it.

"It's been so long since I've seen you. How have you been?"

"Mighty fine, Miz Chandler, mighty fine." The owner of the marina smiled and succeeded in extending the smile to his jowled cheeks. "I s'pose you're here to get the *Starfish* cleaned out. Shore was sorry when your attorney told me you was goin' to rent it out."

"Yes, I know." Her smile faded slightly. Getting rid of the boat seemed to be like closing the final chapter about Blake in her life. "But it was pointless to keep the boat dry-docked here, unused."

"She's a damn fine boat," he insisted, puffing a bit as he stepped inside the shed door and reached for a key. "Never know, someday you might want it yourself."

Dina laughed, a little huskily. "You know I'm not a sailor, Cap'n Tate. I need a whole bottle of motion-sickness pills just to make it out of the harbor without getting seasick!"

"Then you sleep the whole time." He guffawed

32

and started coughing. "I never will forget that time Blake came carrying you off the boat sound asleep. He told me aft'wards that you didn't wake up till the next morning."

"If you will recall, that was the last time he even suggested I go sailing with him." She took the key he handed her, feeling a poignant rush of memories and trying to push them back.

"D'ya want some help movin' any of that stuff?" he offered.

"No, thank you." She couldn't imagine the two of them in the small cabin, not with Cap'n Tate's protruding belly. "I can manage."

"You just give me a holler if you need anything," he said nodding his grizzled head. "You know where she's docked."

"I do." With a wave of her hand, Dina started down the long stretch of dock.

Masts, long, short and medium, stood in broken lines along the pier, sails furled, the hulls motionless in the quiet water. Her steps were directed by memory along the boards. Although she had rarely ever joined Blake after her first two disastrous attempts at sailing, Dina had often come to the marina to wait for his return. But Blake wouldn't be coming back anymore.

The bold letters of the name *Starfish* stood out clearly against the white hull. Dina paused, feeling the tightness in her throat. Then, scolding herself, she stepped aboard. The wooden deck was dull, no longer gleaming and polished as Blake had kept it.

It didn't do any good to tell herself she shouldn't have waited so long to do something about the boat. There had been so many other decisions to make and demands on her time. Plus there had been so many legal entanglements surrounding Blake's disappearance. Those had become knots at the notification of his death. Since his estate wasn't settled, the boat still couldn't be sold until the court decreed the dispensation of his property.

The *Starfish* had been dry-docked since his disappearance, everything aboard exactly the way he had left it after his last sail. Dina unlocked the cabin to go below. The time had come to pack away all his things. Jake Stone, the family attorney, had decided the boat should be leased, even if it couldn't be sold yet, to eliminate the maintenance costs and to keep it from deteriorating through lack of use.

It had occurred to Dina that she could have arranged for someone else to clear away his things and clean up the boat. That was what she planned to do when the attorney had phoned the first of the week to tell her he had received the court's permission to lease the boat. But she was here now and the task lay ahead of her.

Opening drawers and doors, she realized there was a great deal more aboard than she had supposed. The storehouse of canned goods in the cupboards would have brought a smile of delight to any gourmet, but Blake had always been very particular about his food and the way it was prepared. Sighing, Dina wondered how many of the cans were still good. What a waste it would be if she had to throw them all out.

Picking up a can, she quickly set it down. The first order was to get a general idea of what had to be done. She continued her methodical examination of the cabin's contents. The clean, if now musty, clothes brought a smile to her lips. It was funny how a person's memory of little things could dim over such a short time as a few years.

A glance at his clothes brought it all back. Blake had been very meticulous about his clothes, being always clean and well dressed. Even the several changes of denim Levi's kept aboard the boat were creased and pressed. A thin coating of dust couldn't hide the snow-white of his sneakers.

Both seemed something of an extreme, yet Dina couldn't remember a time when she had seem him dressed in a manner that could be described as carelessly casual. It made him sound a bit pompous, but the trait hadn't been at all abrasive.

Blake had been used to good things all his life—a beautiful home, excellent food, vintage wines and specially tailored clothes. Spoiled? With a trace of arrogance? Perhaps, Dina conceded. He had been something of a playboy when she had met him, with devastating charm when he wanted to turn it on. Brilliantly intelligent and almost dreadfully organized, he had been exciting and difficult to live with.

Not at all like Chet, she concluded again. But what was the point in comparing? What could be gained by holding up Blake's smooth sophistication to Chet's easygoing nature? With a shrug of confusion, she turned away from the clothes, shutting her mind to the unanswerable questions.

For the better part of the day she worked aboard the boat, first packing and carrying Blake's belongings to the Porsche, where she stuffed them in every conceivable corner of the small sports car. Then she began cleaning away the years of dust and salt spray, airing the mattresses and cushions, and polishing the interior woodwork.

Dirty and sweaty and physically exhausted, she returned the key to the crusty marina operator. Yet the laborious job had been cathartic, leaving her with an oddly refreshed feeling. Lately all her energy had been expended mentally. The hard work felt good even if her muscles would be stiff and sore tomorrow.

She was humming to herself as the white Porsche rounded the corner onto the street where she lived with her mother-in-law. Ahead was the Chandler home, an imposing brick structure that towered two and a half stories into the air. It was set back from the road by a formal lawn dotted with perfectly shaped trees and well-cut shrubs and a scattering of flower beds. The many windows and double entrance doors were a pristine shade of ivory. At the sight of the half dozen cars parked around the cul-de-sac of the driveway, Dina frowned and slowed the car, forced to park it some distance from the entrance.

There wasn't any dinner party she had forgotten, was there, she wondered to herself. The cars resembled those belonging to close family friends. One, the silver gray Cadillac, was Chet's. She glanced at her watch. He had said he would stop around seven for a drink before taking her out to dinner. It was barely five o'clock.

Her mouth formed a disgruntled line. She had hoped to soak in a tubful of scented bubbles for an hour, but obviously that luxury was going to be denied her. And why hadn't Mother Chandler mentioned she would be entertaining this evening? It wasn't like her.

Puzzled, Dina raised the convertible top of her sports car and rolled up the windows. This was not the time to transport all the items from the car into the house, so she climbed out of the car, her handbag slung over her shoulder, and locked the doors.

Happy voices were talking all over each other from the living room as she entered the house. The double doors of carved oak leading into the room were closed, concealing the owners of the voices. The foyer, with its richly grained oak woodwork complementing pale yellow walls, was empty. The wide staircase rising to the second floor beckoned, its gold carpeted treads like sunlight showing her the path, the carved oak balustrade catching the reflected color. She hesitated, then decided to go for a quick wash and change while her return was still unnoticed.

Only it wasn't unnoticed. As she started to cross the foyer for the stairs leading to the second floor and her bedroom, one of the double doors was surreptitiously opened. Her eyes widened as Chet slipped out, his handsome features strained and tense.

"Where have you been?" There was a hint of desperation in his voice.

If it weren't for the joyful tone of the voices in the other room, Dina might have guessed that some catastrophe had befallen them, judging by Chet's expression.

"At the marina," she answered.

"The marina?" he repeated in disbelief. Again there was that strangled tightness in his voice. "My God, I've been calling all over trying to find you. I never even considered the marina. What were you doing there, for heaven's sake?"

"The *Sarfish*—the boat has been leased. I was getting it cleaned up." The explanation was made while Dina tried to think what crisis could have arisen that Chet would have so urgently needed to contact her about.

"Of all the times—"

Dina broke in sharply. "What's going on?" His attitude was too confusing when she couldn't fathom the reason for it.

"Look, there's something I have to tell you." Chet moistened his lips nervously, his gray blue gaze darting over her face as if trying to judge something from her expression. "But I don't know how to say it."

"What is it?" she demanded impatiently. His tension was becoming contagious.

He took her by the shoulders, his expression deadly serious as he gazed intently into her eyes. Her muscles were becoming sore and they protested at the tightness of his hold.

"It's this . . ." he began earnestly.

But he got no further as a low, huskily pitched male voice interrupted. "Chet seems to think you're going to go into a state of shock when you find out I'm alive."

The floor rocked beneath her feet. Dina managed a half turn on her treacherously unsteady footing, magnetically drawn to the voice. The whole floor seemed to give way when she saw its owner, yet she remained upright, her collapsing muscles supported by Chet.

There was a dreamlike unreality to the moment.

Almost nightmarelike, since it seemed a cruel joke for someone to stand in the doorway of the living room masquerading as Blake, mimicking his voice.

She stared wordlessly at the tall figure framed by the living-room doors. There was much about the chiseled features that resembled Blake—the wide forehead, the carved cheek and jaw, the strong chin and classically straight nose.

Yet there were differences, too. The sun had burned this man's face a dusky tan, making it leathery and tough, giving a hardness to features that in Blake had been suavely handsome. The eyes were the same dark brown, but they wore a narrowed, hooded look as they seemed to pierce into the very marrow of her soul .

His hair was the same deep shade of umber brown, but its waving thickness was much longer than Blake had ever worn it, giving the impression of being rumpled instead of smoothly in place. As tall as Blake, this man's build was more muscled. Not that Blake had been a weakling by any means; it was just that this man seemed more developed without appearing heavier.

The differences registered with computer swiftness, her brain working while the rest of her was reeling from the similarities. The buzzing in her head continued nonstop, facts clicking into place.

But it wasn't her eyes that Dina trusted. What

finally led her to a conclusion was Chet's peculiar behavior before this man appeared; his innate kindness, which would never have permitted a cruel joke like this to be played on her; and the something that he was going to tell before they were interrupted.

Blake was alive. And he was standing in the doorway. She swayed forward, but her feet wouldn't move. Chet's hands tightened in support and she turned her stunned gaze to him. The confirmation was there in his carefully watchful face.

"It's true," she breathed, neither a statement nor a question.

Chet nodded, a silent warning in his eyes. It was then that Dina felt the cold weight of his engagement ring around her finger, and the blood drained from her face. Her hands reached out to cling to Chet's arms, suddenly and desperately needing his support to remain upright.

"It seems Chet was right," that familiar, lazy voice drawled in an arid tone. "My return is more of a shock to you than I thought it would be," Blake observed. The angle of his head shifted slightly to the side to direct his next words over his shoulder without releasing Dina from his level gaze. "She needs some hot, sweet coffee, laced with a stiff shot of brandy."

"Exactly," Chet agreed, and curved a bracing arm around her waist. "Let's find you a place to sit down, Dina." Numbly she accepted his help, aware of his gaze flickering to Blake. "Seeing you standing in the doorway was bound to have been like seeing a ghost. I told you we were all convinced you were dead."

"Not me," Mother Chandler contradicted him, moving to stand beside her son. "I always knew somehow that he was still alive somewhere out there, despite what everyone said."

Fleetingly, Dina was aware of the blatant lie in her mother-in-law's assertion. The thought had barely formed when she realized there were others in the living room. She recognized the faces of close family friends, gathered to celebrate Blake's return. They had been watching the reunion between husband and wife—or rather, the lack of it.

In that paralyzing second, Dina realized she had not so much as touched Blake, let alone joyously fallen into his arms. Her one swaying attempt had been accidentally checked by Chet's steadying hold. It would seem staged and faked if she did so now.

Equally startling was the discovery that she would have to fake it because, although the man in front of her was obviously Blake Chandler, he did not seem like the same man she had married. She felt as if she were looking at a total stranger. He knew what she was thinking and feeling; she could see it in the coolness of his expression, aloof and chilling.

As she and Chet approached the doorway, Blake stepped to one side, giving them room. He smiled down at his mother, his expression revealing nothing to the others that might let them think he found her behavior unnatural under the circumstances.

"If you were so positive I was alive, mother, why are you wearing black?" he chided her.

Color rose in Norma Chandler's cheeks. "For your father, Blake," she responded, not at a loss for an explanation.

41

Everyone was still standing, watching, as Chet guided Dina to the empty cushions of the sofa. After she was seated, he automatically sat down beside her. Blake had followed them into the room.

Every nerve in Dina's body was aware of his presence, although she wasn't able to lift her gaze to him. Guilt burned inside her, gnawing away at any spontaneous reaction she might have had. It didn't help when Blake sat down in the armchair nearest her end of the couch.

The housekeeper appeared, setting a china cup and saucer on the glass-topped table in front of the sofa. "Here's your coffee, just the way Mr. Blake ordered it."

"Thank you, Deirdre," she murmured. She reached for the china cup filled with steaming dark liquid, but her hands were shaking like aspen leaves and she couldn't hold on to it.

Out of the corner of her eye, she caught a suggestion of movement from Blake, as if he was about to lean forward to help her. Chet's hand was already there, lifting the cup to carry it to her lips. It was purely an automatic reaction on Chet's part. He had become used to doing things for her in the past two and a half years, just as Dina had become used to having him do them.

Instinctively, she knew he hadn't told Blake of their engagement and she doubted if anyone else had. But Chet's solicitous concern was telling its own story. And behind that facade of lazy interest, Blake was absorbing every damning detail. Without knowing it, Chet was making matters worse.

The hot and sweetly potent liquid Dina sipped

eased the constriction strangling her voice, and she found the strength to raise her hesitant gaze to Blake's.

"How . . ." she began self-consciously. "I mean when . . . ."

"I walked out of the jungle two weeks ago." He anticipated her question and answered it.

"Two weeks ago?" That was before she had agreed to marry Chet. "Why didn't you let . . . someone know?"

"It was difficult to convince the authorities that I was who I claimed to be. They, too, believed I was dead." There was a slashing line to his mouth, a cynical smile. "It must have been easier for Lazarus back in the Biblical days to return from the dead."

"Are you positive I can't fix you a drink, Mr. Blake?" the housekeeper inquired. "A martini?"

"Nothing, thank you."

Dina frowned. In the past Blake had always drunk two, if not three martinis before dinner. She had not been wrong. There were more than just surface changes in him during the last two and a half years. Unconsciously she covered her hand with her right, hiding not only the wedding rings Blake had given her, but Chet's engagement ring, as well.

"The instant they believed Blake's story," his mother inserted to carry on his explanation, "he caught the first plane out to come home." She beamed at him like the adoring and doting mother that she was.

"You should have phoned." Dina couldn't help saying it. Forewarned, she might have been better prepared for the new Blake Chandler.

"I did."

43

Simultaneously as he spoke, Dina remembered the telephone ringing in the dawn hour as she had left the house. Seconds. She had missed knowing about his return by seconds.

"I'd switched off my extension," Norma Chandler said, "and Deidre was wearing her earplugs. Did you hear it, Dina?"

"No. No, I'd already left," answered Dina.

"When Blake didn't get any answer here," Chet continued the story, "he called me."

"Chet was as stunned as you were, Dina," Blake smiled, but Dina suspected that she was the only one who noticed the lack of amusement in his voice. She knew her gaze wavered under the keenness of his.

"I came over right away to let you and Mrs. Chandler know," Chet finished.

"Where were you, Dina?" Sam Lavecek grumped. He was Blake's godfather and a very old friend of both Blake's mother and father. Over the years he had become something of a Dutch uncle to Blake, later extending the relationship to Dina. "Chet has been half out of his mind worrying about where you were all day. Played hooky from the office, did you?"

"I was at the marina," she answered, and turned to Blake. "The *Starfish* has been leased to a couple, and they plan to sail to Florida for the winter. I spent the day cleaning it up and moving out all of your things."

"What a pity, boy!" Sam Lavecek sympathized, slapping the arm of his chair. "You always did love going out on that boat. Now, the very day you come home, it's being turned over to someone else."

44

"It's only a boat, Sam." There was an enigmatic darkness to his eyes that made his true thoughts impossible to see.

To Dina, in her supersensitive state, he seemed to be implying something else. Perhaps he didn't object to his boat being loaned to someone else—as long as it wasn't his wife. Her apprehension mounted.

"You're right!" the older man agreed with another emphatic slap of his hand on the armchair. "It's only a boat. And what's that compared to having you back? It's a miracle! A miracle!"

The statement brought a surfeit of questions for Blake to answer about the crash and the events that followed. Dina listened to his narrative. Each word that came from his mouth made him seem more and more a stranger.

The small chartered plane had developed engine trouble and had crashed in the teeming jungle. When Blake had come to, the other four people aboard were dead and he was trapped in the twisted wreckage with a broken leg and a few broken ribs. There had been a deep gash on his forehead, still seeping blood, and other cuts and bruises. Dina's gaze found the scar that had made a permanent crease in his forehead.

Blake didn't go into too much detail about how he had got out of the plane the following day, but Dina had a vivid imagination and pictured the agony he must have endured fighting his way out with his injuries, letting the wreckage become a coffin for the mangled lifeless bodies of the others. Not knowing when or if he would be rescued, Blake had been forced to set his own leg.

45

That was something Dina could not visualize him doing. In the past, when there was anything that required professional skill or experience, Blake had always hired someone to do it. So for him to set his own broken bone, regardless of the dire circumstances, seemed completely out of character, something the man she had known would never have done.

When the emergency supply of rations from the plane had run out, Blake had foraged for his food, his diet consisting of fruits and whatever wild animals he could trap, catch or kill. And this was supposed to be the same Blake Chandler who had considered the killing of wild game a disgusting sport and who dined on gourmet cuisine.

Blake, who despised flies and mosquitoes, told of the insects that swarmed in the jungle, flying, crawling, biting, stinging, until he no longer noticed them. The heat and humidity of the jungle rotted his shoes and clothes, forcing him to improvise articles of clothing from the skins of the animals he had killed. Blake, the meticulous dresser, always presenting such a well-groomed appearance....

As he began his tale of the more than two-year-long walk out of the jungle, Dina discovered the crux of the difference. Blake had left Rhode Island a civilized man and had come back part primitive. She stared at him with seeing eyes.

Leaning back in his chair, he looked indolent and relaxed, yet Dina knew his muscles were like coiled springs, always ready to react with the swiftness of a predatory animal. His senses, his nerves were alert to everything going on around him. Nothing

46

escaped the notice of that hooded dark gaze. From the lurking depths of those hard brown eyes, Blake seemed to be viewing them all with cynical amusement, as if he found the so-called dangers and problems of their civilized world laughable when compared to the battle of survival he had fought and won.

"There's something I don't understand," Sam Lavecek commented, frowning when Blake had completed his basically sketchy narrative. "Why did the authorities tell us you were dead after they'd found the wreckage? Surely they must have discovered there was a body missing," he added bluntly.

"I don't imagine they did," Blake answered in a calm, matter-of-fact tone.

"Did you bury their bodies, Blake?" his mother asked. "Is that why they didn't find them?"

"No, mother, I didn't." The cynical amusement that Dina suspected he felt was there, glittering through the brown shutters of the indulgent look he gave his mother. "It would have taken a bulldozer to carve out a grave in that tangled mess of brush, trees and roots. I had no choice but to leave them in the plane. Unfortunately, the jungle is filled with scavengers."

Dina blanched. He sounded so cold and insensitive! Blake had been a passionately vital and volatile man, quick to fly into a temper and quick to love.

What had he become? How much would the savagery in his life in the last two and a half years influence his future? Would his determination become ruthlessness? Would his innate leadership become tyranny? Would his compassion for others become contempt? Would his love turn to lust? Was he a virile man or a male animal? He was her husband, and Dina shuddered at what the answers to those questions might be.

Distantly she heard the housekeeper enter the room to inquire, "What time would you like dinner served this evening, Mrs. Chandler?"

There was hesitation before Norma Chandler replied, "In about an hour, Deirdre. That will be all right for everyone, won't it?" and received a murmur of agreement.

From the sofa cushions beside her, Chet expanded on his agreement to remark, "That will give you ample time to freshen up before dinner, won't it, Dina?"

She clutched at the lifeline he had unknowingly tossed her. "Yes, it will." She wanted desperately to be alone for a few minutes to sort through her jumbled thoughts, terribly afraid she was overreacting. Rising, she addressed her words to everyone. "Please excuse me. I won't be long."

Dina had the disquieting sensation of Blake's eyes following her as she walked from the room. But he made no attempt to stop her, nor offer to come with her to share a few minutes alone, much to her relief.

CHAPTER THREE

THE BRIEF SHOWER had washed away the last lingering traces of unreality. Wrapping the sash to her royal blue terry-cloth robe around her middle, Dina walked through the open doorway of the private bath to her bedroom. She moved to the clothes closet at the far corner of the room to choose what she would wear for dinner, all the while trying to assure herself that she was making mountains out of molehills where Blake was concerned.

There was a click, and then movement in her peripheral vision. She turned as the door opened and Blake walked in. Her mouth opened to order out the intruder, then closed. He was her husband. How could she order him out of her bedroom?

His gaze swept the room, located her, and stopped, fixing her with a stare like a predator would his prey. Her fingers clasped the folds of her robe at the throat, her palms moistening with nervous perspiration. Dina was conscious of the implied intimacy of the room and her own nakedness beneath the terry-cloth material. Blood pounded in her head like a thousand jungle drums signaling danger. Vulnerable, she was wary of him.

The brand-new tan suit and tie he wore gave him a cultured look, but she wasn't taken in by the thin veneer of refinement. It didn't conceal the latent power of that muscled physique, nor soften the rough edges of his sun-hardened features. Blake closed the door, not releasing her from his pinning gaze, and searing alarm halted her breath.

"I've come through hell to get back to you, Dina, yet you can't seem to walk across a room to meet me." The accusation was made in a smooth, low tone rife with sardonic amusement.

His words prodded her into movement. Too much time had elapsed since his return for her to rush into his arms. Her steps were stiff, her back rigid as she approached him. She was cautious of him and it showed. Even if she wanted to, she doubted if she could batter down the wall of reserve she had erected. Stopping in front of him, she searched her mind for welcoming words that she could issue sincerely.

"I'm glad you came back safely," were the ones she could offer that had the ring of truth.

Blake waited . . . for her kiss. The muscles in her stomach contracted sharply with the realization. After a second's hesitation, she forced herself on tiptoe to bring her lips against his mouth in a cool kiss. His large hands spanned the back of her waist, their imprint burning through the material onto her naked flesh. His light touch didn't seem at all familiar. It was almost alien.

At her first attempt to end the kiss, his arms became a vise, fingers raking into her silver gold hair to force her lips to his. Her slender curves were pressed against the hard contours of his body. Her heartbeat skittered madly, then accelerated in alarm.

The hungry demand of his bruising mouth asked more than Dina could give to a man who seemed more of a stranger than her husband. She struggled to free herself of his iron hold and was surprised when Blake let her twist away.

Her breathing was rapid and uneven as she avoided his eyes. "I have to get dressed." She pretended that was her reason for rejecting his embrace. "The others are waiting downstairs."

Those fathomless brown eyes were boring holes into her. Dina could feel them even as she turned away to retrace her steps to the closet and her much-needed clothes. Her knees felt watery.

"You mean Chet is waiting," Blake corrected her with deadly softness.

Her blood ran cold. "Of course. Isn't Chet there with the others?" She feigned ignorance of his meaning and immediately regretted not taking advantage of the opening he had given her to tell him about Chet.

"I've had two and a half years of forced celibacy, Dina. How about you?" The dry contempt in his question spun her around, blue fires of indignation flashing in her eyes, but Blake didn't give her a chance to defend her honor. "How long was it after I disappeared before Chet moved in?"

"He did not move in!" she flashed.

With the swiftness of a swooping hawk, he seized her left hand. His savage grip almost crushed the slender bones of her fingers into a pulp, drawing a gasp of pain from her.

"Figuratively speaking!" His mouth was a thin, cruel line as he lifted her hand. "Or don't you call it moving in when another man's ring joins the ones I put on your finger? Did you think I wouldn't see it?" he blazed. "Did you think I wouldn't notice the looks the two of you were exchanging and the way all the others watched the three of us?" He released her hand in a violent gesture of disgust. Dina nursed the pain-numbed fingers, cradling them in her right hand. "And neither of you had the guts to tell me!"

"Neither of us really had a chance," she responded defensively, her temper flaring from the flame of his. "It isn't an announcement one wants to make in front of others. What was I supposed to say when I saw you standing in the doorway, a husband I thought was dead? 'Darling, I'm so glad you're alive. Oh, by the way, I'm engaged to another man.' Please credit me for having a bit more delicacy than that!"

He gave her a long, hard look. His anger was so tightly controlled that it almost frightened her. It was like looking at a capped volcano, knowing that inside it was erupting, and wondering when the lid would blow.

"This is some homecoming," Blake declared in a contemptuous breath. "A wife who wishes I were still in the grave!"

"I don't wish that," she denied.

"This engagement—" he began, bitter sarcasm coating his words.

"The way you say it makes it sound like something sordid," Dina protested, "and it isn't. Chet and I have been engaged for barely more than a week. At the time that he proposed to me, I thought you were dead and I was free to accept."

52

"Now you know differently. I'm alive. You're my wife, not my widow. You're still married to me." The way he said it, in such cold, concise tones, made it sound like a life sentence.

Dina was trembling and she didn't know why. "I'm aware of that, Blake." Her voice was taut to keep out the tremors. "But this isn't the time to discuss the situation. Your mother is waiting dinner and I still have to get dressed."

For a few harrowing seconds, she thought he was going to argue. "Yes," he agreed slowly, "this isn't the time."

She heard the door being yanked open and flinched as it was slammed shut. If this was a new beginning for their marriage, it was off to a rotten start. They had argued before Blake had disappeared, and now war had nearly been declared on his return. Dina shuddered and walked to the closet again.

Her arrival downstairs coincided with Deirdre's announcement that dinner would be served. Blake was there to escort her into the formal dining room. A chandelier of cut crystal and polished brass hung above the table, glittering down on the Irish linen tablecloth set with the best of his mother's silver and china. An elaborate floral arrangement sat in the center of the buffet, not too near the table so its scent would not interfere with the aroma of the food. Blake was being warmly welcomed home, by everyone but her, and Dina was painfully conscious of the fact.

As they all took their chairs around the Danish styled dining table, the tension in the air was almost electrical. Yet Dina seemed to be the only one who noticed it. Blake sat at the head of the table, the place of honor, with his mother at the opposite end and Chet seated on her right. Dina sat on Blake's left.

Ever since she had come down, Blake had possessively kept her at his side, as if showing everyone that she was his and effectively separating her from Chet. On the surface, he seemed all smiles, at times giving her glimpses of his former devastating charm. But there was still anger smoldering in his brown eyes whenever his gaze was directed to her.

When everyone was seated, the housekeeper came in carrying a tureen of soup. "I fixed your favorite, Mr. Blake," she announced, a beaming smile on her square-jawed face. "Cream of asparagus."

"Bless you, Deidre." He smiled broadly. "Now that's the way to welcome a man home!"

The sharp side of his double-edged remark sliced at Dina. She paled at the censure, but otherwise retained a firm hold on her poise.

The meal was an epicurean's delight, from the soup to the lobster thermidor to the ambrosia of fresh fruit. Blake made all the right comments and compliments, but Dina noticed he didn't seem to savor the taste of the various dishes the way she remembered he had in the past. She had the impression that dining had been reduced to the simple matter of eating. Food was food however it was prepared, and man needed food to live.

Coffee was served in the living room so Deirdre could clear away the dishes. Again Dina was kept at

Blake's elbow. Chet was on the far side of the room. As she glanced his way, he looked up, smoke blue eyes meeting the clear blue of hers. He murmured a quick excuse to the older woman who had him cornered—a Mrs. Burnside, an old school friend of Norma Chandler—and made his way toward her.

Through the cover of her lashes, Dina dared a glance at Blake and saw the faint narrowing of his gaze as Chet approached. The smile on Chet's face was strained when he stopped in front of them. Dina guessed he was trying to find a way to tell Blake of their engagement and she wished there was a way to let him know that Blake was aware of it.

"It seems like old times, Blake," Chet began, forcing a camaraderie into his voice, "coming over to your house for dinner and seeing you and . . . ." His gaze slid nervously to Dina.

"Chet," Blake interrupted calmly, "Dina has told me about your engagement."

The room grew so quiet Dina was certain a feather could have been heard dropping on the carpet. All eyes were focused on the trio, as if a brilliant spotlight were shining on them. She discovered that, like everyone else, she was holding her breath. After the savage anger Blake had displayed upstairs, she wasn't sure what might happen next.

"I'm glad you know. I . . . ." Chet lowered his gaze searching for words.

Blake filled in the moment's pause. "I want you to know I don't bear any ill feelings. You've always been a good friend and I'd like it to continue that way." Dina started to sigh with relief. "After all, what are friends for?"

No one except Dina seemed to pay any attention to the last caustic comment. Chet was too busy shaking the hand Blake offered in friendship. The others were murmuring among themselves about the moment for which they had been waiting all day.

"Naturally the engagement is broken," Blake joked with a smile that contrasted with the sharply serious light in his eyes.

"Naturally," Chet agreed with an answering smile.

And Dina felt a rush of anger that she could be tossed aside so readily without protest. For that matter, she hadn't even been consulted about her wishes.

Immediately she berated herself. It was what she wanted. Blake was alive and she was married to him. She didn't want to divorce him to marry Chet, so why was she fussing? A simple matter of ego, she decided.

After the confrontation over the engagement, the party became anticlimactic. There was a steady trickle of departures among the guests. One minute Dina was wishing Mrs. Burnside goodbye and the next she was alone in the foyer with Blake, his eyes watching her in that steady, measured way she found so unnerving.

"That's the last of them," he announced.

Dina glanced around. "Where's your mother?"

"In the living room helping Deirdre clean up."

"I'll give them a hand." She started to turn away.

But Blake caught her arm. "There's no need." He released it as quickly as he had captured it. "They can handle it by themselves."

Dina didn't protest. The day had been unconscionably long and she felt enervated from the physical and mental stress she had experienced. What she really wanted was a long night of hard, dreamless sleep. She started for the stairs, half aware that Blake was following.

"You didn't return Chet's ring," he reminded her in a flat tone.

Raising her left hand, she glanced at the flowerlike circlet of diamonds. "No, I . . . must have forgotten." She was too tired at this point to care about such a small detail.

When she started to lower her hand, Blake seized it and stripped the ring from her finger before she could react to stop him. He gave it a careless toss onto the polished mahogany table standing against the foyer wall.

"You can't leave valuable things lying around!" Dina instantly retrieved it, clutching it in her hand as she frowned at him—Blake, who insisted there was a place for everything and everything in its place.

"Valuable to whom?" he questioned with cool arrogance.

Her fingers tightened around the ring. "I'll keep it in my room until I can give it back to him." She waited for him to challenge her decision. When he didn't, she walked to the stairs.

"He'll be over tomorrow," Blake stated, speaking from directly behind her. "You can give it to him then."

"What time is he coming?" Dina climbed the stairs knowing she was loath to return the ring when

Blake was around, but he seemed to be leaving her little option.

"At ten for Sunday brunch."

At the head of the stairs, Dina turned. Her bedroom was the first door on the right. She walked to it only to have Blake's arm reach around her to open the door. She stopped abruptly as he pushed it open, her look bewildered.

"What are you doing?" She frowned.

"I'm going to bed." An eyebrow flickered upward as he eyed her coolly. "Where did you think I was going to sleep?"

She looked away, her gaze darting madly around. She was thrown into a trembling state of confusion by his taunting question. "I didn't think about it," she faltered. "I guess I've become used to sleeping alone."

His hand was at the small of her back, firmly directing her into the room. "Surely you don't expect that to continue?"

"I . . . ." Oh, God, yes she did. Dina realized with a frozen start. "I think it might be better . . . for a while." She stopped in the center of the room and turned to face him as he closed the door.

"You do?" Inscrutable brown eyes met her wavering look, his leathery, carved features expressionless.

"Yes, I do."

Her nerves were leaping around as erratically as jumping beans, not helped by the palpitating beat of her heart. She watched with growing apprehension as Blake peeled off his suit jacket and tie and began unbuttoning his shirt.

She tried to reason with him, her voice quivering. "Blake, it's been two and a half years."

"Tell me about it," he inserted dryly.

Her throat tightened to make her voice small. "I don't know you anymore. You're a stranger to me."

"That can be changed."

"You aren't trying to understand, Blake." Dina fought to keep control of herself. "I can't just hop into bed with—"

"Your husband?" he finished the sentence, and gave her a searing look. "Who else would you choose?"

The shirt was coming off, exposing a naked chest and shoulder tanned the same dusky shade as his face. The result heightened Dina's impression of a primitive male, powerful and dangerous, sinewy muscles rippling in the artificial light.

Her senses catapulted in alarm as she felt the force of his earthly, pagan attraction. In an attempt to break the black magic of its spell, she turned away, walking stiffly to her dresser to place Chet's ring in her jewel case.

"No one. That isn't what I meant." She remained at the dresser, her hands flattened on its top, knuckles showing white. He came up behind her and she lifted her gaze. In the dressing-table mirror her wary eyes saw his reflection join with hers. "You've become hard, Blake, a cynic," she said accusingly. "I can imagine what you've gone through...."

"Can you?" There was a faint curl of his lip. "Can you imagine how many nights I held onto my sanity by clinging to the vision of a blue-eyed woman with corn-silk hair?" His fingers twined themselves through the loose strands of her pale gold hair and Dina closed her eyes at the savage note in his voice. "Roughly nine hundred and twenty-two nights. And when I finally see her again, she's clinging to the arm of my best friend. Is it any wonder that I'm hard, bitter, when I've been waiting all this time for her lips to kiss away the gnawing memory of those hours? Did you even miss me, Dina?" With a handful of hair as leverage, he twisted her around to face him. "Did you grieve?"

Her eyes smarted with tears she refused to shed at the tugging pain in her scalp. "When you first disappeared, Blake, I was nearly beside myself with fear. But your mother was even more distraught—losing her husband, then possibly you. I had to spend most of my time comforting her. Then the company started to fall apart at the seams and Chet insisted I had to take over or it would fail. So I was plunged headfirst into another world. During the day I was too busy to think about myself, and at night there was your mother depending on me to be her strength. The only moments I had alone were in this room. And I took sleeping pills so I would get enough rest to able to get through another day. To be truthful, Blake, I didn't have time to grieve."

He was unmoved by her words, his dark eyes flat and cold. "But you had time for Chet," he accused her with icy calm.

Dina winced as the point of his arrow found its target. "It began very innocently. He was your closest friend so it was natural that he kept in touch with your mother and me. Later, there was the company connection. He was always there, bolstering me, encouraging me, and offering me a shoulder to lean on the odd moments that I needed it, without mauling me in return," she explained, refusing to sound guilty. "It grew from there after you were reported killed. I needed him."

"And I need you—now." He drew her inside the steel circle of his hands, flattening her against his chest.

The hard feel of his naked flesh beneath her hands rocked her senses. The warmth of his breath wafted over her averted face, the musky scent of him enveloping her. She pushed at his arms, straining to break out of his hold.

"You haven't listened to a word I've said!" she stormed angrily, inwardly battling against his physical arousal of her senses. "You've changed. I've changed. We need time to adjust!"

"Adjust to what?" Blake snapped. "The differences between a man and a woman? Those are differences we could discover and compensate for very quickly." The zipper of her dress was instantly undone.

"Stop it!" She struggled to keep him from sliding the dress off her shoulders. "You're making me feel like an animal!"

"You are. We both are animals, species Homosapiens." The words were issued in a cold, insensitive tone. "Put on this earth to sleep, eat and breed, to live and die. I learned in the jungle that that's the essence of our existence."

Hysterical laughter gurgled in her throat. "Oh, my God." Dina choked on the sound. "That sounds like 'You Tarzan, me Jane!'"

61

"Eliminate the trappings of society and the pretty words and that's what it comes down to in the end."

"No, our minds are more fully developed. We have feelings, emotions," she protested. "We ...."

The dress was stripped away despite her efforts.

"Shut up!" He growled the order against her mouth and smothered the sounds when she refused to obey.

Leaning and twisting backward, Dina tried to escape the domination of his kiss, but his hands used the attempt to mold her lower body more fully to his length, her hipbones crushed by oak-solid thighs. The silk of her slip was a second skin, concealing and revealing while callused fingers moved roughly around in exploration.

Cruelly, Blake ravaged the softness of her lips. Dina thought her neck would snap under his driving force. Beneath her straining hands she felt the flexing of his muscles, smooth like hammered steel, latent in their sensuality. He was devouring her strength by degrees, slowly and steadily wearing her down. Doubling her fingers, she began hammering at him with her fists, puny blows that had little effect.

The effort seemed to use up the reserves of her strength. Within seconds, a blackness swam in front of her eyes and a dizzying weakness spread through her limbs. Her fingers dug into his shoulders and she clung to him to keep from falling into the yawning abyss that seemed to be opening in front of her.

As her resistance ebbed into nothingness, so did the brutality of his assault. The terrible bruising pressure of his mouth eased, permitting Dina to straighten her neck. Gradually she began to surface from the waves of semiconsciousness, enough to become aware of his loosened hold.

With a determined effort, she broke out of his arms. Gasping in air in panicked breaths, she backed away from him, her knees quivering. Blake swayed toward her, then stopped. A second later she realized why, as her retreat was stopped short by a wall. A cornered animal, she stared at the man who held her at bay. A stranger who was her husband.

She lifted her head, summoning all her pride to beg, "Don't do this, Blake."

Slow, silent strides carried him to her and she didn't attempt to flee. There was no mercy in his eyes and she would not submit to the ignominy of cowering. Her resistance became passive as he undressed, her eyes tightly closed.

"Are you choosing to portray the martyred wife submitting to the bestiality of her husband?" Blake taunted. "This display of frigidity is a farce. My memory wasn't damaged. I remember, too well, what a passionate lover you are."

Dina paled as she remembered, too. A flicker of the old searing fire licked through her veins as he drew her to him and her bare curves came in contact with his nude body. The tiny flame couldn't catch hold, not when the hands fanning it were callused and rough instead of the smooth, manicured hands that had once brought it to a full blaze.

"Don't destroy our marriage," she whispered, trying not to see the curling, sun-bleached hairs forming a pale cloud against the burnished bronze of his chest. "I want to love you again, Blake."

With a muffled imprecation, he buried his face in her hair. "Damn you! Why didn't you say that when I came home?" he muttered thickly in a rasping sound that suggested pain. "Why did you have to wait until now?"

"Would it have mattered?" Dina caught back a sob.

"It might have then." Effortlessly he swung her off her feet into his arms, his jaw set in a ruthless line. "I couldn't care less now. You're mine and I mean to have you."

The overhead light was switched off, throwing the room into darkness. As if guided by animal instinct, Blake carried her to the bed. Without bothering to pull down the covers, he laid her on the bed and towered beside it.

"Blake." There was an unspoken plea in the way she spoke his name, a last attempt to make him understand her unwillingness.

"No," he answered, and the mattress sagged under his weight. "Don't ask me to wait." His low voice was commanding near her ear, his breath stirring her hair. "It's been too long."

And we both have changed, Dina thought, stiffening at the moist touch of his mouth along her neck. *Can't you see the differences, Blake? Physical as well as mental. Haven't you noticed I'm wearing my hair longer?* As his hand slid over her ribs, to cup her breast, she remembered when the roundness had filled it. Now, with maturity, it overflowed.

But Blake seemed intent on discovering the ripeness of her female form, ignoring comparisons. His caressing hands roamed over her with intimate

64

familiarity and she felt her body responding, reluctantly at first. A series of long, drugging kisses soon made her mind blank to all but the demands of her flesh.

Her senses took over, reigning supreme. She gloried in the taste of his lips probing the sensual hollows of her mouth and the brush of the soft, curling hairs on his chest hardening her nipples into erotic pebbles.

The rapidly increasing throb of her pulse was in tempo with the pagan beat of his, building to a climax. And the heady male scent of him, heightened by perspiration and his rising body heat, served to stimulate all her senses until she was filled with nothing but him.

For a time she glimpsed heights she had thought she would never see again. Blake sought all the places that brought her the most pleasure, waiting until she moaned his name in final surrender.

CHAPTER FOUR

DINA LAY IN BED, the covers pulled up to her neck, but she knew the blankets couldn't warm the chill. Her passion spent, she felt cold and empty inside as she stared upward into the darkness of the room. A tear was frozen on an eyelash.

Physically her desires had been satisfied by Blake's skilled knowledge, but she had not been lifted to the rapturous heights of a spiritual union. That only happened when there was love involved. Tonight it had been merely a mutual satisfaction of sexual desires. And that special something that had been missing eliminated the warm afterglow Dina had previously known.

Blake was beside her, their bodies not touching. An arm was flung on the pillow above his head. She could hear the steady sound of his breathing, but doubted that he was asleep. Her sideways glance sought his carved profile in the dim light. There seemed to be a grim line to his mouth, as if he was experiencing the same reaction.

As if feeling her look and hearing her question, he said in a low, flat voice, "There's one argument you didn't make, Dina. If you had, it might have prevented this disillusionment."

"What is it?" she asked in a tight, throbbing voice, longing to know what it was so she could keep this from happening again.

"The real thing can't match two and a half years of expectations."

No, she agreed silently, *not when there are no words of love exchanged, no mating of our hearts nor coming together of our souls.* It had been an act of lust, born out of anger and frustration.

"Passion never can, Blake," she murmured.

He tossed aside the blanket draped across his waist and swung his feet to the floor. Her head turned on the pillow to stare at him in the darkness.

"Where are you going?" she asked softly. Something told her that if Blake would hold her in his arms, the aching void inside her might close.

There was a faint sheen to his sun-browned skin in the shadowy light. She could make out the breadth of his shoulders and the back muscles tapering to his waist. His steps were soundless, silent animal strides.

"Another unfortunate discovery I've made since returning to civilization is that the mattresses are too soft." He spoke in a low voice, a biting, cynical tone. "I'm used to firm beds. That's what comes from spending too many nights sleeping in trees and on hard ground."

She lost him in the darkness and propped herself up on an elbow, keeping the covers tightly around her. "Where are you going?"

"To find a spare blanket and a hard floor." There was the click of the door being opened. "You have part of your wish, Dina," he added caustically. "The bed is yours. You can sleep alone."

As the door closed, a convulsive shudder ran through her. She turned her face into the pillow, curling her body into a tight ball of pain. With eyes squeezed shut, she lay there, aching for the forgetfulness of sleep.

A HAND GENTLY but persistently shook her shoulder. "Mrs. Blake? Wake up, please." Dina stirred, lashes fluttering as she tried to figure out whether or not she was imagining the voice. "Wake up, Mrs. Blake!"

But she wasn't imagining the hand on her arm. Her head throbbed dully as she opened her eyes and rolled over, dragging the covers with her. Her sleepy gaze focused on the agitated expression of the housekeeper hovering above her.

Dina became conscious of several things at once: the rumpled pillow beside her where Blake had lain so briefly, her own naked state beneath the covers, and the clothes scattered around the room—hers and Blake's. *My God, the room is a mess*, she thought.

"What is it, Deirdre?" she questioned, trying to maintain a measure of composure despite the surge of embarrassment.

The older woman bit her lip as if uncertain how to reply. "It's Mr. Blake."

The anxious look on the housekeeper's face brought an instant reaction as Dina propped herself up on her elbows, concern chasing away the remnants of sleep. "Blake? What's wrong? Has something happened to him?"

"No, it's . . . it's just that he's sleeping downstairs—on the floor in the library." A dull red was creeping up her neck into her cheeks. "And he isn't wearing any...any pajamas."

Dina swallowed back a smile, her relief lost in amusement. Poor Deirdre Schneider, she thought, never married in her life nor seriously close to it and probably shocked to her prim core when she found Blake sleeping in the library in the altogether.

"I see," she nodded, and tried to keep her face straight.

"Mr. Stanton will be arriving in just more than an hour." The woman was trying desperately to avoid looking at the bareness of Dina's shoulders. "I thought you should be the one to . . . to wake up Mr. Blake."

"I will," said Dina, and started to rise, then decided against adding to the housekeeper's embarrassment. "Would you hand me my robe at the foot of the bed, Deirdre?"

After handing the robe to her, the housekeeper turned discreetly away while Dina slipped into it. "Mrs. Chandler had a few things sent over yesterday for Mr. Blake," she informed Dina. "There are pajamas and a robe. I put them in the empty closet."

"I'll take them to him." Dina finished tying the sash of her robe. "And, Deirdre, tomorrow I think you'd better make arrangements with Mrs. Chandler to purchase a bed with a very firm mattress, one that's as hard as a rock."

"I will," Deirdre promised as if taking an oath. "Sorry to have awakened you, Mrs. Blake."

"That's quite all right, Deirdre," Dina answered, smiling.

With a brief self-conscious nod, the housekeeper left the room. Dina put on her slippers and walked to the small closet Deirdre had indicated. It was used mostly for storage. Amid the few boxes and garment bags hung three shirts and a brown suit. On the two inside door hooks were the pajamas and matching dressing robe in a muted shade of cranberry silk. Leaving the pajamas, Dina took the robe.

Downstairs, her hand hesitated on the knob of the library door. Tension hammered in her temples and her stomach was twisted into knots. Steeling herself to ignore the attack of nervousness, she opened the door quietly and walked in. Her gaze was directed first to the floor and its open area around the fireplace.

"Deirdre sent in the reserves, I see," Blake's male voice mocked from the side of the room.

Dina turned in its direction and saw him standing near the solid wall of shelves filled with books. A dark green blanket was wrapped around his waist, his naked torso gleaming in that deep shade of tan. Fingers had combed his thick brown hair into a semblance of order, a suggestion of unruliness remaining. Dina's pulse fluctuated in alarm, her head lifted as if scenting danger. He looked like a primitive native, proud, noble and savage.

"Did you hear her come in?" She realized it was a foolish question after she had asked it. Those long months in the jungle had to have sharpened his senses, making them more acute.

"Yes, but I decided it was wiser to pretend I was still asleep rather than shock her sensibilities," he admitted with cynical derision. "I thought she would scamper up the stairs to inform you or my mother of my lewd behavior."

Behind his veiled look Dina felt the dark intensity of his gaze scanning her face—searching for something, but she didn't know what. It made her uncomfortable and she wished she had dressed before coming down.

"I brought you a robe." She held it out to him aware of the faint trembling that wasn't yet visible.

"No doubt at Deirdre's suggestion. She must have been more shocked than I thought." But Blake made no move toward it, forcing Dina to walk to him.

"Deirdre isn't accustomed to finding naked men sleeping on the library floor," she said, defending the housekeeper's reaction and discovering a similar one in herself as Blake reached down to unwrap the blanket from around his waist. Self-consciously she averted her eyes, her color mounting as if it were a stranger undressing in front of her instead of her husband.

There was a rustle of silk, then, "It's safe to look now," Blake taunted, his mouth curving in ungentle mockery.

She flashed him an angry look for drawing attention to her sudden burst of modesty and turned away. The vein in her neck pulsed with a nervousness that she wasn't able to control. His hand touched her shoulder and she flinched from the searing contact.

"For God's sake, Dina, I'm not going to rape you!" he cursed beneath his breath. "Dammit, can't I even touch my wife?"

Her blue eyes were wide and wary as she looked over her shoulder at his fiercely burning gaze. "I

71

don't feel like your wife, Blake," she said tightly. "I don't feel as if I'm married to you."

Immediately the fires were banked in his eyes, that freezing control that was so unlike him coming into play. "You are married to me," he stated, and walked by her to the door. Opening it, he called, "Deirdre! Bring some coffee into the library for my wife and myself." With emphasis on "wife."

"Chet is coming and I still have to dress." Dina reminded him, objecting to spending more minutes alone with him.

"He isn't due for an hour," Blake said, dismissing her protest, and walked to the leather-covered sofa, pausing beside its end table to lift the lid of the ceramic cigarette box. "Cigarette?" He flicked a questioning glance in her direction.

"No, I don't smoke. Remember?" she said with a faintly taunting arch to her voice.

"You might have acquired the habit during my absence," he shrugged.

"I didn't."

Brisk footsteps in the foyer signaled the housekeeper's approach. Seconds later she entered the library with a coffee service and two china cups on the tray she carried. A pink tint was still rouging her cheeks as Deirdre steadfastly avoided looking directly at Blake.

"Where would you like the tray?" she asked Dina.

"The table by the sofa will be fine."

Blake carried the ceramic table lighter to the cigarette in his mouth and snapped the flame to its tip. Smoke spiraled upward and he squinted his eyes against it. Despite his show of disinterest, Dina knew he was aware of the housekeeper's every movement. After setting the tray on the table at the opposite end of the sofa from where Blake stood, Deirdre straightened up erectly.

"Will there be anything else?" Again her query was directed to Dina.

It was Blake who answered. "That will be all," he said, exhaling a thin trail of smoke. "And close the door on your way out, Deirdre."

"Yes, sir." Two red flags dotted her cheeks.

As Deirdre made a hasty exit, firmly closing the door, Blake walked to the tray. Lifting the coffee pot, he filled the two cups and offered one to Dina.

"Black, as I remember, with no sugar," he said in a tone that baited.

"Yes, thank you." Dina refused to bite as she took the cup and saucer from his hand.

Scalding steam rose from the brown liquid and Blake let his cup sit. He studied the glowing tip of his cigarette and the gossamer-thin white smoke rising upward. A wry smile crooked his mouth.

"I'd forgotten how good a cigarette can taste first thing in the morning," he mused.

Dina felt as edgy as a cat with its tail caught in a vise. She couldn't help retorting, "I thought you hadn't forgotten anything."

"Not the important things, I haven't," Blake replied, levelly meeting her irritated glance.

With a broken sigh, she wandered to the library window overlooking the expansive front lawn of the house and the cul-de-sac of its driveway. She was caught by the memory of the last time she had stared out the window in troubled silence. Oddly, it seemed an eternity ago instead of the short time that it was.

"What are you thinking about?" Blake was close, only a scant few feet behind her.

"I was merely remembering the last time I stood at this window." She sipped at the hot coffee.

"When was that?" He seemed only idly curious.

Dina felt his gaze roaming her shapely length as surely as if he touched her, and stiffened to answer bluntly, "The night of my engagement party to Chet."

"Forget about him." The command was crisp and impatient, as Dina guessed it would be.

"It isn't that easy to turn back the clock," she muttered tightly.

The cup nearly slipped from her fingers as she felt the rasping brush of his fingers against her hair. Her throat constricted, shutting off her voice and her breath.

"Have I told you I like your hair this length?" His low voice was a husky caress running down her spine.

He lifted aside the molten gold of her hair, pushing it away from her neck. The warmth of his breath against her skin warned her an instant before she glimpsed the waving darkness of his hair in her side vision.

His unerring mouth sought and found the ultrasensitive and vulnerable spot at the base of her neck. Her heart felt as though it had been knocked sideways, and Blake took full advantage of her Achilles' heel. She felt boneless as her head tipped down and to the side to give him freer access.

The cup rattled in its saucer, but she managed to hold on to it. His arms wound around her waist to mold her back to his muscular length. For a magic second she was transported back to another time. Then a roughened hand slid under the overlapping fold of her robe to encircle the swell of her breast, a callused finger teasing its nipple, and the arms felt suddenly strange.

"Blake, no!" Weakly she tugged at his wrist, no match for his strength.

She gasped as his sensual mouth moved upward to her ear, and desire licked through her veins at the darting probe of his tongue. An all-pervading weakness went through her limbs. It was a dizzying sensation, wild drums pounding in her ears.

"Do you remember the way we used to make love in the mornings?" Blake murmured against her temple.

"Yes," she moaned, the memory all too vivid.

The cup disappeared from her hand, carried away by a fluid movement of Blake's hand. It took only the slightest pressure to turn her around. She was drawn to his side, a muscular, silk-covered thigh insinuating itself between her legs as she was arched against him. She lifted her head, subconsciously braced for the punishment of his rough kisses. Her fingers curled into his shoulders for support.

There was the tantalizing touch of his lips against hers. "After last night, I thought I had you out of my system," he said against them, "but I want you more than before."

A half sob came from her throat at the absence of

any mention of love. In the next second she didn't care, as his mouth closed over hers with sweet pressure. There was no plundering demand, only a persuasive exhorting to respond.

Her lips parted willingly, succumbing to the rapturous mastery of his exploration. The dream world of sensation seemed almost enough. She slid her fingers through the springing thickness of his hair, the scent of him earthy and clean.

As if tired of bending his head to reach her lips, Blake tightened his arm around her waist to lift her straight up, bringing her to eye level. It was another indication of his increased strength, that he should carry her weight so effortlessly. At the moment, Dina was oblivious to this example of his change.

His mouth blazed a moist trail downward to explore the pulsing vein in her neck. "Did Chet ever make you feel like this?" An attempt to exorcise the memory of Chet's kisses from her mind? Had it been motivated by nothing more than that? She pushed out of his hold, staring at him with wounded pride.

"Did he?" Blake repeated, a faintly ragged edge to his breathing.

"You'll never know," she answered in a choked voice. "Maybe he made me feel better."

He took a threatening step toward her, his features dark with rage. There was nowhere for Dina to retreat. She had to stand her ground, despite its indefensibility. Just then there was a knock at the door. Blake halted, casting an angry glance at the door.

"Who is it?" he demanded.

The door opened and Chet walked in. "I'm a bit early, but Deirdre said you were in here having coffee. She's going to bring me a cup." He stopped, as if sensing the heaviness in the atmosphere. "I didn't think you'd mind if I joined you." But it was something of a question.

"Of course not." Dina was quick to use him as a buffer.

"Come in, Chet," Blake continued the invitation. "Speak of the devil, Dina and I were just talking about you."

"Something good, I hope," Chet joked stiffly.

"Yes." Blake's dark gaze swung to Dina, a considering grimness in their depths. "Yes, it was." But he didn't explain what it had been.

She started breathing again, her hand sliding up to her throat. She became conscious of her partially clothed state and used it as an excuse to leave.

"If you two don't mind, I'll leave you to have coffee alone," she said.

"I hope you aren't going on my account," Chet said, frowning.

"No," Dina assured him quickly, avoiding Blake's mocking look. "I was going upstairs anyway to dress before Deirdre serves brunch. I'll be down shortly."

As Dina left, she met Deirdre bringing the extra cup for Chet. The housekeeper's composure was under admirable control now and she was her usual calm-faced self.

Once she was dressed, Dina slipped Chet's ring into the pocket of her dirndl skirt. At some point during the day she hoped to have the chance to return it to him while they were alone. But it was late afternoon before the opportunity presented itself.

THE PRESS HAD LEARNED of Blake's return and the house was in a state of siege for the greater part of the day. Either the doorbell or the telephone seemed to be ringing constantly. Blake had to grant interviews to obtain any peace, but his answers were concise, without elaboration, downplaying his ordeal. As his wife, Dina was forced to be at his side, while Chet adopted the role of press secretary and spokesman for the Chandler company.

Finally, at four o'clock, the siege seemed to be over and a blessed quietness began to settle over the house. Norma Chandler, who had insisted that coffee and sweets be served to all those who had come, was busy helping Deirdre clear away the mess.

The ringing of the telephone signaled a last interview for Blake, one conducted over the phone. Dina had started helping the other two women clean up. When she noticed Chet slip away to the library, she excused herself, knowing she might not have another chance to speak to him alone.

As she stepped inside the library, she saw him pouring whiskey from a crystal decanter over ice cubes in a squat glass. The engagement ring seemed to be burning a circle in her pocket.

"Would you pour me a sherry, Chet?" She quietly closed the door, shutting out Blake's voice coming from the living room.

Chet's sandy blond head lifted, his surprised look

vanishing into a smile when he say her. "Of course." He reached for another glass and a different decanter. Pouring, he remarked, "It's been quite a hectic day."

"Yes, it has." Dina walked over to take the sherry glass from his hand.

Ice clinked as Chet lifted his glass to take a quick swallow of whiskey. "A reporter that I know from one of the local papers called and got me out of bed this morning. He'd gotten wind that there was a shake-up in the Chandler hotel chain and he wanted to know what it was. I pleaded ignorance. But that's why I rushed over here so early, to warn Blake that the onslaught was coming. I knew it was only a matter of time before they found out."

"Yes." She nodded in agreement, glad there had been no announcement of their engagement in the newspaper or the reporters would have turned Blake's return into a circus.

"Blake really knows how to handle himself with the press," Chet stated with undisguised admiration.

"Yes, he does." Dina sipped at her drink.

"And it will make good publicity for the hotels," he added.

"Yes." She was beginning to feel like a puppet whose string was being pulled to nod agreement to everything Chet said—when it really wasn't what she wanted to talk about at all.

"I imagine somebody in the company let it slip about Blake." He stared thoughtfully at the amber liquid in his glass. "I called around to all the major officers yesterday to let them know he was back. That's probably how the word got out."

"Probably," Dina agreed, and promptly took the initiative to lead into her own subject. "Chet, I've been wanting to see you today, alone—" she reached in her pocket to take out the circlet of diamonds "—to return this to you."

He took it from her outstretched hand, looking boyishly uncomfortable. His thumb rubbed it between his fingers as he stared at it, not meeting the sapphire brightness of her gaze.

"I don't want you to get the idea that I was deserting you yesterday." His voice was uncertain, almost apologetic. "But I know how you felt about Blake and I didn't want to stand in the way of your happiness."

With the explanation given for the way he had so readily abandoned their engagement, Chet lifted his head to gaze at her earnestly, a troubled shade of clouded blue in his eyes. Affection rushed through Dina at his unselfishness, sacrificing his wants for hers.

"I understand, Chet."

Relief glimmered in his smile. "You must really be glad to have him back."

"I . . . ." She started to repeat the positive assertion she had been making all day, ready to recite the words automatically, but she stopped herself. Among other things, Chet was her best friend, as well as Blake's. With him she could speak her mind. "He's changed, Chet."

He hesitated for a second before answering, as if her response had caught him off guard and he wanted to word his reply carefully.

"Considering all Blake has been through, it's bound to have left a mark on him," he offered.

"I know, but . . . ." She sighed, agitated and frustrated because she couldn't find the words to explain exactly what she meant.

"Hey, come on now," Chet cajoled, setting his glass down and grasping her gently by the shoulders, his head bent down to peer into her apprehensive face. "When two people care as much about each other as you and Blake do, they're bound to work out their differences. It just can't happen overnight," he reasoned. "Now come on. What do you say? Let's have a little smile. You know it's true that nothing is ever as bad as it seems."

Mountains and molehills. Reluctantly almost, her lips curved at his coaxing words. His steadying influence was having its effect on her again.

"That's my girl!" he grinned.

"Oh, Chet," Dina declared with a laughing sigh, and wrapped her arms lightly around him, taking care not to spill her drink. She hugged him fondly. "What would I do without you?" She drew her head back to gaze at him.

"I hope neither of us has to find out," he remarked, and affectionately kissed the top of her nose.

The knob turned and the library door was pushed open by Blake. At the sight of Dina in Chet's arms he froze, and the same paralysis gripped her. She paled as she saw his lips thin into an angry line.

But the violence of his emotion wasn't detectable in his voice as he remarked casually, "Is this a private party or can anyone join?"

His question broke the chains holding Dina

motionless. She withdrew her arms from around Chet to hold her sherry glass in both hands. Chet turned to greet him, insensitive to the heightening tension in the air.

"Now that you're here, Blake, we can drink a toast to the last of the newspaper reporters," he announced in a celebrating tone, not displaying any self-consciousness about the scene Blake had interrupted.

"For a while anyway," Blake agreed, his gaze swinging to Dina. "What are you drinking?"

"Sherry." There would be no explosion now, Dina realized. Blake would wait until they were alone.

"I'll have the same."

It was late that evening before Chet left. Each dragging minute in the interim honed Dina's nerves to a razor-thin edge. By the time he had left, she could no longer stand the suspense of waiting for the confrontation with Blake.

With the revving of Chet's car coming from the driveway, Dina paused in the foyer to challenge Blake. "Aren't you going to say it?"

He didn't pretend an ignorance of her question, his gaze hard and unrelenting. "Stay away from Chet."

All the blame for the innocent encounter was placed on her, and she reacted with indignant outrage. "And what about Chet?"

"I know Chet well enough to be assured he isn't going to trespass, unless encouraged, on my territory."

"So I'm supposed to avoid him, is that it?" she flashed.

"Whatever relationship you had with him in my absence is finished," Blake declared in a frigid tone. "From now on he's simply an acquaintance of mine. That's all he is to you."

"That's impossible!" She derided his suggestion that she could dismiss Chet from her life with a snap of her fingers. "I can't forget all he's meant to me that easily."

A pair of iron clamps dug into the soft flesh of her arms and she was jerked to him, the breath knocked out of her by the hard contact with the solid wall of his chest. Her lips were crushed by the angry fire of his kiss, a kiss that seared his brand of possession on her and burned away any memory of another's mouth.

Dina was released from his punishing embrace with equal force. Shaken and unnerved, she retreated a step. With the back of her hand she tried to rub away the fiery imprint of his mouth.

"You—" she began with impotent rage.

"Don't push me, Dina!" Blake warned.

They glared at each other in thundering silence. Dina had no idea how long the battle of wills would have continued if his mother hadn't entered the foyer seconds later. Each donned a mask to conceal their personal conflict from her eyes.

"Deidre just told me you'd asked her to bring some blankets to the library, Blake." Norma Chandler was wearing a frown. "You aren't going to sleep there again tonight, are you?"

"Yes, I am, mother," he responded decisively.

"But it's so uncivilized," she protested.

"Perhaps," Blake conceded, for an instant meeting Dina's look. "It's also infinitely preferable to not sleeping."

"I suppose so." His mother sighed her reluctant agreement. "Good night, dear."

"Good night, mother," he returned, and coldly arched an eyebrow at Dina. "Good night."

CHAPTER FIVE

THE LIBRARY DOOR stood open when Dina came down the stairs the next morning. She smoothed a nervous hand over her cream linen skirt and walked to the dining room where breakfast coffee and juice were already on the table. But there was no sign of Blake. Dina helped herself to juice and coffee and sat down.

"Isn't Blake having breakfast this morning?" she questioned the housekeeper when she appeared.

"No, ma'am," Deirdre replied. "He's already left. He said he was meeting Jake Stone for breakfast and going to the office from there. Didn't he tell you?"

"Yes, I believe he did," Dina lied, and forced a smile. "I must have forgotten."

"Mrs. Chandler was most upset about it," the woman remarked with a knowing nod.

Dina frowned. "Because Blake is meeting the attorney?"

"No, because he's going into the office. Mrs. Chandler thought he should wait a few days. I mean, he just came back and all, and right away he's going to work," Deirdre explained.

"He's probably anxious to see how everything is." There was a smug feeling of satisfaction that he would find the entire operation running smoothly knowing that a great deal of the credit was hers.

"What will you have this morning, Mrs. Blake? Shall I fix you an omelet?"

"I think I'll just have juice and coffee, Deirdre, thank you." She wanted to be at the office when Blake arrived to be able to see his face when he realized how capably she had managed in his absence.

"As you wish," the housekeeper sniffed in disapproval.

The morning traffic seemed heavier than usual and Dina chafed at the delay it caused. Still she arrived at the office building well within her usual time. As she stepped out of the elevator onto the floor the company occupied, she was relieved that Chet had already notified the various executive personnel of Blake's return and that she was spared that task. She would have time to go over her notes on the departmental meeting this afternoon and have much of the Monday morning routine handled before Blake arrived.

She breezed down the corridor to her office, keeping her pace brisk while she nodded greetings and returned good mornings to the various employees along the way. She didn't want to stop and chat with anyone and use up her precious time. She felt very buoyant as she entered the office of her private secretary.

"Good morning, Amy," she said cheerfully.

"Good morning, Mrs. Chandler." The young woman beamed back a smile. "You're in good spirits this morning."

"Yes, I am," Dina agreed. Her secretary was going through the morning mail and she walked to her desk to see if there was anything of importance she should know about before Blake arrived.

"Your good spirits wouldn't have anything to do with Mr. Chandler's coming back, would they?" Amy Wentworth inquired with a knowing twinkle. Dina wasn't obliged to make a comment as her secretary continued, "All of us here are so happy he's back safely."

"So am I, Amy," Dina nodded, and glanced over the girl's shoulder for a glimpse at the mail. "Anything special in the mail this morning?"

"Not so far," her secretary replied, returning her attention to the stack of letters.

"Any calls?"

"Only one. Mr. Van Patten called."

"Did he leave a message?" Dina asked, her quick perusal of the mail completed.

"Oh, no," Amy hastened to explain. "Mr. Chandler took the call."

"Mr. Chandler?" she repeated. "Do you mean Blake is already here?"

"Yes, he's in the office." Amy motioned towards Dina's private office. "I'm sure he won't mind if you go right on in, Mrs. Chandler."

For several seconds Dina was too stunned to speak. It was *her* office, her pride protested. And *her* secretary was grandly giving her permission to enter it. Blake had moved in and managed to convey the impression that she had moved out.

Her blue eyes darkened with rage. Turning on her heel, she walked to the private office. She didn't bother to knock, simply pushing the door open and walking in. Blake was seated behind the massive

87

walnut dest—*her* desk! He glanced up when she entered. The arrogantly inquiring lift of his eyebrow lit the fuse of her temper.

"What are you doing here?" she demanded.

"I was about to ask you the same question," countered Blake with infuriating calm.

"It happens to be *my* office and that's *my* secretary outside!" Dina retorted. Her flashing eyes saw the papers in his hands and she recognized the notes as those she had been going to go over for the departmental meeting that afternoon. "And those are *my* notes!"

He leaned back in the swivel chair, viewing her tirade with little emotion. "I was under the impression that all of this—" he waved his hand in an encompassing gesture "—belonged to the company."

"I happen to be in charge of the company," she reminded him.

"You *were* in charge of the company," Blake corrected her. "I'm taking over now."

She was trembling violently now, her anger almost uncontrollable. She fought to keep her voice low and not reveal how thoroughly he had aroused her.

"You're taking over," she repeated. "Just like that!" She snapped her fingers.

"Your job is done." Blake shrugged and fingered the papers on the desk. "And excellently, from all that I've seen this morning."

It was the compliment she had sought, but not delivered the way she had intended it to be. Therefore it brought no satisfaction; the thunder was stolen from her glory.

"And what am I supposed to do?" she demanded.

"Go home. Go back to being my wife." His sun-roughened features wore a frown, as if not understanding why she was so upset.

"And do what?" challenged Dina. "Twiddle my thumbs all day until you come home? Deirdre does all the cooking and the cleaning. It's your mother's house, Blake. There's nothing for me to do there."

"Then start looking for an apartment for us. Or better yet, a house of our own," he suggested. "That's what you wanted before, a place of our own that you could decorate the way you wanted it."

A part of her wanted it still, but it wasn't the motivating force in her life. "That was before, Blake," she argued. "I've changed. If we did have a house and the decorating was all done the way I wanted it, what would I do then? Sit around and admire my handiwork? No, I enjoy my work here. It's demanding and fulfilling."

He was sitting in the chair, watching her with narrowed eyes. "What you're saying is you enjoy the power that goes along with it."

"I enjoy the power," Dina admitted without hesitation, a hint of defiance in the tightness of her voice. "I enjoy the challenge and the responsibility, too. Men don't have a monopoly on those feelings."

"What are you suggesting, Dina? That we reverse our roles and I become the house husband? That I find the house, do all the decorating, cleaning and entertaining?"

"No, I'm not suggesting that." Confusion was tearing at her. She didn't know what the solution was.

"Perhaps you'd like me to take another flight to South America and this time not bother to come back?"

"No, I wouldn't—and stop twisting my words!"

Hot tears flooded her eyes, all the emotional turmoil inside her becoming too much to control. She turned sharply away, blinking frantically at the tears, trying to force them back before Blake saw them.

There was a warning squeak of the swivel chair as Blake rose and approached her. Her lungs were bursting, but she was afraid to take a breath for fear it would sound like a sob.

"Is this the way you handle a business disagreement?" he lashed out in impatient accusation.

Aware that he towered beside her, Dina kept her face averted so he wouldn't see the watery blue of her eyes. "I don't know what you mean," she lied.

His thumb and fingers clamped on her chin and twisted it around so he could see her face. "Do you usually indulge in a female display of tears when you don't get your own way?"

The wall of tears was so solid that Dina could barely see his face. "No," she retorted pushing at the hand that held her chin. "Do you always attack on a personal level whenever someone doesn't agree with you wholeheartedly?"

She heard his long impatient sigh, then his fingers curved to the back of her neck, forcing her head against his chest. An arm encircled her to draw her close. His embrace was strong and warm, but Dina made herself remain indifferent to Blake's attempt to comfort her. She felt the pressure of his chin resting atop her head.

"Would you mind telling me what the hell I'm supposed to do about this?" Blake muttered.

She wiped at the tears with shaking fingers and sniffed, "I don't know."

"Here." He reached inside his suit jacket to hand her his handkerchief. There was a light rap on the door and Blake stiffened. "Who is it?" he snapped, but the door was already opening.

Self-consciously Dina tried to twist out of his arms, but they tightened around her as if closing ranks to protect her. She submitted to their hold, her back to the door.

"Sorry," she heard Chet apologize with a trace of chagrin. "I guess I've gotten used to walking in unannounced."

He must have made a move to leave because Blake said, "It's all right. Come on in, Chet." Unhurriedly he withdrew his arms from around Dina. "You'll have to excuse Dina. She still gets emotional once in a while about my return," he said to explain away her tears and the handkerchief she was using to busily wipe away their traces.

"That's understandable," said Chet, "I came in to let you know everyone's here. They're waiting in the meeting room."

His statement lifted Dina's head with a start. "Meeting?" She picked up on the word and frowned. "There isn't any meeting scheduled on my agenda this morning."

"I called it," Blake announced smoothly, his bland gaze meeting her sharp look. Then he shifted his attention to Chet in a dismissing fashion. "Tell them I'll be there in a few minutes."

"I will." And Chet left.

91

At the click of the closing door, Dina turned roundly on Blake, her anger returning. "You weren't going to tell me about the meeting, were you?" she accused him.

Blake walked to the desk and began shuffling through the papers on top of it. "Initially, no. I didn't see the need to tell you."

"You didn't see the need?" Dina sputtered at his arrogantly dismissive statement.

"To be truthful, Dina—" he turned to look at her, his bluntly chiseled features seeming to be carved out of teakwood "—it didn't occur to me that you would come into the office today."

"Why ever not?" She stared at him in confusion and disbelief.

"I assumed you would be glad, if not grateful, to relinquish charge of the company to me. I thought you saw yourself as a stopgap president and would relish being free of the burdens of responsibility. I thought you would be happy to resume the role of a homemaker."

"You obviously don't know me very well," Dina retorted.

"So I'm beginning to discover," Blake responded grimly.

"What now?" she challenged him.

"No man likes to compete with his wife for a job, and I have no intention of doing so with you," he stated.

"Why not?" Dina argued. "If I'm equally competent—"

"But you are not," Blake interrupted, his eyes turning into dark chips of ironstone.

"I am." Surely she had proven that.

He ignored the assertion. "In the first place, our age difference alone gives me fourteen more years of experience in the business than you. Secondly, my father put me to work as a busboy when I was fifteen. Later I was a porter, a desk clerk, a cook, a manager. Compared to mine, your qualifications are negligible."

His logic deflated her balloon of pride. He made her seem like a fool, a child protesting because a toy was taken away. Dina had learned how to disguise her feelings and she used the skill to her advantage.

"You're probably quite right," she said stiffly. "I'd forgotten how much of a figurehead I was. Chet did the actual running of the company."

"Don't be ridiculous!" Blake dismissed the statement with a contemptuous jeer. "Chet is incapable of making an important decision."

Her eyes widened at the accusation. "How can you say that? He's been so loyal to you all these years, your best friend."

The lashing flick of his gaze laughed at her reference to Chet's loyalty, reminding her of Chet's engagement to her, but he made no mention of it when he spoke. "Just because he's been my friend doesn't mean I'm blind to his faults."

Although puzzled, Dina didn't pursue the topic. It was dangerous ground, likely to turn the conversation to a more personal level. At the moment, she wanted to keep it on business.

"None of that really matters. It still all comes down to the same basic thing—I'm out and you're in."

Blake raked a hand through his hair, rumpling it

into attractive disorder. "What am I supposed to do, Dina?" he demanded impatiently.

"That's up to you," she shrugged, feigning cold indifference while every part of her rebelled at the emptiness entering her life. "If you don't object to my borrowing *your* secretary, a letter formally tendering my resignation will be on *your* desk when you return from your meeting."

"No, I don't object." But Blake bristled at her cutting sarcasm. As she turned on her heel to leave, he covered the distance between them with long strides, grabbing at her elbow to spin her around. "What do you expect me to do?" His eyes were a blaze of anger.

"I don't know—"

He cut across her words. "Do you want me to offer you a position in the administration? Is that it?"

Excited hope leaped into her expression. After Blake had put it into words, she realized that that was exactly what she wanted—to still have a part in running the company, to be involved in its operation.

"Dammit, I can't do it, Dina!" Blake snapped.

Crushed, she demanded in a thin voice, "Why?"

"I can't go around sweeping people out of office so you can take their place. Disregarding the fact that it smacks of nepotism, it implies that I don't approve of the people you hired to fill key positions. The logical deduction from that would be that I believed you'd done an inadequate job of running the company in my absence." His expression was hard and grim. "It's going to be several years before

I can make any changes without them reflecting badly on you."

"That settles it, then, doesn't it?" Her chin quivered, belying the challenge in her voice.

His teeth were gritted, a muscle leaping along his jaw. "If you weren't my wife..." he began, about to offer another explanation of why his hands were tied in this matter.

"That's easily remedied, Blake," Dina flashed, and pulled her arm free before his grip could tighten. She didn't expect it to last long, but he made no attempt to recapture her.

"That's where you're wrong." He clipped out the words with biting precision.

Inwardly quaking under his piercing look, Dina turned away rather than admit his power to intimidate her. "It's immaterial anyway," she said with a small degree of composure. "My resignation will be on your desk within an hour." She walked to the door.

"Dina." The stern command of his voice stopped her from leaving.

She didn't remove her hand from the doorknob or turn to face him. "What?"

"Maybe I can keep you on in an advisory capacity." The stiffness of his words took away from the conciliatory gesture.

"I don't want any favors! And certainly not from the great Blake Chandler!" Dina flared, and yanked open the door.

It closed on a savage rush of expletives. When Dina turned away from the door, she looked into the curious and widened gaze of the secretary, Amy

Wentworth. Dina silently acknowledged that the walls of the private office were thick, but she doubted if they were thick enough to deafen the sound of voices raised in argument. She wondered how much of the aftereffect of her quarrel with Blake was apparent in her face. She strained to appear composed and in command of herself as she walked to Amy's desk.

"Put aside whatever you're doing, Amy," she ordered, trying to ignore the widening look she received.

"But...." The young secretary glanced hesitantly toward the inner office Dina had just left, as if uncertain whether she was to obey Dina or Blake.

Dina didn't give her a chance to put her thoughts into words. "I want you to type a letter of resignation—for me. You know the standard form of these things. Just keep it simple and direct. Effective immediately."

"Yes, Mrs. Chandler," Amy murmured, and immediately removed the dustcover from her electric typewriter.

The connecting office door was pulled open and Dina glanced over her shoulder to see Blake stride through. She could tell he had himself under rigid control, but it was like seeing a predatory animal restrained in chains. The minute the shackles were removed, he would pounce on his prey and tear it apart. And she was his prey.

Yet, even knowing she was being stalked, she was mesmerized by the dangerous look in his gaze. She waited motionless as he walked toward her, the force of his dark vitality vibrating over her nerve ends, making them tingle in sharp awareness.

"Dina, I . . . ." Blake never got the rest of his sentence out.

Chet entered the room through the door to the outer corridor. "Oh, I see you're on your way," he concluded at the sight of Blake. "I was just coming to see how much longer you'd be." His gaze switched its attention to Dina and became a troubled blue as he noticed the white lines of stress on her face.

"Yes, I'm on my way," Blake agreed crisply, and looked back at Dina. "I want you to attend the meeting, Dina." The veiled harshness in his gaze dared her to defy him.

But Dina felt safe in the company of others. "No. It's better for everyone to realize that you're in charge now and not confuse them by having a former head of the company present." She saw his mouth thin at her response and turned away in a gesture of dismissal.

"Dina has a good point," Chet offered in agreement, but a darting look from Blake made him vacillate. "Of course, unless you think it's wiser to—"

"Let's go," Blake snapped.

In a silent storm, he swept from the room, drawing Chet into his wake and leaving Dina feeling drained and colorless. Her nerves seemed to be delicate filaments, capable of snapping at the slightest pressure. When the letter of resignation was typed, her hand trembled as she affixed her signature to it.

"Put it on Mr. Chandler's desk," she ordered, and returned it to Amy.

"It was nice working for you, Mrs. Chandler,"

the young secretary offered as Dina turned to go, the words spoken in all sincerity.

"Thank you, Amy." Dina smiled mistily, then hurried from the room.

Leaving the building, she walked to her car. She knew there was no way she could return to the house and listen to Mother Chandler's happy conversation about Blake's return. With the top down on the white sports car, she removed the scarf from her hair and tucked it in the glove compartment.

With no destination in mind, she climbed into the car and drove, the wind whipping at her hair, which glittered like liquid sunlight in the morning air. Around and through the back streets, the main streets, the side streets of the city of Newport she went.

Half the time she was too blinded by tears to know where she was. She didn't notice the row of palatial mansions on Bellevue Avenue, or the crowds gathered on the wharf for the trial of the America Cup races.

She didn't know who she was, what she was, or why she was. Since Blake's return, she was no longer Dina Chandler. She was once again Mrs. Blake Chandler, lost in her husband's identity. She was no longer a businesswoman, nor did she feel like a housewife, since she had no home and a stranger for a husband. As to the reason why, she was in total confusion.

It was sheer luck that she glanced at the dashboard and noticed the gasoline gauge was hovering at the empty mark. Practicality forced her out of the bewildering whirlpool of questions. They stayed away until she was parked in a gas station and waiting in the building where her tank was being filled.

Then they returned with pounding force and Dina reeled under the power of them. Her restlessly searching gaze accidentally spied the telephone inside the building. She walked blindly to the phone and, from long habit, dialed the number of the one person who had already seen her through so much emotional turmoil.

The impersonal voice of an operator answered and Dina requested in an unsteady voice, "Chet Stanton, please."

"Who is calling, please?"

Dina hesitated a fraction of a second before answering, "A friend."

There was a moment when Dina thought the operator was going to demand a more specific answer than that, then she heard the call being put through. "Chet Stanton speaking," his familiar voice came on the line.

"Chet, this is Dina," she rushed.

"Oh." He sounded surprised and guarded. "Hello."

She guessed at the cause for the way he responded. "Are you alone?"

"No."

Which meant that Blake must be in his office. Dina wasn't certain how she knew it was Blake and not someone else, but she was positive of it.

"Chet, I have to talk to you. I have to see you," she declared in a burst of despair. Glancing at her wristwatch, she didn't give him a chance to reply. "Can you meet me for lunch?"

She heard the deep breath he took before he answered, "I'm sorry, I'm afraid I've already made plans for lunch."

"I have to see you," she repeated. "What about later?"

"It's been a long time since I've seen you." Chet began to enter into the spirit of the thing, however uncertainly. "Why don't we get together for a drink? Say, around five-thirty?"

It was so long to wait, she thought desperately, but realized it was the best he could offer. "Very well," she agreed, and named the first cocktail lounge that came to mind.

"I'll meet you there," Chet promised.

"And, Chet—" Dina hesitated "—please don't say anything to Blake about meeting me. I don't want him to know. He wouldn't understand."

There was a long pause before he finally said, "No, I won't. See you then."

After hanging up the receiver, Dina turned and saw the gas station attendant eyeing her curiously, yet with a measure of concern. She opened the pocketbook slung over her shoulder and started to pay for the gasoline.

"Are you all right, miss?" he questioned.

She glimpsed her faded reflection in the large plate-glass window of the station and understood his reason for asking. Her hair was windblown, and in riotous disorder. Tears had streaked the mascara from her lashes to make smutty lines around her eyes. She looked like a lost and wayward urchin despite the expensive clothes she wore.

"I'm fine," she lied.

In the car, she took a tissue from her bag and wiped the dark smudges from beneath her eyes. A brush put her tangled mass of silky gold hair into a semblance of order before it was covered by the scarf she had discarded.

"You have to get hold of yourself," she scolded her reflection in the rearview mirror.

Turning the key in the ignition, she started the powerful motor of the little car and drove away, wondering what she was going to do with herself for the rest of the day.

CHAPTER SIX

TYPICALLY, THE LOUNGE was dimly lit. Overhead lighting was practically nonexistent and the miniature mock lanterns with their small candle flames flickering inside the glass chimneys provided little more. The dark wood paneling of the walls offered no relief, nor did the heavily beamed low ceiling.

Tucked away in an obscure corner of the lounge, Dina had a total view of the room and the entrance door. A drink was in front of her, untouched, the ice melting. Five more minutes, her watch indicated, but it already seemed an interminable wait.

An hour earlier she had phoned Mother Chandler to tell her she would be late without explaining why or where she was. Blake would be angry, she realized. *Let him*, was her inward response. The consequences of her meeting with Chet she would think about later.

Brilliant sunlight flashed into the room as the door was opened. Dina glanced up, holding her breath and hoping that this time it might be Chet. But a glimpse of the tall figure that entered the lounge paralyzed her lungs. Her heart stopped beating, then skyrocketed in alarm.

Just inside the lounge, Blake paused, letting his eyes adjust to the gloom. There was nowhere Dina could run without drawing his attention. She tried to make herself small, hoping he wouldn't see her in this dim corner of the room. Dina felt rather than saw his gaze fasten on her seconds before his purposeful strides carried him to her table.

When he stopped beside her, Dina couldn't look up. Her teeth were so tightly clenched they hurt. She curled her hands around the drink she hadn't touched since it had been set before her. Despite the simmering resentment she felt, there was a sense of inevitability, too. Blake didn't speak, waiting for Dina to acknowledge him first.

"Imagine meeting you here," she offered in a bitter tone of mock surprise, not letting her gaze lift from the glass cupped in her hands. "Small world, isn't it?"

"It's quite a coincidence," he agreed.

There was a bright glitter in her blue eyes when she finally looked at him. His craggy features were in the shadows, making his expression impossible to see. The disturbing male vitality of his presence began to make itself felt despite her attempt to ignore it.

"How did you know I was here?" she demanded, knowing there was only one answer he could give.

And Blake gave it. "Chet told me."

"Why?" The broken word came out unknowingly, directed at the absent friend who had betrayed her trust.

"Because I asked him."

"He promised he wouldn't tell you!" Her voice was choked, overcome by the discovery that she was lost and completely alone in her confusion.

"So I gathered," Blake offered dryly.

Dina averted her gaze to breathe shakily. "Why did he have to tell you?"

"I am your husband, Dina, despite the way you try to forget it. That gives me the right to at least know where you are."

His voice was as smooth as polished steel, outwardly calm and firm. Her gaze noticed his large hands clenched into fists at his side, revealing the control he was exercising over his anger. He was filled with a white rage that his wife should arrange to meet another man. Dina was frightened, but it was fear that prompted the bravado to challenge him.

"You were in Chet's office when I called, weren't you?" she said accusingly.

"Yes, and I could tell by the guilty look on his face that he was talking to you. After that, it didn't take much to find out what was going on."

"Who did you think I would turn to? I needed him." Dina changed it to present tense. "I need Chet."

Like the sudden uncoiling of a spring, Blake leaned down, spreading his hands across the tabletop, arms rigid. In the flickering candlelight his features resembled a carved teakwood mask of some pagan god, harsh and ruthless and dangerously compelling.

"When are you going to get it through that blind little brain of yours that you've never needed him?" he demanded.

Her heart was pounding out a message of fear. "I don't know you," she breathed in panic. "You're a stranger. You frighten me, Blake."

"That makes two of us, because I'm scared as hell of myself!" He straightened abruptly, issuing an impatient, "Let's get out of here before I do something I'll regret."

Throwing caution away, Dina protested, "I don't want to go anywhere with you."

"I'm aware of that!" His hand clamped a hold on her arm to haul her to her feet, overpowering her weak resistance. Once she was upright, his fingers remained clamped around her arm to keep her pressed to his side. "Is the drink paid for?" Blake reminded her of the untouched contents of the glass on the table.

As always when she came in physical contact with him, she seemed to lose the ability to think coherently. His muscular body was like living steel and the softness of her shape had to yield. Everything was suddenly reduced to an elemental level. Not until Blake had put the question to her a second time did Dina take in what he had asked.

She managed a trembling, "No, it isn't."

Releasing her, Blake took a money clip from his pocket and peeled off a bill, tossing it on the table. Then the steel band of his arm circled her waist to guide her out of the lounge, oblivious to the curious stares.

In towering silence he walked her to the white Porsche, its top still down. He opened the door and pushed her behind the wheel. Then, slamming the door shut, he leaned on the frame, an unrelenting grimness to his mouth.

"My car is going to be glued to your bumper, following you every inch of the way. So don't take any detours on the route home, Dina," he warned.

Before Dina could make any kind of retort, he walked to his car parked in the next row of the lot. Starting the car, she gunned the motor as if she were accelerating for a race, a puny gesture of impotent defiance.

True to his word, his car was a large shadow behind hers every block of the way, an ominous presence she couldn't shake even if she had tried—which she didn't. Stopping in the driveway of his mother's house—their house—Dina hurried from her car, anxious to get inside where the other inhabitants could offer her a degree of safety from him.

Halfway to the door Blake caught up with her, a hand firmly clasping her elbow to slow her down.

"This little episode isn't over yet," he stated in an undertone. "We'll talk about it later."

Dina swallowed the impulse to challenge him. It was better to keep silent with safety so near. Together they entered the house, both concealing the state of war between them.

Mother Chandler appeared in the living-room doorway, wearing an attractive black chiffon dress. Her elegantly coiffed silver hair was freshly styled, thanks to an afternoon's appointment at her favorite salon. She smiled brightly at the pair of them, unaware of the tension crackling between them.

"You're both home—how wonderful!" she exclaimed, assuming her cultured tone. "I was about to suggest to Deirdre that perhaps she should delay dinner for an hour. I'm so glad it won't be necessary. I know how much you detest overcooked meat, Blake."

"You always did like your beef very rare, didn't

106

you, Blake?" Dina followed up on the comment, her gaze glittering at his face with diamond sharpness. "I have always considered your desire for raw flesh as a barbaric tendency."

"It seems you were right, doesn't it?" he countered.

Mother Chandler seemed impervious to the barbed exchange as she waved them imperiously into the living room. "Come along. Let's have a sherry and you can tell me about your first day back at the office, Blake." She rattled on, covering their tight-lipped silence.

IT WAS AN ORDEAL getting through dinner and making the necessary small talk to hide the fact that there was anything wrong. It was even worse after dinner when the three of them sat around with their coffee in the living room. Each tick of the clock was like the swing of a pendulum, bringing nearer the moment when Blake's threatened discussion would take place.

The telephone rang and the housekeeper answered it in the other room. She appeared in the living room seconds later to announce, "It's for you, Mr. Blake. A Mr. Carl Landstrom."

"I'll take it in the library, Deirdre," he responded.

Dina waited several seconds after the library door had closed before turning to Mother Chandler. "It's a business call." Carl Landstrom was head of the accounting department and Dina knew that his innate courtesy would not allow him to call after office hours unless it was something important. "Blake is probably going to be on the phone for a while," she explained, a fact she was going to use to make her escape and avoid his private talk. "Would you explain to him that I'm very tired and have gone on to bed?"

"Of course, dear." The older woman smiled, then sighed with rich contentment. "It's good to have him back, isn't it?"

It was a rhetorical question, and Dina didn't offer a reply as she bent to kiss the relatively smooth cheek of her mother-in-law. "Good night, Mother Chandler."

"Good night."

Upstairs, Dina undressed and took a quick shower. Toweling herself dry, she wrapped the terrycloth robe around her and removed the shower cap from her head, shaking her hair loose. She wanted to be in bed with the lights off before Blake was off the telephone. With luck he wouldn't bother to disturb her. She knew she was merely postponing the discussion, but for the moment that was enough.

Her nightgown was lying neatly at the foot of the bed as she entered the bedroom that adjoined the private bath, her hairbrush in hand. A few brisk strokes to unsnarl the damp curls at the ends of her hair was all that she needed to do for the night, she decided, and sat on the edge of the bed to do it.

The mattress didn't give beneath her weight. It seemed as solid as the seat of a wooden chair. Dina was motionless as she assembled the knowledge and realized that the new mattress and box springs she had ordered for Blake had arrived and hers had been removed.

She sprang from the bed as if discovering a bed

of hot coals beneath it. No, her heart cried, she couldn't sleep with him—not after that last humiliating experience; not with his anger simmering so close to the surface because of today.

The door opened and Blake walked in, and the one thing in the forefront of her mind burst out in panic. "I'm not going to sleep with you!" she cried.

A brow flicked upward. "At the moment, sleep is the furthest thing from my mind."

"Why are you here?" She was too numbed to think beyond the previous moment.

"To finish our discussion." Blake walked to the chair against the wall and motioned toward the matching one. "Sit down."

"No," Dina refused, too agitated to stay in one place even though he sat down with seemingly relaxed composure while she paced restlessly.

"I want to know why you were meeting Chet." His hooded gaze watched her intently, like an animal watching its trapped prey expend its nervous energy before moving in for the kill.

"It was perfectly innocent," she began in self-defense, then abruptly changed her tactics. "It's really none of your business."

"If it was as perfectly innocent as you claim," Blake said, deliberately using her words, "then there's no reason not to tell me."

"What you can't seem to understand, or refuse to understand, is that I need Chet," she flashed. "I need his comfort and understanding, his gentleness. I certainly don't receive that from you!"

"If you'd open your eyes once, you'd see you're not receiving it from him, either," Blake retorted.

"Don't I?" Her sarcastic response was riddled with disbelief.

"Chet doesn't comfort. He merely mouths the words you want to hear. He's incapable of original thought."

"I would hate to have you for a friend, Blake," she declared tightly, "if this is the way you regard friends when they aren't around, cutting them into little pieces."

"I've known Chet a great deal longer than you have. He can't survive unless he's basking in the reflected glory of someone else. When I disappeared, he transferred his allegiance to you, because you represented strength. He's a parasite, Dina, for all his charm," Blake continued his cold dissection. "He lived on your strength. He persuaded you to take charge of the company because he knew he was incapable of leading a child, let alone a major corporation."

"You don't know what you're saying," Dina breathed, walking away from his harsh explanation.

"The next time you're with him, take a good look at him, Dina," he ordered. "And I hope you have the perception to see that you've been supporting him through all this, not the other way around."

"No!" She shook her head in vigorous denial.

"I should have stayed away for a couple more months. Maybe by then the rose-colored spectacles would have come off and you would have found out how heavily he leans on you."

Pausing in her restless pacing, Dina pressed her hands over her ears to shut out his hateful words. "How can you say those things about Chet and still call him your friend?"

"I know his flaws. He's my friend in spite of them," Blake responded evenly. "Yet you were going to marry him without acknowledging that he had any."

"Yes. Yes, I was going to marry him!" Dina cried, pulling her hands away from her ears and turning to confront him.

"Only when I came back, he dropped you so fast it made your head swim. Admit it." Blake sat unmoving in the chair.

"He wanted me to be happy," she argued defensively.

"No," he denied. "My return meant you were on the way out of power and I was in. Chet was securing his position. There was nothing chivalrous in his reason for breaking the engagement. He wasn't sacrificing anything, only insuring it."

"So why did you hound him into admitting he was meeting me today?" challenged Dina.

"I didn't hound him. He was almost relieved to tell me."

"You have an answer for everything, don't you?" She refused to admit that anything Blake was saying made any sense. She fought to keep that feeling of antagonism; without it, she was defenseless against him. "It's been like this ever since you came back," she complained, uttering her thoughts aloud.

"I knew when everyone discovered I was alive, it was going to be a shock. But I thought it would be a pleasant shock," Blake sighed with wry humor. "In your case, I was wrong. It was a plain shock and you haven't recovered from it yet."

Dina heard the underlying bitterness in his tone

111

and felt guilty. She tried to explain. "How did you think I would feel? I'd become my own person. Suddenly you were back and trying to absorb me again in your personality, swallow me up whole."

"How did you think I would react when you've challenged me every minute since I've returned?" His retaliation was instant, his temper ignited by her defensive anger, but he immediately brought it under control. "It seems we've stumbled onto the heart of our problem. Let's see if we can't have a civilized discussion and work it out."

"Civilized!" Dina laughed bitterly. "You don't know the meaning of the word. You spent too much time in the jungle. You aren't even civilized about the way you make love!"

Black fires blazed in his eyes. The muscles along his jaw went white from his effort to keep control. "And you go for the jugular vein every time!" he snarled, rising from the chair in one fluid move.

Dina's heart leaped into her throat. She had aroused a beast she couldn't control. She took a step backward, then turned and darted for the door. But Blake intercepted her, spinning her around, his arms circling her, crushing her to his length.

His touch sizzled through her like an electric shock, immobilizing her. She offered not an ounce of resistance as his mouth covered hers in a long, punishing kiss. She seemed without life or breath, except what he gave her in anger.

Anger needs fuel to keep it burning, and Dina gave him none. Gradually the brutal pressure eased and his head lifted a fraction of an inch. She opened her eyes and gazed breathlessly into the brilliant darkness of his. The warm moistness of his breath was caressing her parted lips.

His hand stroked the spun gold of her hair, brushing it away from her cheek. "Why do you always bring out the worst in me?" he questioned huskily.

"Because I won't let you dominate me the way you do everyone else," Dina whispered. She could feel the involuntary trembling of his muscular body and the beginnings of the same passionate tremors in her own.

"Does it give you a feeling of power—" he kissed her cheek "—to know that—" his mouth teased the curling tips of her lashes "—you can make me lose control?" He returned to tantalize the curving outline of her lips. "You are the only one who could ever make me forget reason."

"Am I?" Dina breathed skeptically, because he seemed in complete control at the moment and she was the one losing her grip.

"I had a lot of time to think while I was trying to fight my way out of that tropical hell. I kept remembering all our violent quarrels that got started over the damnedest things. I kept telling myself that if I ever made it back, they were going to be a thing of the past. Yet within hours after I saw you, we were at each other's throats."

"I know," she nodded.

As if believing her movement was an attempt to escape his lips, Blake captured her chin to hold her head still. With languorous slowness, his mouth took possession of hers. The kiss was like a slow-burning flame that kept growing hotter and hotter.

Its heat melted Dina against his length, so hard and very male. Her throbbing pulse sounded loudly in her ears as the flames coursed through her body.

Before she succumbed completely to the weakness of her physical desire, she twisted away from his mouth. She knew what he wanted, and what she wanted, but she had to deny it.

"It won't work, Blake." Her throat worked convulsively, hating the words even as she said them. "Not after the last time."

"The last time . . . . " He pursued her lips, his mouth hovering a feather's width from them, and she trembled weakly, lacking the strength to turn away. "I hated you for becoming engaged to Chet, even believing I was dead. And I hated myself for not having the control to stop when you asked me not to make love to you. This time it's different."

"It's no good." But the hands that had slipped inside her robe and were caressing her skin with such arousing thoroughness felt very good.

For an instant Dina didn't think Blake was going to pay any attention to her protest, and she wasn't sure that she wanted him to take note of it. Then she felt the tensing of his muscles as he slowly became motionless.

He continued to hold her in his arms as if considering whether to concede to her wishes or to overpower her resistance, something he could easily accomplish in her present half-willing state.

A split second later he was setting her away from him, as if removing himself from temptation. "If that's what you want, I'll wait," he conceded grimly.

"I . . . ." In a way, it wasn't what she wanted; and Dina almost said so, but checked herself. "I need time."

"You've got it," Blake agreed, his control superb, an impenetrable mask concealing his emotions. "Only don't make me wait too long before you come to a decision."

"I won't." Dina wasn't even certain what decision there was to make. What were her choices?

His raking look made her aware of the terry robe hanging loosely open, exposing the cleavage of her breasts. She drew the folds together to conceal the naked form Blake knew so well. He turned away, running his fingers through the wayward thickness of his dark hair.

"Go to bed, Dina," he said with a hint of weariness. "I have some calls to make."

Her gaze swung to the bed and the quilted spread that concealed the rock-hard mattress. "The new box spring and mattress that I had Deirdre order for you came today, and she put it in here. I'll . . . I'll sleep in the guest room."

"No." Blake slashed her a look over his shoulder. "You will sleep with me, if you do nothing else."

Dina didn't make the obvious protest regarding the intimacy of such an arrangement and its frustrations, but offered instead, "That bed is like lying on granite."

There was a wryly mocking twist of his mouth. "To use an old cliché, Dina, you've made your bed, now you have to lie in it."

"I won't," she declared with a stubborn tilt of her chin.

"Am I asking too much to want my wife to sleep beside me?" He gave Dina a long, level look that she couldn't hold.

Averting her head, she closed her eyes to murmur softly "No, it isn't too much."

The next sound she heard was the opening of the door. She turned as Blake left the room. She stared at the closed door that shut her inside, wondering if she hadn't made a mistake by giving in to his request.

Walking over to the bed, she pressed a hand on the quilt to test its firmness. Under her full weight it gave barely an inch. It was going to be quite a difference from the soft mattress she usually slept on, but then her bed partner was a completely different man from the urbane man she had married. Dina wondered which she would get used to first—the hard bed or the hard man?

Nightgowned, with the robe lying at the foot of the bed, she crawled beneath the covers. The unyielding mattress wouldn't mold to her shape, so she had to attempt to adjust her curves to it, without much success. Sleep naturally became elusive as she kept shifting positions on the hard surface trying to find one that was comfortable.

Almost two hours later she was still awake, but she closed her eyes to feign sleep when she heard Blake open the door. It was difficult to regulate her breathing as she listened to his quiet preparations. Keeping to the far side of the bed, she stayed motionless when he climbed in to lie beside her, not touching but close enough for her to feel his body heat.

Blake shifted a few times, then settled into one position. Within a few minutes she heard him breathing deeply in sleep. Sighing, she guessed she was still hours away from it.

CHAPTER SEVEN

A HAND WAS MAKING rubbing strokes along her upper arm, pleasantly soothing caresses. Then fingers tightened to shake her gently.

"Come on, Dina, wake up!" a voice ordered.

"Mmm." The negative sound vibrated from her throat as she snuggled deeper into her pillow.

Only it wasn't a pillow. There was a steady thud beneath her head, and the pillow that wasn't a pillow moved up and down in a regular rhythm. No, it wasn't a pillow. She was nestled in the crook of Blake's arm, her head resting on his chest. She could feel the curling sun-bleached hairs on his chest tickling her cheek and nose.

Sometime in the night she had forsaken the hardness of the mattress to cuddle up to the warm hardness of his body. Her eyelids snapped open at the familiarity sleep had induced. Dina would have moved away from him, but the arm around her tightened to hold her there for another few seconds.

A callused finger tipped her chin upward, forcing her to look at him, and her heart skipped a beat at the lazy warmth in the craggy male face.

"I'd forgotten what it was like to sleep with an octopus," Blake murmured. "Arms and legs all over the place!"

Heat assailed Dina at the intimacy of her position. Sleep had dulled her reflexes. When his thumb touched her lips to trace their outline, Dina was too slow in trying to elude it. As the first teasing brush made itself felt, she lost the desire to escape it. Rough skin lightly explored every contour of her mouth before his thumb probed her lips apart to find the white barrier of her teeth.

It became very difficult to breathe under the erotically stimulating caress, especially when his gaze was absorbing every detail of his action with disturbing interest. Situated as she was, with a hand resting on the hard muscles of his chest, afraid to move, Dina felt and heard the quickening beat of his pulse. Hers was racing no less slowly.

The muffled groan of arousal that came from his throat sent the blood rocketing through her heart. The arm around her ribcage tightened to draw her up. His mouth renewed the exploration his thumb had only begun. With a mastery that left her shattered, Blake parted her lips, his tongue seeking out hers to ignite the fires of passion.

In the crush of his embrace, it was impossible for Dina to ignore the fact that Blake was naked beneath the covers. It was just as impossible to be unaware that her nightgown was twisted up around her hips. It was a discovery his roughly caressing hands soon made.

As his hands slid beneath it, his fingers catching the material to lift it higher, Dina made a weak attempt to stop him. It seemed the minute her own hands came in contact with the living bronze of his muscled arms, they forgot their intention.

More of her bare skin came in contact with his

hard flesh. The delicious havoc it created with her senses only made Dina want to feel more of him. Willingly she slipped her arms from the armholes as Blake lifted it over her head. His mouth was absent from her lips for only that second. The instant the nightgown was tossed aside, he was back kissing her with a demanding passion that she eagerly returned.

Blake shifted, rolling Dina onto her back, the punishing hardness of the mattress beneath her. His sun-bronzed torso was above her, an elbow on the mattress offering him support. His warm, male smell filled her senses, drugging her mind. When he dragged his mouth away from hers, she curved a hand around his neck to bring it back. Blake resisted effortlessly, the burning darkness of his gaze glittering with satisfaction at her aroused state.

At sometime the covers had been kicked aside. As his hand began a slow, intimate exploration of her breasts, waist and hips, Blake watched it, his eyes drinking in the shapely perfection of her female form. The blatant sensuality of the look unnerved Dina to the point that she couldn't permit it to continue. Again came the feeling that it was a stranger's eyes looking at her, not those of her husband.

Gasping back a sob, she tried to roll away from him and reached the protective cover of the sheets and blankets. Blake thwarted the attempt, forcing her back, his weight crushing her to the unyielding mattress that had already bruised her muscles and bones.

"No, Dina, I want to look at you," Blake insisted in a voice husky with desire. "I imagined you like this so many times, lying naked in the bed beside me, your body soft and eager to have me make love to you. Don't blame me for wanting to savor this moment. This time no screech of a jungle bird is going to chase away this image. You are mine, Dina, mine."

The last word was uttered with possessive emphasis as his head descended to stake its first claim, his mouth seeking her lips, kissing them until passion overrode her brief attempt at resistance. A languorous desire consumed her as he extended his lovemaking to more than just her lips. She quivered with fervent longing at the slow descent of his mouth to her breasts, favoring each of them in turn to the erotic stimulations of his tongue.

Under his sensuous skill, Dina forgot the strangeness of his arms and the hardness of the rocklike mattress beneath her. She forgot all but the dizzying climb to the heights of gratification and the dazzling view from the peak. They descended slowly, not finding their breath until they reached the lower altitudes of reality.

Dina lay enclosed in his arms, her head resting on his chest as it had when she had awakened. This time there was a film of perspiration coating his hard muscles and dampening the thick, wiry hairs beneath her head. Dina closed her eyes, aware that she had come very close to discovering her love for Blake again, its light glittered in the far recesses of her heart.

Blake's mouth moved against her hair. "I had forgotten what an almost insatiably passionate little wench you are." His murmured comment suddenly brought the experience down to a purely physical level. What had bordered on an act of love, became lust. "I enjoyed it. Correction, I enjoyed you," he added, which partially brought the light back to her heart.

Crimsoning, Dina rolled out of his arms, an action he didn't attempt to prevent. The movement immediately caused a wince of pain. Every bone and fiber in her body was an aching reminder of the night she had spent in the hard-rock bed.

"How can you stand to sleep in this bed?" Dina was anxious to change the subject, unwilling to speak of the passion they had just shared. "It's awful."

"You'll get used to it." When Blake spoke, Dina realized he had slid out of bed with barely a sound while she had been discovering her aches and pains. Her gaze swung to him as he stepped into the bottoms of his silk pajamas and pulled them on. Feeling her eyes watching him, Blake glanced around. There was a laughing glint in his dark eyes as he said, "It's a concession to Deirdre and her Victorian modesty this morning."

Dina smiled. Even that hurt. "What time is it?"

"Seven," he answered somewhat absently, and rubbed the stubble of beard on his chin.

"That late?"

Her pains deserted her for an instant and she started to rise, intent only on the thought that she would be late getting to the office unless she hurried. Then she remembered she no longer had any reason to go to the office and sank back to the mattress, tiredness and irritation sweeping over her.

"Why am I getting up?" she questioned herself aloud. "It took me so long to get to sleep last night. Why didn't you just let me keep right on sleeping?" Then he wouldn't have made love to her and she wouldn't be experiencing all this confusion and uncertainty, about herself and him.

"You'd be late to work," was Blake's even response.

"Have you forgotten?" Bitterness coated her tongue. "I've been replaced. I'm a lady of leisure now."

"Are you?" He gave her a bland look. "Your boss doesn't think so."

"What boss? You?" Dina breathed out with a scornful laugh. "You're only my husband."

"Does that mean you're turning it down?"

"What? Will you quit talking in riddles?"

"Maybe if you hadn't been so proud and stubborn yesterday morning and attended the meeting as I asked you to, you'd know what I'm talking about."

She pressed a hand against her forehead, tension and sleeplessness pounding between her eyes. "I didn't attend the meeting, so perhaps you could explain."

"We're starting a whole new advertising campaign to upgrade the image of the Chandler Hotel chain," he explained. "We can't possibly compete with the bigger chains on a nationwide basis, especially when most of our hotels are located in resort areas, not necessarily heavily populated ones. We're going to use that fact to our advantage. From now on, when people think of resort hotels, it's going to be synonymous with Chandler Hotels."

"It's a sound idea," Dina conceded. "But what does that have to do with me?"

"You're going to be in charge of the campaign."

"What?" Blake's calm announcement brought her upright, wary disbelief and skepticism in the look she gave him. "Is this some kind of a cruel joke?"

There was an arrogant arch to one dark eyebrow. "Hardly." He walked around the bed to where she stood. "I put the proposal to the rest of the staff yesterday, along with the recommendation that you handle it."

"Is this a token gesture? Something for me to do to keep me quiet?" She couldn't accept that there wasn't an ulterior motive behind the offer. It might mean admitting something else.

"I admit that picking you as my choice to head the campaign was influenced by the tantrum you threw in the office yesterday morning when you discovered I was taking over." His gaze was steady, not yielding an inch in guilt. "But you can be sure, Dina, that I wouldn't have suggested your name to the others if I didn't believe you could handle the job. You can put whatever interpretation you like on that."

Dina believed him. His candor was too forthright to be doubted, especially when he acknowledged the argument they had had earlier. It surprised her that he had relented to this extent, putting her in charge of something that could ultimately be so important to the company. True, she would be working for him, but she would be making decisions on her own, too.

"Why didn't you tell me about this last night?" She frowned. "Your decision had already been made. You just said a moment ago that you told the staff yesterday. Why did you wait until now to tell me?"

Blake studied her thoughtfully. "I was going to tell you last night after we'd had our talk, but circumstances altered my decision and I decided to wait."

"What circumstances?" Dina persisted, not following his reasoning.

"To be perfectly honest, I thought if you knew about it last night you might have been prompted to make love to me out of gratitude," Blake replied without a flicker of emotion appearing in his impassive expression.

There was an explosion of red before her eyes. "You thought I'd be so grateful that I'd . . . ." Anger robbed her of speech.

"It was a possibility."

Dina was so blind with indignant rage that she couldn't see straight, but it didn't affect her aim as her opened palm connected with the hard contour of his cheek. As the white mark turned scarlet, Blake walked into the bathroom. Trembling with the violence of her aroused temper, Dina watched him go.

When her anger dissipated, she was left with a niggling question. If he hadn't made that degrading remark, would she still be angry with him? Or would this have been the first step towards reestablishing the foundation of their marriage, with Blake recognizing that she had the talent and skill to be more than a simple housewife? Hindsight could not provide the answer.

At the breakfast table, their conversation was frigidly civil.

"Please pass the juice."

"May I have the marmalade?"

That fragile mood of shy affection they had woken up to that morning was gone, broken by the doubting of each other's motives.

When both had finished breakfast, Blake set his cup down. "You may ride to the office with me this morning," he announced.

"I would prefer to take my own car."

"It's impractical for both of us to drive."

"If you had to work late, I would be without a way home," Dina protested.

"*If* that should arise, you may have the car and *I'll* take a taxi home," he stated, his demeanor cold and arrogant.

Dina was infuriatingly aware that Blake would have an argument for every excuse she could offer. "Very well, I'll ride with you." She gave in with ill grace.

The morning crush of Newport traffic seemed heavier than normal, the distance to the office greater, the time passing slower, and the polar atmosphere between them colder than ever.

Feeling like a puppy dog on a leash, Dina followed Blake from the parking lot to his office. There she sat down, adopting a business air to listen to specific suggestions that had been offered by Blake and the staff for the campaign. It was a far-reaching plan, extending to redecorating some hotels to meet with their new resort image.

At that one, Dina couldn't help commenting caustically, "I'm suprised I'm not limited to that task. Decorating is woman's work, isn't it?"

The thrust of his frigid gaze pierced her like a cold knife. "Do you want to discuss this program intelligently? Or do you want to bring our personal difficulties into it? Because if you do, I'll find someone else for the job."

Her pride wanted to tell him to find that person, but common sense insisted she would ultimately be the loser if she did. The project promised to be a challenge, and Dina had come to enjoy that. Her pride was a bitter thing to swallow, but she managed to get it down.

"Sorry. That remark just slipped out." She shrugged. "Go on."

There was a second's pause as Blake weighed her words before continuing. When he had concluded, he gave her a copy of the notes from the staff meeting and a tentative budget.

Dina glanced over them, then asked, "Where am I to work?"

"I'll take you to your new office."

She followed him out of the office and walked beside him down the long corridor until they came to the end. Blake opened the last door.

"Here it is."

The metal desk, chair and shelves seemed to fill up the room. Three offices this size could have fit into Blake's office, Dina realized. And that wasn't all. It was cut off from the other staff offices, at the end of the hall, isolated. She could die in there and nobody would know, she thought to herself.

127

Blake saw the fire smoldering in her blue eyes. "This is the only office that was available on such short notice," he explained.

"Is it?" she retorted grimly.

"Yes—" he clipped out the word challengingly "—unless you think I should have moved one of the executive staff out of his or her office to make room for you."

Dina knew that would have been illogical and chaotic, with records being shifted and their exact location possibly unknown for several days. Still, she resented the size and location of her new office, regardless of how much she accepted the practicality of its choice. But she didn't complain. She didn't have to, since Blake knew how she felt.

She looked at the bare desk top and said, "There's no telephone?"

"Arrangements have already been made to have one installed today."

"Fine." She walked briskly into the room, aware of Blake still standing in the doorway.

"If you have any questions—" he began in a cool tone.

Dina interrupted, "I doubt if I will." The banked fires of her anger glittered in the clear blue of her eyes.

His gaze narrowed, his expression hardening. "You can be replaced, Dina."

"Permanently?" she drawled in a taunting kitten-purr voice.

For an instant she thought he might do away with her violently, but instead he exhibited that iron control and pivoted to walk away. There was a tearing in her heart as he left. Dina wondered if she was deliberately antagonizing him or merely reacting to his attempted domination of her.

Pushing the unanswerable question aside, she set to work, taking an inventory of the supplies on hand and calculating what she would need. After obtaining the required items from the supply room, she began making a list of information she would need before drawing up a plan of action for the advertising campaign.

At the sound of footsteps approaching the end of the hallway, she glanced up from her growing list. She had left the door to her office open to lessen the claustrophobic sensation, and she watched the doorway, curious as to who would be coming and for what reason.

Chet appeared, pausing in the doorway, a twinkle in his gray blue eyes, an arm behind his back. "Hello there," he smiled.

"Are you lost or slumming?" Dina questioned with a wry curve to her lips.

He chuckled and admitted, "I was beginning to think I was going to have to stop and ask directions before I found you."

"It's certain I'm not going to be bothered with people stopping by to chat on their way someplace else. This is the end of the line," she declared with a rueful glance around the tiny office. "Which brings me to the next obvious question."

"What am I doing here?" Chet asked it for her. "When I heard you were exiled to the far reaches of the office building, I decided you might like a cup of hot coffee." The arm that had been behind his back moved to the front to reveal the two Styrofoam cups of coffee he was juggling in one hand. "At least, I hope it's hot. After that long walk, it might be cold."

"Hot or lukewarm, it sounds terrific." Dina straightened away from the desk to relax against the rigid back of her chair. "I shall love you forever for thinking of it."

She had tossed out the remark without considering what she was saying, but she was reminded of it as a discomfited look flashed across Chet's face.

"I guess that brings me to the second reason why I'm here." He lowered his head as he walked into the room, not quite able to meet her gaze.

"You mean about not meeting me yesterday and sending Blake in your place," Dina guessed, accurately as it turned out.

"Yes, well—" Chet set the two cups on the desk top "—I'm sorry about that. I know you didn't want me to tell Blake and I wouldn't have, either, except that he was in my office when you called and he guessed who I was talking to."

"So he said," she murmured, not really wanting to talk about it in view of the discussion she had with Blake last night regarding Chet.

"Blake didn't lay down the law and forbid me to go or anything like that, Dina."

"He didn't?" she breathed skeptically.

"No. He asked if you sounded upset," Chet explained. "When I said that you did, he admitted that the two of you were having a few differences and he thought it was best that I didn't become involved in it. He didn't want me to be put in the

130

position of having to take sides when both of you are my friends."

Friends? Dina thought. Just a few days ago, Chet had been her fiancé, not her friend. But he looked so pathetically sorry for having let her down yesterday that she simply couldn't heap more guilt on his bowed head.

Instead she gave him the easy way out. "Blake was right, it isn't fair to put you in the middle of our disagreements. If I hadn't been so upset I would have realized it. Anyway, it doesn't matter now." She shrugged. "It all worked out for the best." That was a white lie, since it almost had, until their blowup that morning.

"I knew it would." The smile he gave her was tinged with relief. "Although I wasn't surprised to hear Blake admit that the two of you had got off to a rocky start." He removed the plastic lid from the cup and handed the cup to her.

"Why do you say that?" she asked.

"The two of you were always testing each other to see which was the stronger. It looks like you still are."

"Which one us is the stronger? In your opinion," Dina qualified her question.

"Oh, I don't know." His laughter was accompanied by a dubious shake of his head. "A feeling of loyalty to my own sex makes me want to say Blake, but I have a hunch I would be underestimating you."

In other words, Dina realized, Chet was not taking sides. He was going to wait until there was a clear-cut winner. In the meantime he was keeping his options open, buttering up both of them.

131

The minute the last thought occurred to her, Dina knew it had been influenced by Blake's comment that Chet was always beside the one in power. But she immediately squashed the thought as small and not deserving of someone as loyal as Chet.

"You're a born diplomat, Chet." She lifted the coffee cup in a toast. "No wonder you're such an asset to this company."

"I try to be," he admitted modestly, and touched the side of his cup to hers. "Here's to the new campaign."

The coffee was only medium hot and Dina took a big sip of it. Chet's reference to the new project made her glance at the papers, notes and lists spread over her desk.

"It's going to be quite a formidable project." She took a deep breath, aware of the magnitude of the image change for the Chandler Hotel chain. "But I can feel it's right and that it will be very successful."

"That's the third reason I'm here."

Her startled gaze flew to his face, her blue eyes rounded and bright with inquiry. "Why?"

Had she made Blake so angry that he was already taking her off the campaign? Oh, why hadn't she held her tongue, she thought, angered by the way she had kept pushing him.

"Blake wants me to work with you on it," Chet announced.

Her relief that Blake hadn't replaced her didn't last long. "Doesn't he think I'm capable of handling it by myself?" Her temper flared at the implied doubt of her ability.

"You wouldn't be here if he didn't believe you

could," he said placatingly. "But after all, you said it yourself. It's going to be a formidable project and you're going to need some help. I've been nominated to be your help. Besides, Blake knows how well we worked together as a team while he was gone."

Dina counted to ten, forcing herself to see the logic of Chet's explanation. But she wasn't sure that she liked the idea. There was still the possibility that Blake had appointed Chet as her watchdog and he would go running to Blake the instant she made a mistake.

She was doing it again, she realized with a desperate kind of anger. She was not only questioning Blake's motives, but making accusations against Chet's character, as well. Damn Blake, she thought, for putting doubts about Chet in her mind.

Chet took a long swig of his coffee, then set it aside. "Where shall we begin?"

"I've been making some lists," Dina readjusted her attention to the project at hand.

She went over the lists with Chet, discussing various points with him. Although Dina was still skeptical of Blake's motives in having Chet assist her, she accepted it at face value until she could prove otherwise. An hour later, Chet left her small office with a formidable list of his own to carry out.

The bulk of the day Dina spent getting the project organized. In itself, that was no easy task. At five o'clock, she was going over the master list again, making notes in the margins while various ideas were still fresh in her mind.

"Are you ready?" Blake's voice snapped from the open doorway.

Her head jerked up at the sound. The lenses of her glasses blurred his image, deceptively softening the toughness of his features. For an instant, Dina almost smiled a welcome, then the sharpness of his demanding question echoed in her mind. Recovering from that momentary rush of pleasure, Dina bent her head over the papers once again.

"I will only be a few more minutes." She adjusted the glasses on the bridge of her nose.

Blake walked in, his dislike at being kept waiting charging the air with tension. He sat in the straight-backed chair in front of her desk. Dina was conscious of his scrutiny, both of her and her work.

"Since when did you wear glasses?" he accused.

She touched a finger to a bow, realizing he had never seen her wearing them. "I began wearing them about a year ago."

"Do you need them?"

"What a ridiculous question!" she snapped. "Of course, I need them."

"It isn't so ridiculous," Blake contradicted with dry sarcasm. "They enhance the image of a crisp, professional career woman who has turned her back on domestic pursuits."

It was a deliberately baiting comment. Dina chose not to rise to the tempting lure. "With all the reading and close work I have had to do, it became too much of a strain on my eyes. After too many headaches, I put my vanity aside and began wearing glasses to read. They have nothing to do with my image," she lied, since the choice of frame styles had been made with that in mind.

"Then you do admit to having an image," he taunted her coldly.

It was no use. She simply couldn't concentrate on what she was doing. It took all of her attention to engage in this battle of words with him. Removing her glasses, she slipped them into their leather case. Dina set her notes aside and cleared the top of her desk.

"You haven't answered my question," Blake prompted in a dangerously quiet voice when she rose to get her coat.

"I hadn't realized your comment was a question." She took her purse from the lower desk drawer, unconsciously letting it slam shut to vent some of her tightly controlled anger.

"Is that how you see yourself, Dina, as a career woman whose life is centered around her work, with no time for a husband?" This time Blake phrased it as a question. The office was so small that when he stood up, he was blocking her path.

"That is hardly true." She faced him, her nerves quivering with his closeness.

"No?" An eyebrow lifted in challenging disbelief.

"Have you forgotten?" It was bravado that mocked him. "I was going to marry Chet, so I must have felt there was room for a husband in my life."

"I am your husband," Blake stated.

"I don't know you." Dina looked anywhere but into those inscrutable dark eyes.

"You knew me well enough this morning, in the most intimate sense of the word that a wife can 'know' her husband," Blake reminded her deliberately.

"This morning was a mistake." She brushed past him to escape into the hallway, but he caught her arm to half turn her around.

135

"Why was it a mistake?" he demanded.

"Because I let myself listen to all your talk about long, lonely nights and I started feeling sorry for you, that's why," Dina lied angrily, because she was still confused by her willingness to let him make love to her this morning when he still remained so much of a stranger to her in many ways.

His mouth thinned into a cruel line, all savage and proud. "Compassion is the last thing I want from you!" he snarled.

"Then stop asking me to pick up the threads of our life. The pattern has changed. I don't know you. The Blake Chandler that spent two and a half years in a jungle is a stranger to me. You may have had to live like an animal, but don't ask me to become your mate. I am more than just an object to satisfy your lust." The words streamed out, flooding over each other in their rush to escape. With each one, his features grew harder and harder until there was nothing gentle or warm left in them.

Blake gave her a push towards the door. "Let's go before you goad me into proving that you're right," he snapped.

Aware that she had nearly wakened a sleeping tiger whose appetites were ravenous, Dina quietly obeyed him. All during the ride back to his mother's house she kept silent, not doing anything to draw attention to herself. Blake ignored her, not a single glance straying to her. The cold war had briefly exploded into a heated battle, but once again the atmosphere was frigid.

Within minutes of entering the house, Blake disappeared into the library. Dina found herself alone in the living room with her mother-in-law, listening to the latest gossip Norma Chandler had picked up at the afternoon's meeting of the garden club.

"Of course, everyone was buzzing with the news about Blake," the woman concluded with a beaming smile. "They wanted to know every single detail of his adventure in the jungle. I thought they were never going to let me leave. Finally I had to insist that I come home to be here when you and Blake arrived."

Dina was certain that Norma Chandler had been the center of attention. No doubt, the woman had reveled in it, even if the spotlight had been a reflection of her son's.

"It was a thoughtful gesture to be waiting at the door when Blake came home from the office," she murmured, knowing some appreciation should be expressed. It was expected.

"I only wish he had waited a few more days before returning to the office," sighed Norma Chandler. "After all he's been through, he was entitled to rest for a few days."

Unspoken was the fact that it would have given her a chance to dote on him, coddle him like a little boy again. But the chance had been denied her and Norma Chandler was protesting. Dina wasn't sure if she was being blamed for Blake's decision to return to work so quickly. In case she was, she decided to set the record straight.

"It wasn't my idea that he had to come back right away. Blake has some bold, new plans for the company. I think he was eager to get back to work so he could put them into operation," Dina explained.

"I am sure you are right, but he isn't giving us much time to enjoy the fact that he is back. There I go," Norma Chandler scolded herself. "I'm complaining when I should be counting my blessings. It's just that I can't help wondering how much longer I'll have him."

"That's a peculiar thing to say," Dina frowned.

"You will probably be moving out soon—into a place of your own, won't you? Then I'll only be able to see him on weekends," she pointed out.

"We have discussed the possibility of getting a place of our own," Dina admitted, choosing her words carefully as she recalled their argument the previous morning. "But I don't think it will happen in the near future. We both will probably be too busy to do much looking. Naturally we don't want to move into just any place," she lied.

It wasn't that Dina had become so career-oriented that she didn't long for a home of her own as she had led Blake to believe. At the moment, she was relieved to live in the Chandler home where his mother and the housekeeper could serve as buffers. She wasn't ready yet to share a home solely with the stranger who was her husband. Maybe she never would be.

"I won't pretend that I'm not glad to hear you say that." Her mother-in-law smiled broadly at the statement. "You know how much I have enjoyed having you live here, Dina. Now that Blake is back, my happiness has been doubled. There is something about having a man around the house that makes it seem more like a home."

"Yes," Dina agreed, if not wholeheartedly.

"I don't like to pry." There was a hesitancy in the woman's voice and expression. "But I have the feeling that there is a bit of tension between you and Blake. If I am wrong, you just say so or tell me to mind my own business. I don't want to become an interfering mother-in-law, but—" Her voice trailed off in the expectancy of a response from Dina.

It was Dina's turn to hesitate. She doubted if Mother Chandler would understand, but she felt a need to confide her fears in someone.

"There is a tension between us," she admitted cautiously. "It's just that Blake has changed. And I have changed. We aren't the same people we were two and a half years ago."

"It's Chet, isn't it?" Norma Chandler drew her own conclusions, hardly listening to what Dina had said. "I know that Blake behaved in front of the others as if he understood and forgave, but it bothered him, didn't it?"

"To a certain extent, yes." But not to the degree that her mother-in-law was implying.

"It is only natural that he'd be upset to find his wife engaged to his best friend, but he'll come around. In a few years, you'll be laughing about it."

"Probably," Dina nodded, but she couldn't help wondering if they would be together in a few years. For that matter, she wondered if they would be together in a few months.

The housekeeper entered the living room. "Dinner is ready whenever you wish," she announced.

"Now is fine, Deirdre," Norma Chandler stated. "Blake is in the library. Would you please tell him?"

Dinner that evening was an awkward meal, one

139

that was made more awkward because Norma Chandler seemed determined to convince Blake how very properly Dina had behaved during his absence. Dina knew it was an outgrowth of their conversation and there was simply no way she could intervene. Blake seemed indifferent to the praise his mother heaped on Dina, which only prompted Norma Chandler to pile more on.

It was a relief to escape to the privacy of the bedroom after coffee had been served. The tension of the day and the evening had tightened her muscles into taut bands. The sight of the bed and the thought of sleeping beside Blake another night increased the tension. She was the captive of a crazy confusion, torn between dreading the idea of Blake making love to her again and looking forward to the possibility.

Dina walked from the bedroom into the private bath that adjoined it. She filled the porcelain tub with hot water and added a liberal amount of scented bubble bath. From her bedroom closet, she brought her robe and hung it on a door hook. Shedding her clothes, Dina stepped into the tub and submerged herself up to her neck in the steamy mound of bubbles.

Lying back in the tub, she let the warm water soak away the tension, and slowly relaxed in the soothing bath. The lavender fragrance of the bubbles wafted through the air, a balm to her senses. The water cooled and Dina added more hot, losing track of time in her watery cocoon.

The bedroom door opened and closed. Dina heard it, but she wasn't unduly concerned that

Blake had come to the room. The bathroom door was closed. She expected him to respect the desire for privacy it implied.

When the bathroom door was opened anyway, Dina sat up straight in a burst of indignation. The sound of sloshing water drew Blake's gaze. Minus his suit jacket and tie, he had unbuttoned the front of his shirt down to his stomach, exposing a disturbing amount of hard muscled flesh and dark chest hairs.

"Sorry, I didn't know you were in here," he apologized insincerely.

The bubbles had been slowly dissipating during her long soak. Only a few bits of foam remained around the uplifting curve of her breasts. The fact did not escape Blake's attention. It kept him from leaving.

Self-consciously Dina grabbed for a handcloth, holding it in front of her. "Now that you've discovered I'm in here, get out."

"I thought you might want me to wash your back, or wouldn't you consider that civilized behavior?" Blake mocked.

"I don't need my back washed, thank you." Dina wasn't sure why she had bothered with the washcloth. It was becoming wet and very clingy. "Please leave," she requested stiffly. "I'm finished with my bath and I'd like to get out of the tub."

"I'm not stopping you. The sooner you are out, the sooner I can take my shower." Blake turned and walked into the bedroom, closing the door behind him.

Not trusting him, Dina quickly rinsed away the

141

bubbles that were drying on her skin and stepped out of the tub. After rubbing herself down with the towel, she slipped into her robe and zipped it to the throat. Another few minutes were spent tidying the bathroom.

When she entered the bedroom, her senses were heightened to a fever pitch. Blake was sitting on the love seat, smoking a cigarette, his posture seemingly indolent. His hooded gaze swept over her.

"It's all yours." Dina waived a hand toward the bathroom.

Blake stubbed out his cigarette and uncoiled his length from the love seat. "Thank you." His response was cool and tauntingly lacking in gratitude.

Dina suppressed a shudder at his freezing politeness and wondered whether their heated exchanges were preferable to this. As he crossed the room, she walked to the closet. At the door, she stopped to glance at him.

It suddenly became imperative that she make him understand that she was not going to let him persuade her to make love, not until she was able to sort out her true feelings for him. She wanted to end this sensation that she was married to a stranger before they shared any further intimacies.

"Blake, I have no intention—" Dina began.

"Neither have I," he cut in sharply and paused at the doorway to the bathroom to pin her with his gaze. His mouth slanted in a cruel line. "I won't be exercising my husbandly rights with you. Didn't you think I was capable of phrasing it politely?" Blake mocked the sudden paleness of her complex-

142

y went. The one in Maine would be done with a
tical flavor. The one in Mexico would have a
y siesta look, complete with mock overhead fans
ning leisurely from the ceiling. The founding
el in Newport already had an elegant yachting
hosphere, which would now be stressed. The
mes varied with each hotel, depending on its
ation.

When the last photograph had been examined
d set aside, Dina looked at her copious collection
notes and sighed at the dollar signs they meant.
e remembered her spiteful comment to Blake
out the interior decorating to be done, remarking
at it was woman's work. Well, there was a moun-
in of it here, one that she doubted Blake would
ve the patience to tackle.

"Now what?" Chet questioned.

"Now—" Dina took a deep breath "—now we
ed to have these notes transferred into sketches."

"Do you want me to start contacting some deco-
ting firms?"

"I suppose so. With the scope of the work that
eds to be done, I'm just wondering how we
ould handle it." She nibbled thoughtfully at her
wer lip. "Something, either major or minor, has to
done at each of the hotels."

"In the past we've always used firms within the
ea of the hotels, in the same city when we could,"
et reminded her.

"Yes, I know." Dina slid the pencil through the
tinum gold hair above her ear. "I checked the
ords last week to get an idea of the possible costs
d noticed that in the past we'd always used local

ion. "Perhaps if I had promised not to rape you, it
would have been more in keeping with your image
of me, wouldn't it?"

Dina turned away from his caustic challenge. "As
long as we understand each other," she murmured
stiffly.

"Just so there isn't any mistake. I won't touch
you again until you come to me. And you will come
to me, Dina." There was something almost threatening in the savagely controlled tone he used.

The closing of the bathroom door left Dina shak-
en. She changed out of her robe into her nightgown
without being aware of her actions. She heard the
shower running in the bathroom and tried not to
visualize Blake standing beneath its spray, all sun-
browned flesh, naked and hard, as paganly virile as
a jungle god.

Shaking away the heady image, she walked to the
bed and folded down the satin coverlet. Dina was
between the silk sheets when Blake came out of the
bathroom, a towel wrapped around his waist. He
didn't glance her way as he switched off the light
and walked around to the opposite side of the bed,
unerringly finding his way in the dark. The mattress
didn't give beneath his weight, but she was aware of
him. The sheets seemed to transmit the heat from
his nude body.

A tidal way of longing threatened to swamp her.
Dina closed her eyes tightly. Blake was fully aware
of what he was doing to her. He had a motive for
everything he did. She didn't believe that he was
denying himself the possession of her out of respect,
any more than she believed he had assigned Chet to

help on the new project purely because she needed competent help. He wanted to undermine her trust in Chet. She vowed he wouldn't succeed.

But the aspersions Blake had made against Chet's character haunted her over the next two weeks. Again and again she cursed in silent protest at the seeds of doubt Blake had planted in her mind. The cold war between herself and Blake neither accelerated in those two weeks, nor was there even a hint of a thaw.

A knock at the opened door brought her out of her gloomy reverie. She had been staring out the dusty pane of the solitary window in her small office. She turned, slipping her reading glasses to a perch on top of her head.

"Hello, Chet." She stiffened at the sight of him and tried to relax, but she had become too self-conscious lately in his company, not feeling the same freedom and trust she had once found with him.

"I've finally got all the interior and exterior photographs of the hotels that you wanted." He indicated the stack of folders he was carrying with both hands. "I thought we should go over them together. Are you too busy to do it now?"

"No, bring them in." Dina began moving the papers from her desk. "Just give me a second to make some room."

Before the actual advertising campaign could begin, there was a lot of groundwork to be done. The most time-consuming part was improving the physical appearance of the hotels.

"I've already looked through them," Chet told her.

"Good," Dina nodded, and be[gan] herself.

The line of her mouth kept grow[ing] grimmer. By the time she reached t[he] stack of photographs, she realized s[he un]timated the amount of time and [it would] take to superficially redo the hotels.

"It's worse than I thought," she si[ghed].

"Yes, I know," Chet agreed, matc[hing her expres]sion.

"Let's take the hotels one by [one, with] notes." She sighed. "The one thing w[e must keep] in mind is that each hotel should b[e] decor indigenous to its location. We [don't want a] vacationer to think that if he's been [in one Chan]dler Hotel, he's been in them all."

"That's right."

"Okay, let's start out with the one[s in]. Dina gazed at the photographs. "I thi[nk they're] the most challenging. I didn't realize [they were so] sterile."

She flipped her glasses into place o[n her nose and] reached for her note pad. 'Here we['ll take advan]tage of the tropical environment. He[re we need] furniture, light and airy colors, no [heavy drapes,] tile floors, and lots of potted plants [and flowers.] Something like the decor in our [Hawaiian hotels] would be good, but without the Poly[nesian touch."

"What about the exterior?"

Dina thought of the budget and [replied, "I think] we can get by with some landscapi[ng. We don't want] to do a major face lift unless there's [a need."]

Down the list of hotels and th[eir]

firms. Before, it had proved to be both economical and good business to trade with a company in the same area as one of our hotels."

"But, since virtually all the hotels are involved, it might not be practical because of all the traveling that would have to be done," he observed. "That cost could eat into whatever savings we might realize by using a local decorator."

"I'm afraid you're right," she agreed with a rueful nod. "We might be better off with a major firm capable of doing all the work. In the long run it might prove to be the more economical choice."

"I tell you what—" Chet leaned forward, his blue gray eyes bright with suggestion "—first let's get these notes typed up. Then why don't I contact two major companies to give us estimates on the work? To get a comparison, I can pick a half dozen hotels that are fairly close to here and obtain bids from local firms. I can use the hotel in Maine, the one here in Newport, naturally, the one in the Poconos—I can check the list."

"That might work," she agreed, turning the idea over in her mind and liking it. It had been a half-formed thought in her own mind, but when Chet had spoken it aloud, it had solidified. "Excellent suggestion, Chet."

"I'll get started on it right away." He began gathering up the notes and the photographs from her desk. "We don't want to waste time."

"Before you go, there's something else I've been thinking about that I wanted to talk over with you to get your opinion," Dina said to detain him.

"What's that?" Chet sat back down.

"To keep this continuity of every hotel being individual, I think we should carry it into the restaurants," she explained.

"But we're doing that." He frowned. "There are going to be decor changes in the restaurants and lounges, too. We just went over them."

"No, I was thinking of extending the idea to the food."

"Do you mean changing the menus?"

"Not completely. We would have to keep the standard items like steaks, et cetera, but add some regional specialities, as well. We do it already along the coast with the seafood."

"I see what you're saying." Chet nodded. "In the Poconos, for instance, we could add some Pennsylvania Dutch foods. We could even carry it down to little touches, like serving genuine johnnycake made out of white cornmeal with the dinner rolls here in Newport."

"Exactly," Dina nodded.

"I'll contact the restaurant managers of all the hotels. Those that aren't already doing this can send us a list of three or four speciality dishes they can add to their menus," he suggested.

"Yes, do that. We can initiate this change right away by simply adding a flyer to the menus until new ones can be printed."

"Consider it done, Dina." He started to rise, then paused. "Is that all?"

"For now, anyway," she laughed.

"I'll be talking to you. And I'll have my secretary send you a copy of these notes," he promised, and gathered the stack of notes and photographs into his arms.

As Chet walked out of the office, the smile left Dina's face and was replaced by a wary frown. She stared at the open doorway, feeling those uneasy suspicions rearing their ugly heads. Then with a firm shake of her head she dismissed them and turned back to the papers she had been working on.

CHAPTER EIGHT

BENT OVER HER DESK, Dina was concentrating on the proposals from the selected advertising agencies. Absently she stroked the eraser tip of her pencil through her hair. Intent on the papers, she didn't hear the footsteps in the hallway or notice the tall figure darkening her open doorway.

"Are you planning to work late?"

The sound of Blake's voice jerked her head up. He stood there, so lithely powerful, so magnetically attractive. The darkness of his tan seemed to have faded little, its bronze hue accentuated by the white turtleneck sweater. Through half-closed lids he looked at her, creating the impression of lazy and friendly interest, yet his expression seemed masked.

As always when he caught her unaware, her pulse accelerated. An odd tightness gripped her throat, leaving her with a breathless sensation. For an instant the room seemed to spin crazily.

It was at moments like these that Dina wanted to let the powerful attraction she felt simply carry her away. But that was too easy and too dangerous. It wouldn't solve any of the differences that had grown in the years they were apart.

His question finally registered. She managed to tear her gaze away from his ever watchful eyes to glance at her wristwatch, surprised to see it was a few minutes before six o'clock.

Then she noticed the silence in the rest of the building. There were no muffled voices coming in from the hallway, no clackety-clack of typewriters. Nearly everyone had left for the day, except herself and Blake.

"I hadn't realized it was so late," she offered in answer to his question. "I just have to clear these things away and I'll be ready to leave."

As she stacked the proposals one on top of the other, preparatory to slipping them into their folder, Blake wandered into the room. He suddenly seemed to fill every square inch of it. Within herself, Dina was conscious of the sensuous disturbance his presence caused.

"How is the campaign progressing?" he inquired, his gaze flicking to the papers in her hand.

Dina had to search for the chilling antagonism that would keep him at a distance. "Hasn't Chet been keeping you informed?"

"No. Was he supposed to?" There was a baiting quality to the blandness of his voice.

"I presumed he would," she retorted, opening a desk drawer to put the folder away.

"If you didn't tell him to keep me up to date, Chet won't," said Blake, hooking a leg over the desk corner to sit on its edge. "He only does what he's told."

The desk drawer was slammed shut. "Will you stop that!" Dina glared at him.

"Stop what?" Blake returned with seeming ignorance.

"Stop making remarks like that about Chet!" The antagonism was there; she no longer had to search for it.

151

Blake made an indifferent shrug. "Whatever you say."

Impatiently she swept the remaining papers and pens into the middle drawer of her desk, leaving the top neat and orderly. Setting her bag on top, she pushed her chair up to the desk. Her sweater was lying on the back of the chair near where Blake stood.

"Hand me my sweater, please." Frigid politeness crept into her voice.

Glancing around, Blake slipped it off the chair back and held it out to her as she walked around the desk to the front. "How are you and Chet getting along?"

"The same as always—very well." Dina gave him a cool look and started to reach for the sweater. "Did you expect it to be different?" It was spoken as a challenge, faintly haughty. A light flashed in her mind and she forgot about the sweater. "You did expect it to change, didn't you?" she accused.

"I don't know what you're talking about."

"That's why you told Chet to give me a hand. I thought it was because you didn't think I could handle the job, but that wasn't it at all, was it?" Her anger was growing with each dawning thought.

Completely in control, Blake refused to react. "You tell me."

"You planted all those doubts in my mind about Chet, then made me work with him, hoping I would become poisoned against him. That's what this was all about, wasn't it?" Dina was incensed at the way Blake had attempted to manipulate her thinking.

"I admit that after our little talk about Chet, I

152

hoped the blinkers would come off and you would see him as he really is." There wasn't a trace of regret in his expression or his voice that his motive had been uncovered.

"That is the lowest, dirtiest thing I've ever heard!" she hissed.

Trembling with rage, she was completely unaware of her hand lashing out to strike him until it was caught in a vise grip short of its target. She gasped in pain as he twisted her arm to force her closer. He had straightened from the desk to stand before her, the sweater cast aside on the desk top.

"The last time you slapped me, I let you get away with it because I might have deserved it. But not this time," Blake told her flatly. "Not when I'm telling the truth."

"But it isn't the truth!" Dina flared, undaunted by his implied threat. "Not one word you've said against Chet is true. It's all lies. None of it is true!"

That darkly piercing look was back in his eyes as they scanned her upturned face. "You know it's true, don't you?" he breathed in a low, satisfied voice. "You've started to see it for yourself—that's why you're so angry."

"No, it isn't true," she denied. "I haven't seen it."

"You have. Why don't you admit it?" Blake insisted with grim patience.

"No," Dina continued to resist and strained to break free of his hold. "And I'm not going to stay here and listen to you tear Chet down anymore."

He increased the pressure of his grip and issued a taut denial. "I am not trying to make him appear less of a man. I'm trying to make you see him the way he is and not the way you've imagined him to be. Why can't you understand that what I'm saying is not a personal attack on him?"

Suddenly, unexpectedly, she did understand and she believed him. The discovery took the heat out of her anger. Dina stopped fighting him and stood quietly.

"All right," she admitted.

"All right what?" Blake lowered his gaze to her mouth, watching her lips as they formed the answering words.

"I have noticed a few things," Dina admitted further.

"Such as?"

"The way he takes a suggestion and elaborates on it until you're almost convinced the idea was his in the first place."

"He's done that?"

"Yes. Today, when I mentioned an idea I had about adding regional dishes to the restaurant menus." She wished Blake would stop watching her talk. It was unsettling, heightening her senses. "He's already contacting the restaurant managers to see about starting it."

"Chet is very good at organizing and carrying out a suggestion," Blake agreed. "What else?"

"I don't know. A lot of little things." The compliment Blake had given Chet prompted Dina to mention another conversation that had bothered her. "When I didn't take a stand today about having a local or a major decorating firm redo the hotels, Chet didn't either. He suggested getting comparison bids from both and avoided offering a concrete

154

opinion. In the last two weeks, I honestly can't remember Chet making a decision or offering a proposal of his own."

Looking back, she realized that his proposal of marriage had been an outgrowth of a conversation about whether she would marry again or not. When she had coneded the possibility, Chet had asked if it would be someone like Blake she would choose. Her negative answer had then led to Chet's suggesting himself, after first testing out his ground.

That was hardly the mark of the strong, dependable man she had believed him to be. His reliability was limited to the times when someone else told him what to do.

Lost in her thoughts, Dina was unaware of the silence that had fallen between them until Blake spoke. "I have another equally selfish reason for wanting Chet to work with you on this project." His fingers were lightly stroking the inside of her wrist, a caressing motion that was disturbing.

A tingling warmth spread up her arm, her nerves fluttering in awareness of how close she stood to him. "What is it?" There was a breathless catch to her voice. She looked into his eyes, nearly overcome by the sensation that she could willingly drown in the dark pools.

"Because I know that eventually this project is going to entail a good deal of traveling and I wanted to make certain it wasn't my wife who went on these trips."

"I see." She couldn't think of anything else to say.

"You might as well know this, Dina," he said.

"You and I are never going to be separated for any reason."

The ruthlessly determined note underlying his statement made her shiver. There was a sense of being trapped, a feeling that his wishes were inescapable. Whatever Blake wanted, he got. But not from her, her pride protested—not unless it was her own decision to agree.

With a degree of reluctance, she withdrew from his touch, turning to the desk to pick up her sweater and handbag. "I'm ready to leave now," she said, aware of the conflicting magnetic currents between them, alternately pulling and repelling.

Blake didn't make a move to leave. He just stood there looking at her, making her feel more uncomfortable and unsure of her own wants and needs.

"Sooner or later you're going to have to make a decision," he told her.

"I know. Sooner or later," she echoed softly.

"Why are you waiting? What is holding you back?" he questioned. "It isn't Chet anymore, so what's left?"

"I don't know." Dina shook her head uncertainly.

Needing to move, she started for the door. With that animal silence she was beginning to associate with him, Blake came up behind her, his hands sliding over her shoulders. The mere touch of him stopped her in her tracks.

"Decide now," Blaked ordered in a low murmur.

The silvery gold length of her hair was secured in a bun low on the back of her head. She felt the warm stirring of his breath on the exposed skin of her neck, sensitive and vulnerable. The sensuous pressure of his lips exploring that special pleasure point sent a delicious tremor through her.

His hands slid down to her forearms, crossing them in front of her as he molded her shoulders, waist and hips to the hard contours of his body. Dina felt as pliable as putty, willing to be shaped into anything he wanted. Primitive passions scorched through her veins.

She struggled out of the emotional upheaval going on within her to protest, "Blake, I can't!"

"You want to." His mouth moved to her ear, his teeth nibbling at its lobe. "You know you do."

"I don't know anything," she breathed raggedly.

"Then feel," Blake instructed.

That was the problem. She felt too much and it blocked out her thinking processes. She didn't want to make a decision in the heat of an embrace. And certainly not in this inferno that was consuming her now.

"Blake, no!" She swallowed and pushed his hands from around her waist.

She took a step away from his tempting embrace and stopped, shaking and weak with desire. Her head was lowered, her chin tucked into her throat. She felt his gaze boring into her shoulders.

"Blake, no!" He mimicked her words with a biting inflection. "That's always your answer. How much longer are you going to keep giving it?"

"Until I'm absolutely sure that I know what I'm doing," Dina answered.

"And how long will that be?" Blake was striving for control. It was evident in the clipped patience of his tone.

"I don't know," she sighed. "I just know it's easy to surrender to passion now and not so easy to face tomorrow."

"Then you're a hell of a lot stronger than I am, Dina," he snapped, "because I don't give a damn about tomorrow!" He slipped a hand under her elbow. Her first thought was that he intended to ignore her uncertainties and kiss her into submission, something that would not be too difficult to do. Instead his hand pushed her forward. "Let's go," he muttered.

His long, ground-eating strides made it impossible for Dina to keep up with him without half running. The rigid set of his jaw kept her from drawing attention to herself or her plight. He didn't slow down until he reached the parking lot, where she struggled to catch her breath as they walked to the car.

Without looking directly at her, Blake unlocked the passenger door and held it open for her, slamming it shut when she was safely inside. Walking around the car, he unlocked his own door and slid behind the wheel. He put the key in the ignition, but didn't start the car.

Resting his hands on the steering wheel, he stared straight ahead for several long seconds, a forbiddingly hard line to his mouth. Dina grew increasingly uneasy at the silence and felt pinned when his dark glaze finally swung to her. It wasn't a pleasant sensation.

"The first day I was back," Blake said, "you claimed we needed time to get to know each other again—that we had to become adjusted to each other again. You felt we should talk."

"I'm surprised you remember," she remarked, and could have bitten off her tongue for issuing such caustic words.

"Believe me, I remember everything you've said," he returned with dry weariness, his attention shifting to the windshield in front of him. Dina shifted uncomfortably in her seat, but remained silent. "The point is, Dina, that we aren't getting to know each other again. We aren't talking. The only place we spend any time together alone is in the bedroom. And we both know there isn't any communication taking place there, physical or otherwise."

"So what are you suggesting? That we should communicate on a physical level and work on from there?" Dina questioned stiffly, her pulse quickening in a reaction that did not reject the idea.

"No, that isn't what I'm suggesting—" there was a cynical twist to his mouth "—although I know you're convinced that my instincts have become purely primitive."

A slight flush warmed her cheeks. "Then what are you suggesting?"

"That we spend more time together, as you wanted."

"That's a bit difficult with both of us working."

"Neither of us works on the weekend," Blake reminded her.

"You're forgetting we live in your mother's house." And Mother Chandler had still not got over her son's miraculous return. She still hovered around him every possible moment she could.

"No, I'm not," Blake returned calmly. "The key word is alone—no friends, no relatives, just you and

I. I realize that can't be accomplished in my mother's home. That's why I've decided we'll spend the weekend at Block Island so we can have the time alone together that you claim we need."

"Block Island." Dina repeated the name of the resort island located roughly fourteen miles off the Rhode Island coast.

"That's what I said. Any objections?" He turned his head to look at her, a challenging glitter in his dark eyes.

"None." How could there be when he had cornered her with her own words?

"There is one thing more, Dina." Blake continued to study her, aware of her reluctant agreement—although why it was reluctant, Dina didn't know.

"What's that?" She was almost afraid to ask.

"I want this clearly understood before we go. If you haven't made up your mind about us by Sunday night, I'm not waiting any longer." At the sight of her paling complexion, he smiled without humor. "And I don't care whether you consider that a threat or a promise."

"You can't make a deadline like that," she protested.

"Can't I?" Blake had already turned away to start the car, ignoring her now that he had stated his intentions.

"All you're doing is turning this weekend into a farce," Dina retorted.

"Call it what you like," Blake said indifferently. "Just be sure to pack a suitcase and bring it to the office with you Friday morning. We'll catch the ferry to Block Island after work."

As THE FERRY LEFT the protected waters of Narragansett Bay for the open waters of the Atlantic heading for the porkchop-shaped island offshore, Dina stared sightlessly at the Brenton Reef Light Tower. She and Blake had barely exchanged five words with each other since leaving the office, and the silence was growing thicker.

She knew the reason her lips were so tightly closed. Blake's Sunday night ultimatum had made her feel as if he was pointing a gun at her head. So how could she look forward to the weekend ahead of them? He had already foreordained the outcome, so what was the purpose? She should have refused to come. Why hadn't she?

Pressing a hand to her forehead, she tried to rub away the dull throb. The pills she had taken to stave off the sea sickness were working, but they clouded her thinking processes. At least she had been spared the embarrassment of being sick all over the place, even if she did feel slightly drugged.

Sighing, she glanced at Blake standing a few yards away talking to a fellow passenger. Their attention was on the low-hanging, dull gray clouds overhead. There was nothing menacing about them, but they added to the gloom Dina felt.

The two were obviously discussing the weather, because Dina overheard the man remark, "I hope you're right that it's going to be sunny and clear at the island. I don't know anything about ocean currents and how they affect the weather. All I know is that I want to get a weekend of fishing in."

Blake's prediction of good weather on Block Island proved correct. They were within sight of their destination when the clouds began to thin, permitting glimpses of blue sky and a sinking yellow sun. When the ferry docked at the Old Harbor landing, there were only patches of clouds in the sky.

But the silence between Dina and Blake didn't break. Despite that, she felt her spirits lift as they drove off the ferry onto the island, named after Adrian Block, the first European to explore it. The island's atmosphere was refreshing and Dina understood why it had been a fashionable health spa in the Gay Nineties.

She became absorbed in the scenery as Blake drove across the island to the picturesque resort village of New Harbor stretched along the banks of the Great Salt Pond. It had once been an inland lake, but a man-made channel now linked it to the ocean, providing a spacious harbor for both pleasure craft and commercial fishing boats.

Much of the previous tension returned when Blake parked in front of a hotel. It seemed different somehow to share a hotel room. Just why, Dina couldn't say, since they'd been sharing a bedroom almost ever since Blake had returned. She felt self-conscious walking beside him into the lobby.

Blake glanced down at her, his gaze inspecting the discomfited look on her face. "How are you feeling?"

"Fine," Dina rushed out the answer.

"No leftover nausea from the ferry trip?"

"None. Actually I never felt I was going to be sick. Except for a slight headache, I'm fine," she insisted. "Either the pills are getting stronger or I'm finally outgrowing my sea sickness."

"Good." His smile was somewhat grim. "Excuse me. I'll go check on our reservation."

As he walked to the desk to register, she lingered near a rack of postcards, pretending an interest in their colorful pictures. There was a curling sensation in her stomach when she saw the porter take their bags. Blake walked toward her and she immediately picked a card from the rack, ostensibly to study it more closely.

"Were you planning to send a postcard to someone?" The cynically amused query didn't help her fluttering stomach.

"No." She quickly returned it to the rack. "I was just looking at the picture."

"Tomorrow we'll take a look at the real thing."

Dina had to glance at the postcard. She had been so conscious of Blake she hadn't noticed what the subject of the card had been. Now she saw it was a lighthouse.

"It looks interesting," she offered, just to be saying something.

"Yes," Blake agreed dryly, as if aware that she hadn't previously known what it was. "Shall we go to our rooms?"

"Rooms?" In the plural, her eyes asked.

"Yes, two," he answered. Dina was surprised by the gentle, almost tender expression of patience that crossed his usually hard features. "We have adjoining bedrooms. I intend to give this weekend every chance of proving whatever it is that you feel needs proving, Dina."

There didn't seem to be any response she could make. Strangely, this seemed more of a concession

163

than all the nights when Blake had shared her bed without forcing an intimacy—perhaps because he was granting her the privacy to think without his presence to disturb or influence her.

When he handed her one of the keys in his hand, she managed a quiet, "Thank you."

"When a man is desperate, he'll try anything," Blake returned cryptically, but Dina thought she caught a glimmer of humor in his dark eyes. It made him seem more human.

They walked to their rooms in silence, but it was no longer as strained as it had been. Blake hesitated outside his door, catching her eye for an instant before he turned the key in his lock and walked in.

Entering her room, Dina noticed her suitcase lying on the luggage rack and walked over to it, intending to unpack. Instead, she paused at the interior door that connected the two bedrooms. Blake was on the other side of it. Unconsciously she reached for the doorknob. It refused to turn; the door was locked. Regret conflicted with relief as she walked back to her suitcase and unpacked.

An hour later she had showered and was dressed in a wheat-colored shirtwaist dress that was elegantly casual. Blake hadn't said whether he would meet her at the restaurant for dinner or go down with her. She debated whether she should wait in the room or go to the restaurant, then decided to wait and she sat down on the bed.

Instantly a smile curved her lips. The mattress was blissfully soft, sinking beneath her weight like feather down. It was going to be a wonderful change from Blake's rock-firm mattress at the house.

Just then there was a knock at her door and Dina rose to answer it, the smile lingering on her lips. Blake stood outside, his eyes warming to a dark brown at her expression.

"You look pleased at something," he commented.

"My bed," Dina explained, a pair of dimples etching grooves in her cheeks. "It's soft."

His chuckle of understanding was soft, almost silent—a disarming sight and sound. Her heart skipped a beat, then refused to return to an even tempo.

"Shall we go to dinner?"

It was more of a statement than a question as Blake held out his hand for hers. Self-consciously she let her fingers be engulfed in his hand, but he continued to block the doorway, not permitting her to step out. His hold on her hand shifted, raising the inside of her wrist to his mouth.

"Have I told you how very beautiful you are?" he murmured.

"Blake, please," Dina protested, her lashes fluttering down at the heady touch of his warm lips against the sensitive area of her wrist.

"It's simply a compliment," he interrupted with a wry smile as he brought her hand away. "All you have to do is say 'thank you.'"

"Thank you," she repeated in a tight little voice, more disturbed than she cared to acknowledge by the effect he had on her.

"That's better." Blake moved to the side, leading her out of the room and reaching behind her to close the hotel-room door.

Fresh seafood was the natural selection to make

from the menu. Once that decision had been made, Dina sat in the chair opposite from Blake. Inside she was a bundle of twisted nerves, but she forced herself to be still.

Without the steady chatter of Mother Chandler to lead a table conversation, she couldn't think of anything to say. It seemed an indication of how far she and Blake had grown apart. Her tongue was tied into knots.

"I'm going to have to make a trip to the bookstore soon," Blake commented with seeming idleness. "I have a lot of reading to catch up on."

"Yes, I suppose you do." Dina wanted to cry at how stilted her response had been.

But Blake either didn't notice it or deliberately ignored it. "It sounds a little crazy, I know, but reading was one of the things I really missed. More than good meals and clean clothes. I never considered it a necessity before."

"I doubt if I have, either," she admitted, forgetting her self-consciousness at his provocative comment.

"Any new titles you'd like to recommend?"

Dina hesitated, then suggested, *Roots*.

Before she realized what was happening, she found herself becoming engrossed in a discussion of new books that had been published in Blake's absence, and titles they had both read in the past. From reading, their conversation drifted to movies and Broadway shows. It seemed a natural progression to tell him about things she had done while he was gone, decisions she had been forced to make, such as subletting their apartment and sorting their furnishings.

166

When Blake later signaled their waiter for the check, Dina was astounded to discover that it was after ten o'clock and there had not been one awkward moment between them, not a single remark that had been in any way argumentative. She hadn't thought it was possible. She wondered if Blake had noticed it, but was afraid to ask. She didn't want to risk breaking whatever kind of temporary truce they had established.

They both seemed to be in a reflective mood as they retraced their way to their rooms. Dina was conscious of his hand lightly resting on the back of her waist, a faintly possessive air to his guiding touch, but she didn't object to it in the least.

"Do you know what this reminds me of?" Blake questioned her when they paused in front of her door.

"What?" Dina looked up, curious and thoughtful.

"All those times I used to walk you to the door of your sorority house and kiss you good night in a dark corner of the building." He glanced around the hallway, "Of course, here there aren't any dark corners." His gaze returned to her face. "But I *am* going to kiss you good night."

His head bent and Dina lifted hers to meet him halfway. The kiss was searingly light and questing, both seeking answers to unknown questions. Each seemed to realize that it would take only the slightest provocation to deepen the embrace to one of passion. Yet neither made it, merely testing the temperature of the water without becoming submerged in it.

With obvious reluctance they both withdrew from the embrace, gazing silently at each other. Blake took a step back, a closed look stealing over his face.

"Do you have your key?" he asked.

"Yes." Dina unfastened her clutch purse and took it out.

He hesitated a fraction of a second. "Good night, Dina." He moved toward his own door.

"Good night, Blake," she murmured, and entered her hotel room alone.

CHAPTER NINE

DINA DIDN'T SLEEP WELL that night. The irony of it was that it was because the mattress was too soft. She was wakened from her fitful dozing by a knock on the door and stumbled groggily across the room to answer it.

"Who is it?" She leaned tiredly against the door, her hand resting on the locked night latch.

"Blake," was the answer. "Are you ready for breakfast?"

Dina groaned. It couldn't possibly be morning already.

"Are you all right?" His tone was low and piercing.

"Fine," she mumbled, adding silently, *I just need some sleep.*

The doorknob rattled as he attempted to open it. "Unlock the door, Dina," he ordered.

She was too tired to think of a reason to refuse and too tired to argue if she had one. Slipping off the night chain, she unlocked the latch and stepped aside as Blake pushed the door open. Concern was written all over his expression, but she didn't notice.

"I don't want breakfast," Dina was already turning to make her way back to the bed. "You go ahead without me."

Blake's arm went around her to turn her back.

He pushed the tangle of corn-silk hair behind her ear and held it there, his hand cupping the side of her head and tipping it up. His strength was a glorious thing and Dina willingly let him support her weight, too weary to stand on her own.

"What's the matter, Dina? You look exhausted." Blake was frowning.

"I am," she sighed. "My beautifully soft bed was too soft. I barely slept all night."

He laughed softly. "Why didn't you take a pillow and blanket off the bed and sleep on the floor? Or was that too uncivilized for you?" He mocked her in a gently teasing voice.

"I suppose that's what you did?" Dina lifted her tired lashes to glance at him. He looked disgustingly refreshed and rested.

"Yes," he nodded.

"And probably slept like a baby," she added enviously.

"I didn't sleep all that well," Blake denied.

"Why not?" Dina slid her arms around his hard, warm body and rested her head against his shoulder, closing her eyes.

"I haven't liked sleeping alone since I met you."

His provocative statement sailed over her sleepy head. Dina was only aware of how very right it felt to be in his arms, so comfortable and so warm. She snuggled closer.

"Why don't you just hold me for a while and let me sleep?" she suggested in a sleepy murmur.

"I don't think so." The arm that had been around her withdrew to press a hand against her rib cage just below her breast to push her away. "If I hold

170

you much longer, I won't be thinking about sleep," Blake stated, a half smile curving one corner of his mouth. "Why don't you shower and dress? I'll go get some coffee to help you wake up before we go to breakfast."

Dina didn't have a chance to agree or disagree. One minute she was in his arms and the next he was walking to the door, leaving her swaying there unsteadily. The closing of the door goaded her into movement. She looked longingly at the bed, but knew it was no use. Even if she could go back to sleep, Blake would be back shortly to waken her. Following his suggestion, she walked to the bathroom.

It was shortly after midmorning by the time Blake and Dina finished their breakfast and started out on a leisurely tour of the island, dotted with freshwater ponds. It was not the first visit for either of them, but it had been several years since their last.

There was little noticeable change on the island, with the possible exception that a few more trees had been planted by property owners. The young saplings looked forlorn in a landscape that was remarkably devoid of trees. Early settlers had long ago cut down the native ones for lumber to build their homes. Reforestation was a new and slow process.

Stone fences crisscrossed the rolling terrain. The rocks had been deposited on the island by glaciers from the Ice Age and stacked, probably long ago by slave labor, to erect property boundaries of early farms. They were a picturesque touch on the island,

171

called by an early Italian navigator God's Little Isle.

On the southeastern shore Blake parked the car on Mohegan Bluffs. The picture-postcard lighthouse sat on the point of the bluffs, the rustic house and tower looking out to sea. Its navigational beacon was one of the most powerful on the New England coastline.

The salty breeze off the ocean was cool. Dina zipped the coral windbreaker up to her neck while Blake locked the car. Screeching seagulls soared overhead as they walked together past the lighthouse to the steep path leading down the headland to the beach.

A fisherman stood knee-deep in the surf, casting a fly line into the whitecaps. He nodded a friendly acknowledgment to them as they strolled by. Blake's arm was around Dina's shoulders, keeping her close to his side. She stepped over a piece of driftwood and turned her gaze up to his face. His features were relaxed with a look of contentment about them.

"Why are we getting along so well?" she mused, more to herself than to him.

"Maybe it's because we've stopped looking at each other," Blake suggested.

"What?" A bewildered frown creased her forehead, confusion darkening the blue of her eyes.

"It does sound a bit strange, doesn't it?" A faint smile touched his mouth when he glanced at her, then he directed his gaze ahead of them, a contemplative look about his expression. "What I think I mean is that we've stopped trying to see the flaws in each other, the differences. We've started looking outward together."

"Do you suppose that's it?" Dina, too, shifted her gaze to the beach in front of them.

"Why bother to analyze the reason?" he countered. "Why not just enjoy it?"

"That's true." She scuffed a canvas toe against a stone. "Except that I like to know the why of things."

"So I remember," Blake murmured dryly. "Like the time I gave you your engagement ring and you wanted to know what made me decide to propose to you."

Dina laughed. "And you said it was because I would make such a beautiful ornament in your home." The laughter died as she gave him a guarded look. "Is that the way you regard women? As ornaments?"

There was a hint of exasperation in his impatient glance. "You should know me better than that, Dina."

She was silent for several paces. "That's the problem, I guess—I'm not certain anymore how well I know you. You always seemed so cultured. Now—" she lifted her hand in a searching gesture "—you are so...earthy."

"I suppose I learned that the basics of life are more important. The rest is just window dressing. Fundamentally I don't believe I've changed."

"Perhaps I was so busy looking for the window dressing that I didn't recognize you," she wondered aloud.

"Perhaps," Blake conceded. He flashed her a

173

quick smile. "How did we get started on such a serious discussion?"

His lightning switch from a pensive mood to one that was lightly teasing was infectious. Dina responded immediately, "I don't know. You started it."

"No, I didn't. You did," he corrected her in the same light vein, "when you questioned why we weren't arguing."

"You didn't have to answer me, so therefore it's all your fault," she shrugged.

"Logic like that could only come from a woman," Blake declared with an amused shake of his head.

"Are you making disparaging remarks against my sex again?" she demanded in mock anger.

"I'm just stating facts," he insisted.

Dina gave him a sideways push with her shoulder. Knocked off balance, his arm slipped from around her and he had to take a step to one side to recover. Their aimless pace had taken them closer to the water's edge than either had realized, and when Blake took that step, his foot—shoe, sock and trouser cuff landed in salt water—Dina gasped in a laugh at the one wet foot.

"So you think its funny, do you?" He took a playfully threatening step toward her.

Unconsciously she began to retreat. "Honestly, Blake, I'm sorry." She was trying hard not to laugh, but it bubbled in her voice. "I didn't know. I didn't mean to push you in the water, honestly."

Blake continued to approach her. "Let's see if it's so funny when you get wet."

"Blake, no!" Dina kept backing up, swallowing

the laughter as she negatively shook the silver gold mane of her hair.

The wicked glint in his eye warned her that words would not appease him. Turning, she ran, sprinting for the rock bluff at a safer distance from the lapping ocean waves. Blake chased her, his long strides eating up her short lead. Any moment he would overtake her, Dina knew, and she spared a laughing glance over her shoulder.

A piece of driftwood in her path tripped her and sent her sprawling headlong onto the beach. Her outstretched arms broke most of her fall. Unharmed, she rolled onto her back, out of breath but still trying not to laugh, as Blake dropped to his knees beside her.

"Are you all right?" he asked, half smiling and half concerned.

"Fine," she managed to gasp.

Sitting on his heels, Blake watched silently as she caught her breath. But as her breathing slowed, her heartbeat increased. An exciting tension was leaping between them, quivering over her nerve ends in lightning stimulation.

Blake moved forward as if to assist her to her feet, but as he moved closer, arms bracing him above her, her lips parted, glistening moistly. Dina lifted her hands to his chest as if to resist him, but instead they slid around his neck, pulling him down.

Fire ignited at the hard pressure of his mouth, hungry and demanding. It spread through her veins, her bones melting under the intense heat. The weight of his body crushed her to the rocky sand. It was an exquisite pain. No part of her was immune to the fire Blake was arousing so thoroughly.

Reeling under the torrid assault of his desire, she knew she had lost control. She made no attempt to regain it, willing to let his lips dominate hers for as long as he chose. With each breath, she drew in the intoxicating scent of him, warm and magic, a fuel for the fire that consumed her.

Never had Dina felt so alive. Every corner of her heart was filled with love, overflowing and spilling out like a volcano. Any differences were burned away by the fiery embrace that transcended physical limits.

"Hey, mister?" She heard a child's voice when previously she had only been able to hear the pagan rhythms of their matching heartbeats. "Hey, mister!" This time the voice was more insistent and Blake dragged his mouth from hers to roll onto his side. "Have you seen my puppy?"

A young boy of six stood beside them, knees dirty, a baseball cap on his light brown hair, staring at them innocently. Dina could feel Blake gathering the control to answer him.

"No, son, I haven't." His reply was tight and brief to conceal the raggedness of his breathing.

"He's white and black with a red collar," the boy explained.

"Sorry, we haven't seen him," Blake repeated patiently.

"If you do, would you bring him back to me?"

"Sure."

"Thanks." And he trotted off, disappearing around a jutting promontory on the beach.

Blake stared in the direction the boy had taken. "A few more seconds and it could have been embarrassing," he remarked grimly. "Come on." Rolling to his feet, he caught at Dina's hand to pull her along with him.

"Where are we going?" There was a faint pink to her cheeks.

"Back to the hotel."

"Why?"

"You're forgetting," he answered accusingly, flashing her a look that still had the smoldering light of desire. "I have a wet shoe, sock and pant leg."

Slightly subdued, Dina offered, "I'm sorry about that."

"I'm not." His finger touched her lips, tracing their outline, warm and still throbbing from his possession of them. "If that's what I get for a wet foot, I can't help wondering what would happen if I'd been drenched from head to toe." She breathed in sharply, wanting to tell him he didn't have to wait to find out, but she simply couldn't say the words. Blake didn't wait for her to speak, removing his fingers from her lips to encircle her hand. "Let's go, shall we?"

Dina nodded in silent agreement.

The magic moment lay between them on their return trip to the hotel, the irrevocable change it had made unspoken. But it was there in the looks they exchanged, in the things they didn't say and in the way they avoided physical contact with each other. They each seemed to know how combustible a touch could be and were not ready to start a false fire.

Neither of them was willing to acknowledge the change in the relationship. At the same time, they couldn't go back to the cold hostility that had preceded the visit to the island. They each played a waiting game.

After a late lunch in the hotel restaurant, they entered the lobby. Blake stopped short and turned to Dina. "We're checking out and going home," he announced.

"It's only Saturday," she protested.

"Yes. I know," he agreed with a hint of impatience. "But I'm not looking forward to spending another night here."

Dina hesitated, uncertain of his meaning. Finally she acknowledged. "The beds aren't very comfortable."

His mouth twisted wryly. "Yes, they're too soft."

"Do we have time to catch the ferry?"

"If you don't waste too much time packing, we do," he told her.

"I won't," she promised.

"I'll check out while you get started," said Blake.

During the ferry crossing neither mentioned the abrupt change of plans that had them returning early. They talked around it as if unwilling to delve too deeply into the reason. When the ferry docked in Newport they stopped talking altogether, both absorbed in their own thoughts.

It was several seconds before Dina noticed that Blake had missed a corner. "You were supposed to turn at that last block," she reminded him.

"We aren't going back to the house right away," he said.

Dina waited for him to tell her their destination. When he didn't, she asked, "Where are we going?"

"There's something I want to show you," was all he answered.

After several more blocks, he turned onto a tree-shaded street, branches arching overhead, nearly touching. He slowed the car down, seeming to read the house numbers as he drove down the street. Dina's curiosity grew with each second of his continued silence. Finally he turned into a driveway and stopped the car, switching off the engine.

Dina glanced at the large white house surrounded by a green lawn with lots of trees and flowering shrubs. She didn't recognize the place.

"Who lives here?" she asked.

Blake was already opening his car door and stepping outside. "You'll see."

She flashed him a look of irritation as he came around to open her door. He was carrying all this mystery business just a little too far. But she said nothing and walked ahead of him along the winding sidewalk to the front door.

There was a jingle of metal behind her and she turned. Blake was taking a set of keys from his pocket. Selecting one, he stepped ahead of her and inserted it in the front-door lock. Suspicion glittered in her eyes.

Pushing the door open, he motioned to her. "Go on in."

Her gaze swerved to the opened door as she moved forward to cross the threshold. On her right, carved oak posts ran from floor to ceiling to partition the mock entryway from the spacious living room beyond. Although the room was sparsely furnished, the items that were there Dina recognized as furniture stored from their apartment.

"What is this supposed to mean?" Unable to look at him, she thought she already knew the answer, and his high-handedness made her tremble with anger.

"Do you like it?" Blake ignored her question to ask one of his own.

"Am I to presume you bought this house without consulting me?" she demanded accusingly in a low, shaking voice, barely able to control her ire.

"As I recall, you were too busy to be bothered with looking for a place for us to live or furnishing it," he reminded her in an expressionless tone. "But to answer your question—no, I haven't signed any documents to purchase this house."

"If that's true, what is all our furniture doing here?" Her hand waved jerkily to the sofa and chairs.

"I obtained permission from the owner to have it brought in to see how it would fit in the rooms and to give the decorator an idea of what still has to be done."

Dina turned on him roundly, her eyes flashing fire. "In other words, you're presenting me with an accomplished fact! It doesn't matter what I want! You've decided on this house and if I don't like it, that's just too bad, isn't it?"

"Your opinion does matter." A muscle was twitching along his jaw, the only outward sign that he felt the lashing of her words. "That's why I brought you here."

There was a skeptical lift of her chin, disbelief glittering in her eyes despite his smooth denial. "Why not? Why not before? All this furniture wasn't just brought here and arranged overnight."

"No, it wasn't," Blake agreed.

"Then why now?" Dina repeated her demand.

"Because I had the impression you were ready to start looking for a place we might share together."

His narrowed gaze was piercing, impaling her on its point until she wanted to squirm under his sharp scrutiny. She averted her attention to the room, unable to admit that it might have been more than an impression.

"Was I wrong, Dina?" Blake questioned.

She didn't want to answer that question—not yet, not until she had more time to think about it. She didn't want to be manipulated into a commitment.

"Since I'm here, you might as well show me through the rest of the house," she said with forced indifference.

Blake hesitated, as if to pursue the answer to his question, then gestured with his hand. "The dining room and kitchen are this way," he directed.

As Dina toured the house, she realized it was everything they had ever talked about in a home of their own. Spacious without being too large, with ample room for entertaining, a study for Blake where he could work undisturbed in the evenings, a large patio in back, and plenty of closets.

"Since you're working, I thought we could arrange to have a maid to come in and do the housework," Blake explained as they walked down the hallway from the master bedroom to the main living area of the house.

"Yes," Dina agreed absently. At the open doorway of one of the two empty rooms, she paused to look inside again. The spare bedrooms were smaller than the master bedroom, but stil adequately large.

"There is one thing I haven't asked you." Blake stopped beside her.

"What's that?" She turned to meet his gaze.

"I haven't asked how you felt about having children."

Slightly flustered, Dina looked back to the empty room, visualizing it not as a guest bedroom but as a children's room. "We've talked about it before." They had discussed having two children, possibly three, she remembered.

"That was several years ago," Blake pointed out, "before you became a career woman."

"Working women raise children." She hedged, avoiding a direct answer and speaking in generalities instead.

"And there are some working women who prefer not to have children," he added. "I'm asking what you prefer, Dina."

He seemed to silently demand that she look at him. Reluctantly she let her gaze swing back to him, but she was unable to look any higher than his mouth. There were no soft curves to it; it was strong and firm and masculine. Dina had the impulse to raise her fingertips to it and trace the strength of its outline.

"I would like to have children, yes." Her reply was soft, almost inaudible.

"Do you have any objections to my being their father?" There was a husky quality to his voice.

The movement of his mouth when he spoke broke the spell and Dina looked away, her heart pulsing erratically. She didn't make a response. She couldn't seem to speak. Something was blocking her voice.

"Do you?" Blake repeated. When she remained silent, his fingers turned her chin to force her to look at him. "Was I mistaken this afternoon on the beach?" His steady gaze didn't waver as he looked deeply into her eyes, seemingly into her very soul. "Did you give me your answer, or was it a fleeting surrender to passion?"

"I don't know." Dina wanted to look away, but she couldn't. Her mind was reeling from his touch, incapable of coherent thought. "I...I can't think."

"Just this once, don't think" Blake requested. "Tell me what you're feeling."

His hands slipped to her shoulders, tightening for a fraction of a second as if he wanted to shake the answer out of her, but they relaxed to simply hold her. Dina stared into the bluntly chiseled features, leather-tanned, and those compelling dark eyes. This was Blake, a man, her husband, and not quite the stranger she had thought him to be.

She swayed toward him and he gathered her into his arms, prepared to meet her more than halfway. Her lips parted under the plundering force of his mouth, taking the prize she so readily surrendered to him. As if it had never been away, her soft shape molded itself to the hard contours of his body.

His roaming hands caressed and shaped her ever closer to his solidly muscled flesh. Their combined body heat melted them together, fusing them with

183

the glorious fire of their love. His driving male need made Dina aware of the empty aching in the pit of her stomach, which only he could satisfy.

Soon the torrid embrace was not enough. It was unable to meet the insatiable needs of their desires. Bending slightly, Blake curved an arm under her knees to lift her bodily and carry her to the master bedroom and the bare mattress of their old marriage bed.

As he laid her on the bed, the twining arms around his neck pulled him down to join her. Nothing existed for either of them but each other—not the past and not the future, only the moment, eternally suspended in time.

The inital storm of their passion was quickly spent. When Blake came to her a second time, their lovemaking was slow and languorous. Each touch, each kiss, each intimate caress was enjoyed and prolonged, savored and cherished.

The beauty of it brought tears to Dina's eyes, jewel-bright and awesomely happy. Blake kissed them away, gently, adoringly. Never had it been like this between them, as near to perfection as mere mortals can get.

Blake curved her to his side, locking his arms around her. Dina sighed in rapturous contentment and snuggled closer, not wanting to move, never wanting to move. Here was where she belonged, where she would always belong.

CHAPTER TEN

BLAKE STROKED HER HAIR, absently trailing his fingers through the silken ends, watching the fairness of its color glisten in the light. Her eyes were closed in supreme contentment.

"Would you say it now, Dina?" His huskily caressing voice rumbled from deep within his chest.

"Say what?" she questioned in equal softness, not sure words could express anything close to what she was feeling.

"Welcome home, darling." He supplied the words he wanted to hear.

Tipping back her head, she looked up to his face, love bringing a dazzling brilliance to the blue of her eyes. "Welcome home, darling." She repeated the words in a voice that trembled with the depth of her meaning.

A strangled moan of a torment ending came from his throat as he lifted her the few inches necessary to plant a hard, possessive kiss on her lips. Then his trembling fingers moved over her lips as if to apologize for hurting them.

"I've been waiting so long to hear that." There was a sad, almost wistful curve to his strong mouth. "Now, it doesn't seem nearly as important."

"A thousand times I've wondered if it might not have been different if I'd known you were alive before I saw you at the house," Dina whispered, her heart aching at the time together they had lost. "I thought it was someone's twisted idea of a joke."

"I should have made more of an effort to get hold of you or have the authorities reach you before I came back," Blake insisted. "I knew it would be a shock. Chet tried to convince me to let him break the news to you, but I didn't listen, not even when my own mother was so stunned that she didn't believe it was me. I was expecting too much not to think you would react the same way. In the end I went to my mother, but I tried to make you come to me."

"It wasn't just shock," she explained. "It was guilt, because I'd become engaged to Chet. And there you were, my husband. I wanted to run to you, but I couldn't. Then suddenly, you seemed so different—a stranger, someone I didn't know. It was window dressing," Dina sighed.

"Subconsciously I didn't want to admit there'd been any changes in either of us," he murmured with a rueful smile. "I wanted everything to be the way it was, as if I'd never been gone."

"Still, everything might have been different if I hadn't been engaged to Chet." Dina turned to rest her head again on his bronzed chest and listen to the strong rhythm of his heartbeat.

"It might have made us less wary of each other, but we still would have had to adjust to our growth as human beings. It would have been painful under any circumstances," he insisted.

"Yes, but Chet—" Dina started to argue.

Blake interrupted. "He was never a threat to our

relationship. Even if I hadn't come back, I'm convinced you would never have married him. You might have drifted along with the engagement for a year, but you're much too intelligent not to eventually have seen that it wouldn't work."

She relaxed, suddenly knowing he was right, and the last little doubt vanished. Smiling, she slid her hand over his flat, muscular stomach, as smooth and hard as polished bronze.

"Weren't you just a little bit jealous of Chet?" The question was half teasing and half serious.

"No, I was never jealous of him," he chuckled, and tugged at a lock of hair.

"Never?" Dina was almost disappointed.

"Never," Blake repeated in an absolutely positive tone. "There were times, though, when I was envious."

"Why?"

"Because you were so natural with him, so warm and friendly, trusting him, relying on him, and turning to him when you were confused. I wanted it to be me," he explained. "A man's instinct to protect is as strong as the maternal instinct in a woman. That's why I was envious of Chet—because you wouldn't look to me for security."

"I feel very secure now." Dina hugged him. "I love you, Blake. I've never stopped loving you."

"That's what I really wanted to hear." His arms tightened around her, crushing her ribs. "Welcome home was just a substitute for I love you."

"I love you," she repeated. "You don't have to prompt me into saying that. I shall keep saying it until you get sick of it."

"Never, my love." He shook his head.

There was a long silence as they reveled inwardly at the rediscovery of their love and the eloquently simple words that expressed so much.

"I hate to bring up something so mundane," Dina whispered, "but where are we going to sleep tonight?"

"I don't even want to go to sleep," said Blake.

"Aren't you tired?" Her sleepless night on the soft mattress was beginning to catch up with her, aided by the dreamy contentment of his embrace.

"Exhausted," he admitted with a smile in his voice. "But I'm afraid if I go to sleep, I'll wake up and find none of this has happened. Or worse, that I'm still in the jungle."

"If you are, I'm going to be there with you," she declared, and poked a finger in his chest. "You Tarzan, me Jane." Blake chuckled and kissed her hair. "Seriously, Blake, are we going back to the house tonight?"

"Not if the storage boxes in the garage have any blankets in them. Do they?" he questioned.

"Did you take everything out that I had in storage?"

"Every single solitary thing," he confirmed.

"Then there are blankets in the boxes in the garage," she promised. "As a matter of fact, there's everything there needed to set up housekeeping."

"Is that what you'd like to do?" Blake asked. "Stay here tonight?"

"I thought you'd already decided we were."

"I'm asking if that's what you want to do," he explained patiently.

"I must remember that and mark it on the calendar," Dina murmured. "Blake asked me what I wanted to do instead of telling me what I was going to do."

"All right, troublemaker," he laughed. "You know what I'm really asking."

"You want to know whether I like the house?" Dina guessed, propping herself up on a elbow beside him.

"Do you?"

"Yes. As a matter of fact, I love it," she smiled. "It's everything we ever said we wanted in a house."

"Good. That's what I thought, too. Monday morning I'll have the agent draw up the papers for us to sign. In the meantime, I don't think he'll mind if we start unpacking the boxes in the garage."

"What if he sells it to somebody else?"

"He won't. I put earnest money down to hold it until you saw it and, I hoped, approved of my choice."

"Were you so positive I'd like it?"

"As positive as I was that you'd love me again," Blake answered.

"Conceited!" Dina teased. "It would serve you right if I hadn't liked it."

"But you do, and now you can take over the decorating of it."

"It might end up looking like a hotel," she warned.

"It better not," he laughed, and pulled her into his arms.

THERE WAS A SCATTERING of snowflakes outside her office window, falling from pearl gray clouds. A serenely joyful light was in Dina's eyes as she smiled at the telephone receiver she held to her ear.

"Thank you, I'll tell him," she promised. "Merry Christmas."

Hanging up, she let her attention return to the papers on her desk while absently humming a Christmas carol. The interoffice line buzzed and she picked up the telephone again.

She had barely identified herself when Blake ordered crisply, "I want you in my office immediately."

"What's it about?"

"We'll discuss it when you get here."

An eyebrow arched at his sharpness. "Very well," Dina agreed calmly. "Give me about fifteen minutes."

"I said now," he snapped.

"You're forgetting it takes that long to walk from my little cubbyhole to your office," she reminded him dryly.

"Now, Dina!" And the connection was broken.

Breathing in deeply, she stared at the dead phone before finally replacing it on its cradle. She took a few precious seconds to put her desk into some kind of order, then walked into the corridor, closing her office door as she left.

Her statement of fifteen minutes was an exaggeration. Eight minutes later, Amy Wentworth glanced up from her typewriter and motioned her into Blake's office with a greeting wave of her hand. Dina knocked once on the connecting door and opened it to walk in.

Blake sat behind his desk leaning back in his

chair when Dina entered. The bluntly male features still retained much of his tropical tan, but they were drawn into coldly harsh lines to match the temperature outdoors. Anger glittered in his dark eyes and Dina had no idea why.

"You wanted to see me, Blake?" She walked to his desk, smiling warmly at her husband, but it didn't thaw his expression. "Am I being called on the carpet about something?"

"You're damned right you are!" He reached forward to shove a paper across his desk toward her, his glittering and watchful gaze never leaving her face for an instant. "What's this all about?"

Dina reached for the paper and glanced over it. "This is the revised budget request," she answered, frowning as she recognized it. "Where did you get it?"

"From Chet," Blake snapped.

Her mouth became a straight line of grim exasperation. "He wasn't supposed to give it to you. I wanted to go over it with you when I submitted it."

"He didn't give it to me, I took it. And you can go over it with me now," he ordered. "This is the—what—third or fourth budget revision?"

"The third." Dina was determined not to match his biting tone. "And if you'd told me why you wanted to speak to me, I could have brought some suppporting papers."

"I'm not interested in supporting papers, I want an explanantion. What's the cause for the increase this time? And don't tell me it's inflation."

"It's a combination of things," she began. "We had to change advertising agencies for the cam-

191

paign because the original firm wasn't able to produce due to some internal problem. That meant an increase in the cost."

"You should have checked more thoroughly into the first company," he rebuked her.

"Their difficulties occurred after we'd signed a contract with them," she replied sharply to his criticism.

There was disbelief in his look, but he didn't pursue that aspect. "What else?"

"We had to revise the cost figures on revamping the hotels. The—"

"I knew it," he declared through clenched teeth. "The redecorating costs for the hotels have escalated every time you've submitted a budget. Are you redecorating them or rebuilding?"

The slow-burning fuse of her temper was lit. "There are times when I'm not so positive myself," she said, simmering. "Have you seen that hotel in Florida? It looks like a hospital. We've tried landscaping and painting, but it needs a whole new facade."

"Why don't you just arrange to tear it down and build a new one?" he flashed.

"That's the best suggestion I've heard yet!" she retorted. "Why don't you bring that up to the expansion department?"

"At the rate you're going, it might be the most economical decision!" With controlled violence, Blake pushed out of his chair, standing behind the desk to glance at her. "I should have known this would happen. You put a woman in charge and give her a free hand, and right away she thinks it means she has a blank check!"

Hot tears burned her eyes. "If that's what you think—" pain strangled her voice "—why don't you take over? I never asked for the job in the first place! If you think a man can do so much better, go ahead!"

"And don't think I couldn't!"

"The great Blake Chandler. Oh, I'm sure you could do a much better job," Dina issued sarcastically, and turned away, hugging her arms in front of her in a mixture of disgust and hurt. "I don't know what ever made me think I'd want your baby."

"I don't know, either!" Blake snarled behind her. "It's a lucky thing you have a choice, isn't it?"

"That's the whole point! I don't have a choice anymore," she cried bitterly.

Her sentence hung in the air for a long, heavy second before Blake broke the silence with a low demand. "What did you say?"

"Didn't I tell you?" She tossed the question over her shoulder, her chin quivering with the forced attempt at lightness. "I'm going to have a baby."

In the next second his hands were on her shoulders to gently turn her around. Dina kept her chin lowered, still angry and hurt by his barbed attack.

"Are you sure?" he asked quietly.

"Yes, I'm sure." She closed her eyes to try to force back the tears. "Doctor Cosgrove called me a few minutes ago to confirm the test results."

"Why didn't you tell me?" His tension was exhaled with the question.

"How could I when you've been yelling at me for the past five minutes?" Her eyes flared open to glare at him.

His fingers lightly touched her cheek before he cupped it in his hand. "I was, wasn't I?" There was a rueful twist to his mouth.

"Yes, you were." But her assertion didn't carry any sting of anger.

"I lost my perspective for a moment, the order of importance. I could lose everything I have and it wouldn't matter as long as I didn't lose you."

The glow radiating from his face was warm and powerful and Dina basked in the love light. That serene joy she had known before their argument returned with doubled strength.

"No, it doesn't matter as long as I have you," she agreed, and turned her lips to his hand to press a kiss into his open palm.

His head lowered, his mouth claiming hers in a sweetly fierce kiss that rocked her senses. She clung to him, reveling in the possessive embrace that gathered her close to his male length. A wild, glorious melody raced through her veins, its tune timeless, the universal song of love.

She was breathless when the kiss ended, and the sensation remained as Blake buried his face in the silver gold hair, his mouth trailing a blazing fire to the sensitive skin of her neck. She felt the tremors vibrating through his muscular form and knew she disturbed him as sensually as he disturbed her.

When he finally lifted his head, there was a disarming smile softening his roughly carved features. His hands moved to tangle his fingers in her hair and hold her face up for his gaze to explore. Dina knew this was a moment she would treasure forever in her heart.

"We're really going to have a baby?" There was a faintly marveling look in his eyes as Blake turned the statement into a near question.

"Yes," Dina nodded.

"Are you all right?" he frowned.

"I'm fine." She smiled. With a sighing shake of her head, she asked, "Why do we argue so much, Blake?"

"It's our nature, I guess." He smiled wryly in return. "We'd better get used to the fact, because we'll probably do it the rest of our lives."

"Always testing to find out which of us is stronger." Dina recalled Chet's explanation for their constant quarrels.

"Don't worry, honey, I'll let you be stronger once in a while," he promised.

"Blake!" She started to protest indignantly at his superior remark.

"Can you imagine what our children are going to be like?" he laughed. "Pigheaded, argumentative little rebels, more than likely."

"More than likely," Dina agreed, "And we'll love every battling moment of raising them."

"The same as every battling moment you and I have together." He kissed her lightly and gazed into her eyes. "When's the baby due?"

"July."

"The new campaign will be in full swing by then. I can just see you directing operations from the maternity ward," Blake chuckled.

"You mean that I still have the job?" Dina arched a mocking brow at him.

"Of course," he returned with an arrogant smile.

"Aren't you glad you have an understanding boss who will let you set your own hours or work at home, if that's convenient?"

"I'm very lucky." She slid her arms around his neck, rising on tiptoes. "Lucky in more than one way."

"Dina." Blake spoke her name in an aching murmur against her lips.

WILD AND WONDERFUL

"I WONDER IF HE'D
PLAY HIS ACE OF HEARTS."

"Ace of hearts?" Glenna frowned. "My father doesn't know I'm here."

"Then this was all your idea," Jett concluded.

"Yes." Her eyes pleaded with him as she went on, "You were his last hope, Jett. It isn't just the mine he's going to lose, but his home, everything he's worked for all his life. He's given up. Can't you reconsider?"

"You don't know what you're asking, Glenna." Jett shook his head with an angry kind of weariness.

"He needs you. What do I have to say or do to make you listen to me?"

"What if I told you to take off your robe?" His glance flicked to the satin bow with raw challenge.

And Glenna slowly raised a hand to untie the front bow....

CHAPTER ONE

THE FIRE-RED PORSCHE convertible hugged the twisting, curving road through the West Virginia mountainscape, a splash of scarlet on the gray ribbon of concrete winding through the spring-green country. With the car's top down, the driver was exposed to the lingering sun and the billowing white clouds in the light blue sky.

Rounding a curve, Glenna Reynolds briefly lifted her face to the warmth of the sun. The teasing fingers of a speed-generated breeze tugged at her dark auburn hair, whirling its long curls away from her shoulders. A pair of owl-round sunglasses shielded her gray green eyes from the angling glare of the late afternoon sun. Contentment was etched in her vital and expressive features, a contentment born from a day spent pursuing journalistic pleasures.

On the passenger seat of the sports car, a camera was concealed in its leather case, along with a notebook containing scribbled impressions. Together the two contained a collection of springtime images that continued to float in Glenna's mind.

The wildly beautiful mountains and valleys of West Virginia had revealed its May treasures to her. Wildflowers were blooming at their peak, from the delicate lady's slipper to the flame azalea, their multicolored displays of beauty trapped in film. Jotted notations reaffirmed the camera's record of fox pups playing outside their den, tiny chipmunks darting about the forest floor, and the young fawn camouflaged and hidden at a meadow's edge.

Noted, too, were the sensations of being able to hear the new leaves growing, the fragile spring green rivaled only by the flowering red maple. Another time the hush of the woods had been broken by the drumming of a ruffed grouse. The camera shutter hadn't been quick enough to catch the jeweled flash of a scarlet tanager flitting through the trees, but hastily scribbled phrases had recorded the sighting on the pages of her notebook.

Captivated by the charm of spring, Glenna had tarried longer than she had intended. A glance at her watch increased the pressure of her foot on the accelerator pedal. The last thing she wanted was for her father to become concerned about her whereabouts. She regretted that she hadn't left him a message warning him that she might be late.

Since his heart attack this last winter, his second one, Orin Reynolds had become more conscious of her absences from him. Her father's attitude was not at all possessive. It was more an awareness of the shortness of his time to spend with her, something Glenna reciprocated in full. Even though he was as fully recovered from the attack as he would ever be, Glenna knew how slim the chance was that he would survive a third major attack.

She no longer took his presence in her life for granted and had adjusted her life-style and career to allow more time with her father. When he had been released from the hospital this last time, Glenna had wanted to give up everything to stay at home and take care of him. Orin Reynolds had rejected her suggestion, insisting that a temporary nurse and their housekeeper-cook, Hannah Burns, could take adequate care of him, and wisely informing her that she would need to escape into her writing. His advice had proved over and over again to be correct. If she needed further proof of it, the exhilarating flow of thoughts and ideas from today's outing provided it.

Braking, Glenna slowed the car to make the turn onto the graveled lane leading to the large white house nestled on the mountain slope amid the trees. It was a graceful old building, once the main house of a large estate, but the fertile valley land had been sold off some years ago. All that remained of the former land was the immediate grounds of the house and the few nontillable acres surrounding it.

Glenna recognized the car parked in the driveway and smiled wryly. Although the doctor had limited the amount of time Orin Reynolds was allowed to spend at the office of his coal-mining operation to three days a week, her father had insisted on daily reports when he wasn't there.

Hence, Bruce Hawkins's car was a familiar sight.

The garage was separate from the house, a small stable converted some sixty years ago to hold automobiles. Its double set of doors beckoned to the red Porsche, but Glenna stopped the car short of its protection. There was time enough later to put it away.

Tipping her sunglasses atop her head, she collected the camera case and notebook from the passenger seat and left the car keys in the ignition for the time being. Her long legs swiftly climbed the veranda steps to the front door.

There was a pause in her stride as she entered the foyer, pushing the door shut behind her and turning to the study that had orginally been the front parlor of the old house. The solid oak doors slid open at the touch of her hand, bringing the conversation within to an abrupt end.

Her heart was squeezed by the harrowed and worried lines that aged her father's face twenty years. The instant his gaze lighted on her face, his expression underwent a transformation—the tension smoothing into a welcoming smile of false unconcern. This sudden attempt to mask his feelings puzzled and frightened Glenna. What was he trying to hide?

Walking toward his chair, Glenna fixed a smile on her mouth while her eyes searched his face. But her poker-playing father revealed none of his inner thoughts. If she had knocked at the study door she wouldn't have seen even that brief glimpse of his inner anxiety.

"Had you started to wonder where I was?" Her voice was cheerful as she deposited her camera and notebook on the sturdy oak desk before she reached his chair. Resting a hand on the chair arm, Glenna bent down to brush her lips to the pallor of his cheeks, a color that had become natural to his complexion.

"I hadn't," Orin Reynolds insisted with a bright sparkle in his eyes. "I knew you would wander in sooner or later, but I think Bruce was becoming concerned whether you were going to show up."

Glenna straightened and looked in the direction her father had glanced. Bruce Hawkins was standing beside the fireplace, a shoulder leaning against the marble mantlepiece. His blue gaze was warmly admiring in its inspection of her, taking in the wind-tossed curls of her chestnut hair, the loose-fitting velour sweater the color of butter cream draping the swelling mounds of her breasts, and the slimness of her hips and long legs in her brushed-denim jeans. The frank appreciation in his look held a hint of reserve, out of respect for her father's presence.

"Where have you been?" Bruce asked the question her father hadn't. There was nothing interrogating in it, just casual interest.

"Communing with Mother Nature," Glenna replied.

Her gray green eyes swept his straw-colored hair and square-jawed face. Bruce was good-looking, intelligent, and ambitious. Since her father's first attack more than two years ago, he had assumed more and more responsibility for the operation of the Reynoldses' coal mine.

It was really only after her father's first heart attack that Glenna had become acquainted with him. The relationship between them had grown slowly until it had reached its present point where they were more than friends but not quite lovers.

Glenna was fully aware that she was the one unwilling to let their relationship progress any further. Her hesitancy was something that confused Glenna. Bruce appeared to represent all that she desired in a man, yet some vital ingredient seemed to be missing. Its lack kept her from making any firm commitment.

Sometimes she thought it was a loyalty to her father that made her hold back. Other times, like now, Glenna simply didn't know why she was reluctant. One word from her, one indication of acceptance, and she knew Bruce would propose.

"Communing with nature," Bruce repeated her answer. "With your eye on the plan to write a series of articles, I'll wager."

"You guessed right," Glenna agreed, leaving the uncertainty of her feelings toward Bruce to be examined at a later time. "That's one thing about free-lancing; I can slant an article so many different ways that I can sell the same story line to several different periodicals."

"And your head is buzzing with all of the ideas," her father surmised.

The softness of her throaty laugh was an affirmative answer, because it had been true when she entered the study although a whole new set of thoughts had subsequently supplanted the ideas for the nature-oriented articles.

"There's some coffee in the pot yet. Would you like a cup?" Bruce offered, moving to the china coffee service sitting on the oblong coffee table in front of the sofa.

Briefly, Glenna resented this extension of hospitality in her own home, but she quelled it. Bruce's familiarity was something both she and her father had invited. Besides, there was a certain thoughtfulness in his request. She wondered at her sudden sensitivity to the situation.

"I'd love some, thank you." She took a seat on the sofa while he poured a cup and handed it to her. Black, with no sugar, the way she liked it. Bruce sank his lean frame onto the cushion beside her, an arm automatically seeking the backrest of the sofa behind her head, but he didn't touch her.

"How are things at the mine?" The question from Glenna was an absent one, issued automatically, a polite inquiry because it was Bruce's province.

Glenna glanced over the rim of her coffee cup in time to see Bruce dart a sharp look at her father. Then he replied, too blandly, "Fine."

Instantly she knew there was a problem. A serious one. She sipped at her coffee, using the action to hide her knowledge while her mind raced back to the anxious expression on her father's face when she had entered the room.

"I invited Bruce to dinner this evening," her father informed her with a subtle change of subject. "Hannah assured me the main dish would stretch to feed four. The way she cooks I can never decide whether she is trying to fatten us up or trying to feed an army. The woman always cooks enough for ten people."

"Heaven knows you need some fattening up," Glenna observed, commenting on his weight loss that had made his usually brawny frame appear gaunt. But she knew he disliked any discussion of his health and turned to Bruce. "You are staying?" The lilt of her voice changed the statement into a question.

"I never turn down an invitation for a home-cooked meal or the company of a lovely young woman." His casually worded answer was at war with the flattering intensity of his look.

Glenna teased him deliberately. "I shall have to warn Hannah that you have designs on her, as well as her cooking."

Bruce chuckled, amused by her response. The movement of her father's hand distracted her attention. He was reaching automatically into the breast pocket of his shirt for a cigarette. Orin Reynolds had quit smoking after his first heart attack. Only in moments of severe stress did the habit reassert itself. His shirt pocket no longer held a pack of cigarettes. Glenna noticed the faint tremor of his hand when it was lowered to the armrest. It was not a withdrawal symptom from smoking.

"After two years, you can't still want a

cigarette, dad," she chided to make him aware she had seen his action. It didn't prompt the reaction she wanted.

Just for a second the facade of well-being slipped to reveal an expression that appeared supremely tired and defeated. A chill raced down Glenna's spine at the sullenness in his gray eyes before he laughed gruffly. Something was very wrong. Glenna only wished that she knew what it was.

"After two years I am craving the taste of tobacco. There are times when heaven to me is a smoke-filled poker room with whiskey and cigarettes amid a raucous backdrop of fiddle music instead of fluffy clouds, halos, and harps," he joked. "There are times when the quality of life outweighs the quantity."

"That is a rather morbid observation, dad." Glenna forced a smile, but she was aware that there was very little color in her cheeks. She saw the grain of truth in his words, but her father had always been a fighter, battling the odds stacked against him. His remark had smacked of surrender. It wasn't something she could understand, even issued in jest.

"I suppose it is, but sometimes I...." He stopped and breathed out a sigh. His mouth twitched into a rueful smile, vitality dancing back to glitter in his eyes. "I guess I'm tired."

"Why don't you lie down for a few minutes before dinner?" Glenna suggested. "I'll keep Bruce company."

"Did you hear that, Bruce?" her father

mocked. "She sounds so concerned about me, doesn't she? But a father knows when his daughter doesn't want him around."

Her fingers tightened on the curved handle of her coffee cup. It was action designed to keep Glenna from leaping to her feet to help her father out of the chair. He hated any acknowledgment of the weakness of his muscles. It was a slow process, but he rose, unaided, to walk stiffly from the room.

Her throat was hurting by the time she heard the study door slide shut behind him. She stared at the coffee in the china cup she was holding so tightly. There was a stony clarity to her eyes—eyes that had become strangers to tears.

"What is wrong at the mine, Bruce?" she demanded without looking up.

A second of pregnant silence was followed by a hollow laugh. "I don't know what you are talking about. Nothing is wrong at the mine."

"It must be very serious for both you and dad to lie to me." Glenna set the cup on the table with a briskness that rattled it against its saucer.

She rose so abruptly that she dislodged the sunglasses from their perch atop her head. Impatiently she removed them and folded the bows with a decisive snap before setting them on the table, too.

Heavily fringed with lashes, her eyes narrowed their gaze on Bruce. "I want to know what it is."

"There isn't anything you can do." He looked grim.

"You don't know that," she retorted. "I haven't heard any talk of a wildcat strike. And I can't believe the miners would walk out on dad like that, anyway. If it's a labor problem, surely dad can iron it out if you can't."

"It isn't labor." He avoided her gaze, his jaw hardening.

Glenna frowned. With that possibility eliminated, she was at a loss to guess the cause. "Then what is it? You are a mining engineer so it can't be anything technical."

"It's the government." The hint that his skill was being questioned forced Bruce into supplying the reason.

"What? Taxes?" She couldn't imagine her father getting into a position where he was delinquent in employee taxes.

"Nothing so simple," Bruce replied in a scoffing breath and pushed to his feet. He shoved his hands into the hip pockets of his slacks, an action that pushed his shoulders back and stretched the material of his blue shirt across the sinewed width of his chest. "The mine failed its safety inspection."

"How bad is it?" Glenna heard the dullness in her voice, the feeling of dread sweeping over her.

"They are issuing an injunction to shut the mine down within thirty days if the necessary steps aren't taken immediately to correct the situation," he announced in a voice as leaden as her own.

"Surely you can appeal the ruling—gain more time," she argued.

"That's what I've been doing for the last year and a half," he snapped in a sudden blaze of temper. "We ran out of time. There won't be any more postponements."

Parallel furrows ran across her forehead. "If you knew it was coming, why didn't you take steps to correct the problem?" Glenna challenged in a spate of responding anger. "Why did you leave it until the last minute? I suppose you just dumped this all on dad this afternoon—when it's practically too late to do anything to stop it. No wonder he acted so defeated. He isn't well. He trusted you to—"

"Orin has known from the start!" Bruce interrupted sharply. "If I'd had my choice, I would have begun implementing and installing new safety measures. But I didn't have any say in the matter."

"Are you implying that my father knowingly endangered the lives of the miners?" The accusation brought a pronounced silver glitter to her eyes, making them icy and more gray than green.

"For God's sake! He had no more choice in the matter than I did."

He turned away to rest an arm on the mantle of the fireplace, bending his head to rub his hand over his mouth and chin in a gesture of exasperation and futility.

Her anger dissipated at his attitude of helplessness. "What do you mean? Why didn't he have a choice?" Glenna frowned. "You said yourself that the solution was to comply."

"That costs money, Glenna," Bruce sighed and straightened to look at her. "That's why the initial ruling was appealed to gain time to raise the capital to make the changes and install the necessary devices."

"He could borrow it. The bank would loan him the—"

"No. Orin took out second and third mortgates on everything he owned to pull the mine through the strike we had two and a half years ago. Once he could have borrowed on his reputation alone, but after these last two heart attacks he's had—" Bruce filled the pause with an expressive shrug of his shoulders "—the lending institutions regard him as an uninsurable risk with overextended credit."

Dark clouds of despair began to enfold her in their arms. Glenna felt chilled and struggled to elude their murky envelopment. Her gaze clung to Bruce's handsome features.

"Surely there has to be someone who will help dad." She tried to sound calm, and not nearly as desperate as she felt.

In her mind the thoughts kept turning over and over. If the mine was closed it would ultimately mean bankruptcy. They would lose the house and everything of any value. The effect such a situation would have on her father was something Glenna didn't want to contemplate. She barely succeeded in suppressing a shudder.

"On your father's instructions, I sent out feelers to see if Coulson Mining would be interested in a merger with your father's company—on the chance they might see some tax advantages.'' Bruce shook his head grimly. "Their reply was a flat 'not interested.' ''

"Coulson Mining," Glenna repeated. "Jett Coulson's company? The coal magnate."

"Coal, gas, you name it and he's rolling in it—including gold," Bruce nodded.

With startling clarity Glenna recalled the mental picture of a grainy newspaper photograph she had seen of Jett Coulson when she had been reading a trade journal to her father shortly after his first heart attack. The man's hair and eyes had appeared as black as the shining coal that had built his fortune. At the time of the photograph he had been in his midthirties, yet his features had been lined with a toughness beyond his years.

To Glenna, Jett Coulson had seemed all rough, raw manhood. Yet her father had spoken of him with respect, she remembered. What she had viewed as ruthlessness in his features, her father had regarded as strength. Jett Coulson's lack of polish and refinement made him a man the miners could understand and believe, even when they disagreed. It was said that Jett Coulson never lied. The standing joke was that a lot of people wished he would.

"Did you talk to Jett Coulson?" she asked, clinging to the one tantalizing straw Bruce had offered.

"Are you kidding?" he laughed harshly. "I'm nothing but a manager—a mining engineer. I talked to one of his underlings."

212

"There wasn't even a crumb of interest," Glenna persisted.

"Be realistic, Glenna," Bruce sighed. "Why should Coulson agree to a merger when he'll probably be able to pick the mine up for nothing in a few months. Why should he bail your father out of this mess? He's never had a reputation for being a good samaritan. It's unlikely he'll have a change of heart at this late date."

"No, I suppose not." Her shoulders slumped in defeat. She turned away to walk to a front window to gaze sightlessly at the shadows gathering on the lawn. "What's going to happen to daddy?" She wasn't aware she had murmured the aching question aloud.

Approaching her from behind, Bruce rubbed his hands over her arms. "Glenna, I'm sorry. I wish there was some way I could help...something I could do to prevent this."

She heard the echo of futility in his voice, the forlorn emptiness of his offer. When his arms curved around her and his jaw rested against her hair, there was no comfort in his embrace.

"I haven't got much money, but when the mine closes—" he began.

"*If* the mine closes, not *when*, Bruce," Glenna quickly corrected him and moved out of his arms and away from the window. Her back was ramrod straight when she turned to regard him. "It will be thirty days, you said, until the injunction takes effect. A lot can happen in thirty days."

"You sound like your father." He eyed her sadly. "Don't be a fool, Glenna."

His remarks only served to make her more determined. If her father hadn't given up hope yet, neither would she. Her patrician features took on an air of resolve. The sunlight glinting through the window set the deep auburn hue of her brown hair afire, as if reinforcing her purpose.

"A Reynolds doesn't give up without putting up one helluva fight first. Dad isn't the type to lie down and let the world step on him. And neither am I."

"I don't think you understand what you are up against." Bruce shook his head, but didn't attempt to argue too strongly. "There is a time for pride...and a time to be sensible. I should know, Glenna. I've fought this day for a year and a half. You can think what you like about me, but after a year and a half of butting my head against a stone wall, I know when to quit."

"Is that what you are going to do? Quit?" Her lip curled in a contemptuous challenge.

"Not literally. No, I'll see this thing through to the bitter end." There was absolutely no doubt in his expression about what the end would be. Turning, he walked to the desk and picked up the briefcase lying atop it. "I think it would be better if I took a rain check on the dinner invitation tonight. I don't think either of us would be very good company. Make my apologies to Orin, will you?" he murmured quietly.

"Of course." Glenna accepted his decision

with a curt nod and made no attempt to walk with him to the front door.

His glance was faintly mocking when he crossed the room and paused at the sliding oak doors. "I'll show myself out," he said, taunting her lack of courtesy.

"I know you will," she replied coolly.

CHAPTER TWO

THE TINGLING SHOWER SPRAY drummed out some of her tension. The raking wire claws of the hairbrush eliminated more of it while untangling her wind-snarled hair. Makeup and a floral, silk shirtwaist bolstered her spirits.

When she met her father in the dining room she felt capable of taking on any obstacle—including the stone wall Bruce had referred to. Which was just as well because she was subjected to her father's sharp-eyed scrutiny the minute she entered the room.

"Hannah tells me Bruce decided not to stay for dinner. Did you two have a lover's quarrel?" He sat in his accustomed chair at the head of the claw-footed dining-room table.

"We aren't lovers so that isn't possible." She pulled out the chair on his right and sat down. She denied his allegation with ease, not at all upset by the presumption he had made concerning her relationship with Bruce.

An iron-gray eyebrow was raised. "You obviously had a difference of opinion about something."

"We did." Glenna agreed with a quick smile

as she spread the Irish-linen napkin across her lap. "It was over the closing of the mine. He regarded it as inevitable. I didn't." She saw the look of consternation spread across his face and turned her attention to the housekeeper entering the room with a tureen of soup. "Hmm, that smells good, Hannah." She sniffed the air appreciatively, the warm aroma of chicken stock wafting from the china serving bowl.

"Homemade. I spent all afternoon fixing the noodles," the plump woman retorted with her usual sassy spirit. "And you'd better do more than pick at my food tonight, Orin Reynolds, or else I'll stick you in a high chair and spoon-feed you. If you think I can't do it, you just try me," she threatened and set the tureen on the table near Glenna with a decisive thump.

Her father barely noticed the housekeeper, who had practically become an adopted member of the family. Aware that his silence was generated by her reference to the trouble at the mine, Glenna took over the task of ladling the homemade chicken soup into the individual bowls.

"Dad loves your homemade egg noodles, Hannah," Glenna assured the woman sternly eyeing Orin Reynold's bowed head. "Don't you?" she prompted and set a bowl of the steaming soup in front of him.

"How did you find out about the mine?" He lifted his gaze to her face. His expression was a little stunned, a little disbelieving and tinted with relief.

"Did you really think you could keep it from me?" she chided and dished a bowl of soup for herself. "I simply asked Bruce outright what the problem was at the mine. I saw how worried you looked when I first came in. Bruce isn't as good a poker player as you are. It was a simple deduction that whatever was bothering you, it had to do with the mine. After that it was a simple matter of putting a few pointed questions to Bruce." She shrugged her shoulders in an indication of how easy it had been to get the answers from him.

The curving line of his mouth held faint bemusement. "I doubt if it was hard to get the answers from him. You have Hawkins wrapped around your little finger. He'd do or say anything to please you, you know that, don't you?"

It wasn't really a question so much as it was an observation. Glenna flicked him a dry glance, reading between the lines of his comment.

"Don't decide to try any matchmaking, dad." She filled the last soup bowl and leaned across the table to set it where Hannah would be sitting. "I'll choose my own future husband, thank you." Moving the soup tureen to the center of the table, Glenna returned the conversation to its original topic, the coal mine and its problems. "Why didn't you tell me about the trouble you were having?"

"I didn't want to cause you any needless worry." He picked up his soupspoon and dipped it into the bowl, but made no attempt to lift a spoonful to his mouth. "I never thought it would come to this point," her father admitted as Hannah returned to the dining room with a basket of homemade saltine crackers to go with the soup. "I was positive that between us, Bruce and I would come up with a solution that would keep the mine from being shut down. I wasn't really trying to keep it from you. I just didn't want you worrying over something you couldn't do anything about. You have enough on your mind."

"What's this about the mine being shut down?" Hannah demanded. A frown of concern narrowed her eyes. "When did all this come about? And eat your soup. Stop playing with it," she ordered without a pause.

"The mine doesn't meet the safety standards. Unless it complies, the government is shutting it down," Glenna explained quickly and a little absently since it was old news to her. She barely noticed the faint shock that spread across Hannah's face as the plump woman sank into the chair opposite her. Challenge glinted in the look Glenna cast at her father. "So what are you going to do? Quit? That seems to be the opinion Bruce has."

"We have exhausted just about every avenue of hope," Orin sighed. Leaving the spoon in the bowl, he rested his elbows on the table and clasped his hands together to form an upright triangle with the table top, pressing his fingers to his mouth. There was grim resignation in his features. "I'm at a complete loss to know which way to turn."

The housekeeper glared at him. "Orin Reynolds, I have never known you to give up."

He lifted his head, sending the frazzle-haired woman an irritated look. "Who said I was? I just don't know where to go from here."

Glenna smiled at the fighting spirit displayed by that response. It was reassuring, and reinforced her own determination. To her father the future wasn't as dark and foreboding as Bruce regarded it.

"Bruce indicated that was the way you felt," she said. "So do I."

They exchanged glances. The underlying strain that had tautened his features faded at her supportive remark. His expression became touched with a reminiscent warmth and affection.

"There are times when you remind me so much of your mother. God bless her soul," he murmured. "She always stood beside me no matter what." After a touching pause he added, "I miss her."

The sighing comment was a needless admission. The love her parents shared had been one of the greatest securities of Glenna's childhood. She was aware how keenly her father had felt the loss of his wife to cancer three years ago. It had been mercifully swift, but Glenna suspected that her mother's death had precipitated his heart attack a short year later. For a while she had feared he had a subconscious death wish to join his beloved Mary, but his will to live was strong.

"What on earth are you going to do?" the housekeeper questioned, then grimaced. "The soup is getting cold. If you had terrible news like this, why did you wait until I had food on the table before bringing it up? It would have been so much easier, Orin, if you had talked about this before dinner...or afterward, but not in the middle of a meal." She sent him a disgruntled look. "You haven't answered my question. What are you going to do?" Hannah ignored the fact that she hadn't given him an opportunity to reply.

"I don't know." He shook his head and reached for the spoon resting in his soup bowl. "We seem to be up against a brick wall."

"If you can't knock it down, there has to be a way to go around it, under it, or over it," Glenna reasoned.

"I thought we had a way around it," he agreed with her logic, his mouth twisting ruefully. "Unfortunately it turned out to be a dead end."

"You are referring to merging with Coulson Mining?" she guessed.

The spoon he held was poised in midair, halfway to his mouth, the broth dripping off the edge into the bowl as Orin shot her a quick look. "You know about that, too?" he said with faint surprise. "It doesn't sound like Bruce left anything out."

"Not much," she admitted.

He carried the spoon the rest of the way to his mouth and swallowed the soup broth it contained. Returning the spoon to the bowl, he reached for one of Hannah's crackers and began buttering it, as if he needed something to do with his hands.

"Did Bruce also tell you that he suggested a meeting with the miners to let them know about the situation and the possibility the mine will be closed in a month?" His gaze slid from the cracker to Glenna.

She attacked her soup, angered again by Bruce's defeatist attitude. "I certainly hope you put him straight on that score," she stated in a vigorous rejection of the plan.

"I agreed with him." Her father didn't meet her stunned look as he took abnormal interest in evenly spreading the butter over his cracker. "He's setting the meeting between shift changes tomorrow afternoon."

The announcement shocked Glenna. It seemed to indicate a surrender to the inevitable, which was a direct contradiction to all of his previous statements. She returned the soupspoon to its place beside the rest of the silverware, mindless of the broth stain it made on the tablecloth.

"You aren't serious," she protested incredulously.

"It is the only fair thing to do, Glenna." His voice was patiently reasoning. "If—" He paused to reemphasize the qualifying word. "If the mine is going to be closed, the miners should know about it before it happens so they have a chance to prepare for the layoff.''

''But you are going to try to find a way to keep it operating, so why tell them?'' She didn't understand.

''I feel we should prepare them for the worst that could happen.'' It was an unequivocal statement of his belief. Put that way, it didn't sound quite so bad. A heavy sigh brought an air of sadness to her father. ''It wouldn't be so tragic if I was the only one who would suffer from the closing of the mine, but so many people's lives are involved. The economy of this whole community revolves around the Reynolds Mine. We'll have our own minature depression in this valley.''

''It isn't as if you aren't trying to do something to prevent it.'' Glenna refused to let him blame himself for any repercussions that might occur.

''I know.'' He smiled at her encouragement. ''I'm fighting just as hard for myself as I am for them. After all, I stand to lose everything including this house where Mary and I spent so many wonderful years—'' The tightness in his throat cut the sentence short as his gaze made a sweep of the room. It ended its arc to linger on the housekeeper. ''Even you would be affected by the closing of the mine, dear Hannah.'' He reached out to cover the housekeeper's hand with his own, a gesture that revealed the affection he felt toward the irascible woman. ''You would be out of a job and a place to live. I had always intended for you to have a tidy pension to retire on, but I doubt if I could afford to give you severance pay.''

''Don't you go trying to force your charity on me, Orin Reynolds.'' Hannah pulled her hand from beneath his, rejecting his apology, but the gruffness of her voice revealed how deeply moved she was by his remarks. ''I can look out for myself. I always have, haven't I?''

''Of course,'' he smiled benignly.

''The mine isn't shut down, and we haven't been turned out of this house yet.'' Glenna felt the need to point that out. ''So let's concentrate our attention on trying to prevent it, instead of deciding what we will do if it happens.''

''Any suggestions?'' It wasn't a taunting request from her father, merely an acknowledgment that he could think of no more avenues to explore.

''Aren't there other mining companies that might be interested in a merger besides Coulson? Just because Coulson isn't interested doesn't mean another company might not be,'' she reasoned.

''Considering the mine's indebtedness and the investment capital needed to bring it up to standard, only a large corporation could absorb us—a company that could take advantage of the tax benefits. The only company that fits that bill is Jett Coulson's. And you know what his answer was,'' he murmured dryly.

''It wasn't his answer,'' Glenna remembered.

"It came from one of his underlings. Bruce said so."

"But I'm sure it came down from him."

"You don't know that."

Her father studied her for a minute, silently following her train of thought. "You think I should get the answer straight from the horse's mouth, so to speak."

"Why not?" she shrugged. "You haven't personally spoken to him. Neither has Bruce. As competent as Bruce might be as a manager, that doesn't mean he's equally as competent to present your merger proposition." She watched him mulling over her comment.

"You could be right," he conceded thoughtfully. "Maybe I should arrange a meeting with Jett Coulson."

"Absolutely," Glenna nodded as she watched the hope being reborn in his gray eyes. "What have you got to lose?"

"Absolutely nothing." He spooned some homemade soup into his mouth and tasted its flavor for the first time. His bright gaze darted to the housekeeper, a smile of approval curving his mouth. "This is delicious, Hannah."

"Of course it is," the housekeeper sniffed, as if there could be any doubt she would serve less than the best.

LATE THE FOLLOWING AFTERNOON, Glenna was in her bedroom. One corner of the room was a miniature study, a small desk cubbyholed amid the bookshelves. A portable typewriter sat in the

225

center of the orderly chaos, a sheet of paper in its carriage, and her notes from the previous day's outing scattered around the desk top.

A knock at the door intruded on Glenna's frowning concentration, turning her head from the scribbled handwriting she was trying to decipher. Before she could respond to the summoning knock, the door opened to admit her father.

"We're in luck," he announced, entering the room with more buoyancy to his stride than she had seen in a long time.

She pushed all thoughts of the article she was trying to write from her mind and directed all her attention to him. A faint smile touched her mouth as she studied his jovial mood.

"What kind of luck are we in?" Glenna joked and tucked the thickness of her auburn hair behind an ear. "Good or bad?"

"Anything would have to be an improvement over what we've had so it must be good." Despite his surface vigor, he sought out the plump armchair covered in toasted-gold corduroy. It was an indication of how fleeting his strength was, his lack of stamina.

Glenna was careful to ignore it. "Are you going to tell me what this good luck is, or keep me in suspense?"

"I just found out in a roundabout way that Jett Coulson is going to be entertaining some of his lobbyists at Greenbrier this weekend." His smile fairly beamed from his face.

His announcement merely drew a frown from

Glenna. "And that is the good luck?" She failed to see what was so wonderful about it.

"It certainly is. Meeting him there will allow a casual approach," he explained. "If I made an appointment to see Coulson at his office there would undoubtedly be a hundred and one interruptions, and his time would be limited. At the inn, I'll have more than one chance to discuss it with him."

It sounded very logical but Glenna saw a problem. "But if he's entertaining, won't he—"

"It's only an excuse to party. Coulson will have plenty of free time," her father assured.

"Are you sure this is the course you should take?" She wasn't convinced. "Wouldn't it be wiser to meet him in an atmosphere more conducive to business?"

Her father chuckled. "More business deals are consummated at social gatherings than are ever accomplished in a corporate office. Once an agreement is reached, it's up to the attorneys to work out the fine details. A handshake from Coulson over the dinner table is as good as cash in the bank."

"You certainly know more about such things than I do," Glenna conceded and shifted in her chair to hook a leg beneath her.

"How long do you think it will take to drive from here to White Sulphur Springs? I'd like to arrive around noon on Friday."

"It shouldn't take more than two or three hours," she guessed.

"You will be my chauffeur, won't you?" her

father asked, well aware that his doctor would be against him driving that distance alone.

"I'm certainly not going to let you go by yourself." Then she hesitated. "Are you sure you wouldn't rather have Bruce with you?"

"That would be much too obvious." He shook his head, rejecting her suggestion. "I want it to appear to be a father-daughter outing, all very casual. A weekend vacation will be good for you anyway. Besides, you can pick up a lot of material for your writing."

"I'm sure I could, but—" Glenna paused uncertainly, eyeing her father with concern. "Dad, do you think we can afford this?"

"At this point a few hundred dollars isn't going to keep us out of bankruptcy court." His expression became serious. "This is the last roll of the dice. We might as well shoot our whole wad and go out in style."

"You have always been a first-class gambler, dad." She observed with a faint smile that held warmth but no humor.

"Be sure to pack our best clothes." Her father stood up, the decision made and irrevocable now. "We don't want to look like a pair of beggars when we meet Coulson."

THE WHITE MAGNIFICENCE of the Greenbrier was nestled in an upland Allegheny valley. Its forested lawns and mountain backdrop provided the beauty of natural surroundings. The famed spa and its predecessor, Old White, obtained its initial notoriety from the soothing mineral waters that smelled like an egg that was half boiled and half spoiled. Yet its guest register over the years included an impressive list of celebrities.

This was not Glenna's first visit to the famous West Virginia resort, but she was still awed by its stately elegance and aura of steeped tradition. The many-storied facade was pristine white with a columned portico entrance worthy of the grandest and noblest of guests.

After they had registered and been shown to their adjoining rooms, she and her father had split up. Glenna had wanted to do some exploring and familiarize herself again with the hotel complex while her father wanted to make inquiries and learn the most logical place to "bump into" Jett Coulson.

Her wandering walk brought Glenna into the facility housing the indoor tennis courts. She paused to watch a match being played on the near court, two couples playing a game of mixed doubles. The good-natured ribbing that was exchanged back and forth between the pairs brought a smile to her face.

A shouted reference to the time directed her glance at her watch. It was a few minutes past three o'clock. By the time she returned to her room and changed into her swimsuit, she would have an hour to swim before meeting her father. The fairness of her skin, the complexion of a true redhead, forced Glenna to avoid the sun during the middle of the day when its burning rays did the most damage.

As she started to move away from the near

tennis court, a hoot of laughter attracted her attention. Turning her head, she glanced over her shoulder. In the split second when she wasn't watching where she was going, she nearly walked into another player. Her forward progress was halted by a pair of hands that stopped her before she ran into him.

Her attention was jerked to the front; a hurried apology forming on her lips. It froze there for a full second as Glenna stared at the tall sunbronzed figure of a man in white tennis shorts and white knit top. A black pair of eyes were returning her stunned regard with a shimmer of bemusement as he removed his hands from her shoulders.

Glenna was struck by the irony of the situation. She had accidentally run into the man that her father was contriving to bump into. A smile played with the corners of her mouth, attracting his interest.

"I'm sorry, Mr. Coulson," she apologized smoothly. "I'm afraid I wasn't paying attention to where I was going."

An eyebrow flicked upward at the use of his name. All the toughness was there in his features, just as she had remembered from the photograph she had seen. But the photograph hadn't captured the perpetual gleam in his dark eyes—the gleam of a rogue wolf.

"Have we met before?" Like his gaze, his voice had a certain directness to it. Glenna was subjected to the boldness of his sweeping glance. "I can't believe I would have forgotten meeting you."

The line was delivered smoothly, so smoothly that Glenna found it hard to question its sincerity. "We've never been introduced. I recognized you from a newspaper photograph," she explained and felt warmed by the slow smile that spread across his mouth.

"You must have a very good memory. It's been some time since there have been any articles about me, Miss—" He paused deliberately to invite Glenna to fill in the blank.

"Reynolds. Glenna Reynolds." She found herself becoming intrigued by this man that she had once labeled as ruthless. There was a reckless gambler's charm about him that she hadn't expected. This, plus the unwavering determination etched in his craggy features, made a potent combination. She began to feel the force of it exerting its influence on her. She hadn't anticipated being sexually disturbed by Jett Coulson.

"That name sounds familiar to me. Glenna Reynolds." He repeated it as if to jog his memory, his eyes narrowing faintly.

"Perhaps you have—" She started to explain who her father was, but Jett Coulson interrupted her with a snap of his fingers in recollection.

"Glenna Renolds was the by-line on an article that was in the magazine section of the Sunday paper. Was that yours?" His look became thoughtful, a degree of aloofness entering his expression.

"Yes, it was," Glenna admitted with faint astonishment. "I'm flattered that you read it... and remembered it."

"I remembered it because of the way you managed to take a boring subject and made it appear interesting," he replied diffidently.

"Thank you...I think." She qualified her statement because she wasn't sure that his remark hadn't been a backhanded compliment. It irritated Glenna to think he might be mocking her behind his poker-smooth exterior.

"Is this a business trip or pleasure?" His observing gaze seemed to take note of the turbulence clouding her gray green eyes, yet he had shifted the subject so smoothly that Glenna wondered if she hadn't imagined the gibe in the last.

"Both," she admitted.

"The Greenbrier has been written about many times."

"Then my challenge will be to do it differently." There was a defensive tilt to her chin, elevating it a degree. She became conscious of his superior height and his unshakable self-assurance.

"I enjoy a challenge myself," he murmured. Then he inclined his head in a slight nod. "Excuse me, but I have a tennis date to keep."

His comment prompted Glenna to move to one side as if she had been blocking him, which she hadn't. His tanned and sinewed legs carried him past her with long strides. Her gaze followed him for several seconds, taking note of the narrowness of his waist and hips tapering out to the breadth of his ropy shoulders. There was little doubt in her mind that Jett Coulson was a breed of man she had never encountered before—and was unlikely to meet again. He was one of a kind.

CHAPTER THREE

ORIN REYNOLDS was at the poolside when Glenna climbed the ladder out of the swimming pool. She sensed an air of urgency about him as she walked, leaving a trail of water behind her, to the deck chair where she'd left her towel and flowered robe.

"Hi!" When she greeted him, she was slightly out of breath from the swim, but exhilarated by the activity. Within seconds after leaving the pool, the evaporation of water cooled her skin and began raising goosebumps. Glenna shook out the towel and began briskly rubbing herself down. "What's up? I thought we were going to meet in the room."

"I tipped the bellboy. He told me that Coulson usually has a cocktail in the lounge before dinner. I wanted to be sure we got there before he did so we could spot him coming in."

Unsnapping her bathing cap, she took it off to let her auburn hair tumble free. "I bumped into him—literally—at the tennis court this afternoon."

"Coulson?" Her father appeared to need reassurance that they were talking about the same person.

"The one and only." She used the towel to blot the excess moisture from her swimsuit, a sleek one-piece suit of sea green.

"What did he say?" Her father was keenly alert, studying every nuance of her expression. "Does he know who you are?"

"He doesn't know that I'm your daughter—at least I didn't tell him I was. But he had read one of my articles and remembered my name from that." Which was something she was still a little surprised about. "That was just about the extent of our conversation."

"Mmm." Orin Reynolds seemed to digest that information while Glenna slipped into the loose-fitting floral robe and hooked the wide belt around her slim waistline. "Do you have shoes?"

"Under the chair." She knelt to remove the fashionably heeled slip-ons from beneath the chair. Using his arm for balance, she stepped into first one, then the other.

"Let's go to the lounge." He took her arm and started to lead her away.

Glenna stopped in stunned protest. "I can't go to the lounge like this."

"Nonsense. It's informal. There will be people there in tennis shorts. You are certainly more fully clothed than that." He dismissed her protest.

Glenna didn't attempt to argue about her wearing apparel. "But I haven't any lipstick—any makeup on." Her fingers touched the damp tendrils of curling hair. "And my hair—"

"Nothing you could do would improve on perfection." Deliberately he was too lavish in his praise, mocking her vanity.

"Dad, be serious," she sighed, unable to stay upset by his high-handedness.

"If you are determined to spoil that ·fresh clean look, use the powder room to comb your hair and put on some lipstick," he conceded with an indulging smile. "But don't take long. I don't want to miss him."

After Glenna had made the necessary repairs to her appearance she met her father at the entrance to the lounge. It was just beginning to fill with the happy-hour crowd. Orin Reynolds guided her to a table strategically located to permit him to observe the door. Their drink order was served—a glass of white wine for Glenna and a Perrier with a lime twist for her father. She had taken her first sip of the wine when Jett Coulson entered the lounge alone. She touched her father's arm to draw attention to the man inside the doorway, but it was unnecessary. Orin had already spotted him.

Those gleaming dark eyes were making a slow inspection of the room, not in search of anyone as far as Glenna could tell, but simply taking note of who was present. Her father stood up, attracting Jett's attention. His gaze narrowed as it touched Glenna, then returned to her father.

"Mr. Coulson." Without raising his voice from its pleasant pitch, her father succeeded in summoning Jett to their table. "I haven't had the pleasure of meeting you formally. My name is Orin Reynolds, of the Reynolds Mine.''

There was a firm clasping of hands as Jett murmured a polite, ''How do you do, Mr. Reynolds.''

If her father's name or that of his coal mine, meant anything to Jett, Glenna didn't see any recognition register in his expression. But she was coming to mistrust those hardened features to reveal his inner thoughts.

''I believe you met my daughter Glenna earlier this afternoon,'' her father said, by way of acknowledging her presence.

''Yes, we...bumped into each other.'' The faint pause carried an inflection of dry amusement as Jett nodded to her. ''Hello, again, Miss Reynolds.''

''Hello, Mr. Coulson.'' There was a husky pitch to her voice, and Glenna wasn't sure exactly where it had come from. She seemed to be holding her breath, too, without knowing why.

No longer dressed in his tennis clothes, he had changed into a pair of navy slacks and a silk shirt in a subdued blue design against a cream background. The untamed thickness of his hair held a sheen of dampness, prompting Glenna to surmise he had probably showered. She had been so fully prepared to dislike him; now she found herself wondering why she didn't.

''Sit down,'' her father invited. ''Let me buy you a drink.'' Then he paused, as if suddenly realizing. ''Were you meeting someone?''

"No." He chose to sit in the empty chair beside Glenna, across the table from her father.

"What will you have to drink?" Orin signaled to the cocktail waitress.

"Scotch, neat, on the rocks," Jett ordered and her father passed the information on.

"Who won your tennis match?" Seated this close, Glenna inhaled the tangy scent of his after-shave with each breath she took. It stimulated her senses, awakening them to his rough brand of masculinity.

"I did." The reply was neither a boast nor a brag, merely a simple statement of fact.

"Naturally," she murmured dryly, goaded by the sheer confidence of his statement.

He turned his head to regard her with those gleaming, but impassive black eyes. "I always play to win."

"Don't you ever play simply for the fun of competing?" Even as she asked the question she remembered her first conclusion that he could be ruthless.

"That's the rationale of a loser." A half-smile tugged at the corners of his mouth, taunting her. Then he let his gaze slide back to her father. "I would never have guessed she was your daughter, Mr. Reynolds."

"Please, call me Orin," her father insisted and cast a smiling glance at her. "No, there isn't much of a resemblance between us. Thankfully, Glenna takes after her mother, God rest her soul. She was a strikingly beautiful woman, like Glenna."

"Don't mind him. He's prejudiced." For the first time she was embarrassed by her father's compliments. Usually when he made such remarks about her looks in front of friends or strangers, she just smiled and let them pass by without comment. This time they made her uncomfortable. Or was it the dark and knowing regard of the man sitting beside her?

Jett's Scotch was served. The interruption allowed conversation to drift to another topic, much to Glenna's relief.

"Tell me, Orin, what brings you here?" Jett questioned with mild interest. "Your daughter mentioned that she was here on a combination of business and pleasure. Is that true for you, too?"

Glenna hastened to explain. "I told Mr. Coulson of my intention to write a travel article about Greenbrier."

"Glenna has quite a talent with words. I believe she said you had read some of her work," her father attempted to dodge the initial question.

"Yes, I have," Jett admitted but didn't repeat the comment he'd made to Glenna when they'd met before. "Do you help with the research?"

"No," Orin denied with a throaty laugh. "She does everything herself. I don't know which of us is chaperoning the other. I can't say that this is strictly a pleasure trip for me since a businessman never escapes his responsibilities, not even for a weekend. I'm sure you know what I mean."

Jett nodded. "I understand."

"What brings you here?"

Glenna marveled at the bland innocence of her father's expression as if he didn't have the vaguest idea why Jett was at the inn. His face held just the right touch of curiosity and interest. She sipped her wine, wondering if Jett Coulson realized he was being bluffed.

"I'm entertaining some lobbyists from Washington." He took a swallow of straight Scotch without flinching.

"I thought I recognized some familiar faces in the lobby. That explains it," her father stated with just the right note of discovery, but Glenna was suspicious of the look Jett gave him. "I wish there were some strings they could pull for me," he sighed heavily. "The government's threatening to shut down my mine at the end of the month."

"That's too bad." The remark did not invite a further disclosure of Orin's troubles.

"Sorry, dear." Her father reached over and patted her hand. It was all Glenna could do to keep from jumping in surprise. "I promised not to bring up that subject this weekend, didn't I?"

It took her a full second to recover, during which she was careful not to look at Jett Coulson. She doubted that she was as adept as these two men were at concealing their thoughts.

"You did promise," she lied in agreement. "But I don't think I ever expected you to be able

240

to keep it." She added the last so her father could reintroduce the subject.

"Glenna suggested this weekend excursion to distract me from the problems at the mine," her father explained. "But you're here...and the coal lobbyists. Which proves, I suppose, that a person can never run away from their problems."

"Not for long, at any rate." Jett rested his arms on the table, his silk-clad elbow brushing her forearm.

The contact swerved his gaze to her. Glenna realized why his regard was so deliciously unnerving. He looked at her as if she were the only woman in the entire room. The enigmatic glow in his dark eyes seemed to say that he knew a lot about her already, and wanted to know a lot more. His appeal was a devastating combination of virile charm and ruthless determination. Glenna could feel it slowly crumbling her resistance.

"How has your company been affected by the new government regulations?" Her father's inquiry released her from Jett's gaze. "I know you strip-mine the majority of your coal and have the Reclamation Act to contend with, but I'm referring specifically to the underground coal that can't be strip-mined."

The two men talked about mining in general for a while—its politics, new technology, and its future potential. Glenna became aware that her father was slowly steering the conversation in the direction he wanted it to take, subtly dropping facts and figures about his mine. When he nudged her with his foot, she took the hint.

She pushed her chair back from the table and smiled under Jett's questioning regard. "You and dad will probably talk 'coal' for another hour or more. In the meantime I think I'll go to my room to shower and change for dinner. If you'll excuse me."

As she rose so did Jett Coulson. At first she thought his action was prompted by courtesy until she saw him glance at his watch.

"It is getting late...and I have to change before dinner, too," he announced with casual indifference.

Glenna silently applauded the absence of frustration and disappointment on her father's face, two emotions that he had to be feeling. Instead he was smiling quite broadly.

"Well, I'm certainly not going to sit here and drink alone." Placing both hands on the table, he pushed to his feet. "I'll come with you, Glenna, and change for dinner, too."

When she noticed his legs appear wobbly from sitting for such a long time, she absently hooked an arm through her father's to give him support without it appearing that it was her purpose. Taking her time Glenna strolled in the direction of the lounge exit while she continued to help her father.

"Thank you for the drink, Orin." Jett Coulson kept pace with them. "And for the interesting conversation."

"I enjoyed talking to you," her father returned. "We'd like you to have dinner with us tonight. You are more than welcome to join us, if you're free."

"As I mentioned I'm entertaining guests this weekend." As he paused his gaze strayed over each of them. "You and your daughter are welcome to sit at my table this evening."

"We wouldn't want to intrude," Glenna was surprised to hear her father resist the invitation.

"You won't be intruding. Everyone at the table will probably be talking coal anyway," Jett shrugged.

"In that case—" her father made a pretense of hesitating as he glanced at her "—we'll be glad to accept."

As they left the lounge and walked to the elevator, Jett explained that he had made reservations to dine at eight o'clock in the formal dining room. By the time they reached the elevators, her father was steady enough on his feet that he no longer needed Glenna's support. She released his arm to enter the elevator first. There wasn't any opportunity to talk during the ride up to their floor since other guests had crowded into the elevator, too.

When the elevator stopped at their floor, she was surprised to discover that Jett had disembarked with them. She glanced at her father, who was also frowning in bewildered astonishment.

"Is this your floor, too?" he asked.

"Yes," Jett nodded with barely a change in his expression.

"Isn't that a coincidence?" her father declared on an incredulous laugh. "It's ours, too."

"Yes, it certainly is." The dry inflection of his voice seemed to doubt it, but Glenna couldn't be sure. "I'll see you in the dining room at eight."

As he moved off down the hall, Glenna walked with her father to their adjoining suites. Suspicion reared its head, but she didn't voice it until Jett Coulson was out of hearing.

"Did you know he had a room on this floor?" she questioned.

"Of course." He unlocked his door and Glenna followed him into his suite. "Every gambler knows he has to even the odds if he can."

"Jett Coulson plays poker, too, dad."

Her remark sent a serious look chasing across his tired face. "Yes, I noticed. And he's damned good at it, too. I never once suspected that he would decide to leave when you got up to go." Then he shrugged. "It doesn't matter. I'll have another chance."

At the moment she wasn't concerned about the missed opportunity. "Why don't you rest for an hour? You have plenty of time to get ready for dinner."

"Yes, I think I'll do that." He moved woodenly toward the bed and stretched his gaunt frame atop the bed cover.

Glenna studied him for a worried second,

then unlocked the connecting door to her separate suite of rooms. She slipped quietly inside and leaned against the closed door. Had she been wrong to suggest this battle to save the mine, their home, everything? For the first time she doubted her father's ability to sway Jett Coulson onto his side.

When she dressed for dinner later that evening, she recalled her father's remark that they would go out in style. In a month they may not have a place to live, but tonight she was going to be dressed as elegantly as any woman in the room.

The jade green silk of her dress was an exotic foil to the burnished chestnut of her hair, swept atop her head in a mass of ringlets and secured by jeweled combs that had belonged to her mother. The jade material encircled her throat, leaving her shoulders and arms bare. It was nipped in tightly at the waistline, then flared into a skirt. With it she carried a crocheted shawl of silver threads.

When she knocked on the connecting door, her father was fighting with the knot of his tie. She tied it for him, noting how much good the short rest had done him. Together they went downstairs, arriving at the dining room precisely at eight o'clock. All but two of Jett's party were already there.

Glenna was aware of the curious glances she received as she was introduced to the men around the table. Their silent speculation increased when Jett seated her in a chair to his right. Her father was given the chair next to her, which put Glenna between the two men. Her position and the other guests at the table virtually negated her father's chances to talk privately with Jett.

The conversation around the dinner table was lively, focused mainly on coal as Jett had predicted. Her father included himself in the discussion quite easily. Mostly Glenna just listened to the stimulating and intelligent exchanges. She couldn't help noticing how bluntly Jett stated his opinions, never couching his replies in diplomatic terms. In contrast everyone else appeared to be the epitome of tact, phrasing their remarks so they wouldn't offend anyone.

It was a trait, she discovered, that was not limited to business discussion when Jett inquired, "Are you bored with the conversation?"

The others were busy talking and appeared unaware of the question he had addressed to Glenna. "No, I'm not bored." She lifted her gaze briefly from the prime rib she was cutting to the velvet sheen of his glance. "Dad and Bruce usually sit at the dinner table talking about daily coal production, grades and tonnage. I'm used to it."

"Bruce?" His voice carried an aloof curiosity for the identity of this unknown person.

"Bruce Hawkins," Glenna supplied the rest of his name. "He manages the mine for dad." She thought she felt his gaze boring into her, but she looked up as Jett was making a leisurely sweep of the guests.

"Does it bother you being the only female at the table?" He idly speared a piece of meat on his fork and carried it to his mouth.

Glenna let her own fork rest on the china dinner plate, bewildered by the question that had nothing to do with the subject they had previously been discussing. This confusion was reflected in her eyes.

"Why should it bother me?" she asked with a slight frown.

"I didn't say it 'should,'" he corrected smoothly. "I asked if it did."

"No, it doesn't." But she still didn't understand the point of the question.

"Perhaps you enjoy being the object of so many admiring glances?" Jett suggested.

She wasn't going to deny that she had received some. "I'm flattered, but—" Glenna didn't bother to finish the sentence, abandoning the defensive to counter. "Maybe I should ask you that first question. Does it bother you that I'm the only female at a table with all these men?"

"Not as long as you're sitting beside me it doesn't." He didn't have to hesitate over his answer, issuing it smoothly without as much as a glance in her direction.

A question from one of the other guests ended the personal conversation as Jett responded to it. The vaguely possessive ring that had been in his voice seemed to confirm that she was being singled out for his attention by this forthright and virile man. And that bothered Glenna, creating fluttering butterflies in her stomach, because she was beginning to regard him as a man rather than just as someone her father wished to do business with.

This change in attitude prompted her to notice more details about him. She studied his hard angular features, taking note of the straight bridge of his nose, the flat planes of his cheeks, his strong chin and clean jawline. On either side of his mouth arcing indentations were grooved to soften the harshness of its thin line. Sun creases fanned out from the corners of his eyes, tilting upward to emphasize the enigmatic and smiling gleam that was always in his dark eyes.

His hands and fingers were long and strong boned, but there was nothing slender or delicate about them. As Glenna watched their deft and competent movements, her imagination began weaving fantasies about their skill in a lover's caress and the sensations they might arouse on her sensitive skin. That thought was one step away from imagining the persuasive force of his mouth on hers. At that point Glenna brought her wayward thoughts to a screeching halt. No purpose would be served except to heighten her already overstimulated libido.

Distraction was provided when the dinner plates were removed and coffee was served. Jett took out a pack of cigarettes and offered one to her. She shook her head in silent refusal.

"Do you mind if I smoke?" An eyebrow was quirked in accompaniment to his question.

"I don't mind." Glenna shook her head again.

Jett started to light it, then paused to glance at her father. "Would you care for a cigarette, Orin?"

"No." His was a reluctant refusal. "The doctor made me quit smoking three years ago when I had my heart attack." But he made no mention of his recent one.

"You seem to have enjoyed a full recovery." Jett exhaled a trail of smoke, studying her father through its grayness.

Glenna was surprised to hear her father admit, "But I'm not the man I once was."

When the waiter returned a few minutes later to refill their coffee cups, a debate began among the guests whether to have more coffee or to visit the lounge for after-dinner drinks. The majority decided on the lounge, which started a general exodus from the table.

"Will you be joining us in the lounge?" Jett asked as her father courteously pulled back her chair for Glenna to stand.

The glance she exchanged with her father indicated they were both of the same mind, but he was the one who spoke. "No, thank you. It's been a long day and I need my rest."

"Thank you for dinner, Mr. Coulson," Glenna added.

"It was my pleasure."

"We enjoyed the meal...and the company."

Her father inserted his expression of gratitude. "Good night."

"Good night." His gaze touched each of them, lingering for a pulsing second on Glenna.

Outside the dining room Glenna and her father separated themselves from the others to walk toward the elevators. Glenna was fully aware that she possessed too much nervous energy to go to sleep yet. She would simply toss and turn if she went to bed now.

"If you don't mind, dad, I'm not coming up with you. I think I'll take a walk outside and enjoy a little of the night air before turning in," she explained.

"I certainly don't mind," he assured her. "I'll see you at breakfast in the morning."

"Good night." She brushed a kiss across his cheek, then left him to walk to a door exiting the inn.

She was nearly to the door when she saw Jett Coulson approaching. She felt the excited fluttering of her nerve ends, her pulse altering its rhythm to an uneven patter.

"Going for a stroll, Miss Reynolds?" The mildness of his tone made it less of a question and more of a complacent guess.

Glenna stopped to respond just the same. "I thought I'd walk off some of the dinner before turning in."

He paused beside her, dangerously attractive in his dark evening clothes. "That was exactly my intention. Shall we go together?"

The levelness of his gaze held a silent challenge. Alarm bells rang in her head, sending out dire warnings of the consequences in accepting. Glenna knew exactly what would happen if she took a moonlight stroll with this man. So did he. If she didn't want to know what it would be like in his arms, this was the time to say no.

"Why not?" she agreed with an expressive lift of a shoulder and returned the directness of his look.

CHAPTER FOUR

Outside the briskness of the night air prompted Glenna to lift the silver shawl to cover the bareness of her shoulders and arms from the slight chill. The touch of coolness seemed to heighten her senses, making her keenly aware of the male figure walking a scant half step behind her.

By silent consent Jett had allowed her to set the pace and the direction of their stroll. Glenna led him away from the stately white hotel onto the tree-shaded grounds. Once they had escaped the bright lights shining on the building, Glenna slowed her pace still more to wander beneath the trees.

Overhead the cloudless sky was a patchwork of stars. A misty moon sent its beams to illuminate the lawn wherever the newly leafed trees failed to shade it. Nature's creatures were offering their night songs to the breezeless air.

Glenna paused beneath a tree and leaned carefully against its rough trunk to gaze through vee openings of its branches at the sequin-studded sky. The shawl was hugged tightly around her, not in defense of the slight chill but to hold onto the enchantment of the scene.

Unbidden, the opening lines of a song came to her mind. "Almost heaven," she unconsciously murmured them aloud. The sound of her voice echoed in her ears, stirring her to the realization that she had spoken her thoughts. Straightening from the tree trunk she glanced at Jett. He was watching her, his stance relaxed. "Do you remember the song 'Country Roads'?"

"Mmm." It was an affirmative response.

Glenna wandered to the edge of the shadow the tree cast in the moonlight. The ground beneath her feet was uneven so she moved carefully.

"West Virginia is my idea of 'almost heaven,'" she explained softly while her gaze continued to admire the night sky and the soothing night sounds.

"Is it?" Jett came up behind her, stopping at a point near her right shoulder. "The slogan on the license plate is a more apt description of West Virginia—wild and wonderful. Or is that your idea of 'almost heaven?'"

She sent him a sidelong glance, angled slightly over her shoulder. "Perhaps. But I've never attempted to define it."

His head inclined slightly toward her. "What's that perfume you're wearing? That fragrance has been tantalizing me all evening."

Glenna wasn't prepared for the sudden switch of topics. Her mind raced to make the transition while her senses erupted with the intimation of his words.

"It's a new scent by Chanel. I've forgotten

253

the name of it.'' It didn't seem important as she
half turned to answer him. Raw warmth spread
through her in anticipation of his next move.

Glenna wasn't disappointed as his hand
found the curve of her neck to tip her head back
while his mouth made a steady descent to her
lips. His kiss was sensually sure and softly exploring, his mouth moving back and forth
across her lips with deliberate ease. Reaching
out, his hand clasped her waist and turned her
the rest of the way around to bring her fully into
his embrace.

The warmth of his arms enfolded her, lan-
guidly heating her body with his. Under the
masterful persuasion of his kiss resistance never
entered her mind. The sensations he was
creating within her were much too enjoyable to
want them to end. This absence of force was
seduction in its purest and most dangerous
form.

Her eyes were closed in dreamy contentment
as his mouth wandered over her cheek to the
lobe of her ear. The sliding caress of his hand
along her neck succeeded in pushing her shawl
off one shoulder. He bent his head to let his
warm lips more intimately explore the rounded
bone.

''Your skin reminds me of the creamy smooth
petal of a magnolia,'' Jett murmured against
her skin, then slowly straightened.

Reluctantly Glenna raised her lashes to look
at him, wishing he hadn't stopped so soon. His
unfathomable black gaze wandered over her up-

turned face in a caressing fashion, yet managed to convey the impression that she was a very special lady.

"Why do I have the feeling that your father is setting me up for something?" It was a full moment before his casually worded question penetrated her sensually induced state of vulnerability.

Shock ran through her as Glenna realized his timing had been deliberate. Even now, while she was stiffening in his arms, his hand continued to trace the curving arc of her shoulder and neck, a thumb drawing circles on her sensitive skin. Her lips parted in a wordless and angry protest at the accusation, but her voice was temporarily lost to her.

But Jett didn't seem unduly perturbed that she failed to answer him. He continued to regard her with lazy alertness. "Your father is trying to hustle something. I haven't been able to decide whether it's his coal company...or if he's hustling you. If it's you, I might find it tempting."

When his head began a downward motion, as if to kiss her again, Glenna lashed out with her hand, slapping his face in a flash of temper. Without pausing, she pivoted out of the loose hold of his arms to stand rigid, her back to him. She expected retaliation or pursuit.

Instead Jett responded to her assault with an amused taunt. "What happened? Did I come too close to the truth?"

"No!" Swinging her head around, she denied

it too quickly and too vigorously. Instantly she realized that her anger had been born partly because Jett had so accurately seen through her father, and partly because he could think so clearly while holding her in his arms. She and her lightning-quick temper had overreacted. Bowing her head she took a calming breath.

"I lost my temper." She grudgingly offered him an apology. "I'm sorry I slapped you."

"In that case—" his voice was thick with restrained laughter as his hands reached out to turn her around and span her waist "—let's kiss and make up."

Glenna flattened her hands against his chest to brace herself away from him, but he overpowered this resistance with little effort. His hands spread up her spine to shape her to his length, the slickness of her dress offering little protection from the searing impression made by his hard muscled body.

Unable to elude his embrace, Glenna attempted verbal abuse to gain her release. "You are the most—"

His soft throaty chuckle foretold the futility of that. "I've heard all the adjectives before."

His hand cradled the back of her head to hold it still while his mouth covered her tightly compressed lips. Glenna was frustrated by the lack of brutality in his embrace. There was no punishment in his kiss, only a devouring kind of passion that ate away at her defenses. Neither was she bruised by his hands. It would have been so much easier for her to be repulsed by his embrace if he had been hurting her. Jett didn't need brute force to undermine her resistance.

When Glenna reached the point where she could no longer remain stiff in his arms and let her body become pliant against his, Jett eased his mouth from her lips. "Shall I turn the other cheek so you can slap it?"

She lowered her gaze from his sensually expert mouth to the white collar of his dress shirt, its paleness standing out sharply against the tan of his throat and the dark material of his suit. Her heartbeat was slow to return to its normal rate; so was her breathing.

"If you knew my father, you wouldn't have made the insinuation that angered me into slapping you the first time." Her voice was low, its pitch still disturbed by his kisses. "My father never 'hustled' anyone in his life."

"Perhaps 'hustle' was a bad choice of verbs," Jett conceded and loosened the enclosing circle of his arms to permit more breathing room between them. "But I know when I'm being primed."

Glenna felt a prickle of discomfort because she knew it was true. "I'm not certain that I know what you mean by that, but my father is an honest man." She could look him in the eye and say that.

"I don't recall implying that he wasn't," he returned evenly and let his gaze run over her face. "Mainly I'm curious what part you play in his plans."

"None. I'm just here if he needs me," Glenna

shrugged because moral support was the limit of her involvement. She had never taken an active part in his business affairs. It would be a poor time to become involved now when skillful negotiations were required, and she was a bungling amateur.

Jett didn't appear totally convinced by her reply, but seemed willing to withhold judgment. The corners of his mouth deepened in a dry smile as his arms slid from her to let her stand free.

"Do you think he will need you?" he mused.

Without the warmth of his body heat, Glenna shivered. She was beyond coping with his double-edged questions. "It's getting cool. I think I'll go in now."

If she expected a protest from Jett there was none forthcoming. "I'll walk with you."

They retraced their path to the inn in silence. He stayed at her side until she reached the elevator. He saw her safely inside and punched the button to her floor.

"Good night, Glenna." He used her given name easily, but she didn't have time to reciprocate before the doors slid closed.

In her room Glenna knocked once on the connecting door to her father's suite. There was only silence on the other side. She hesitated, then opened the door to look in. She tiptoed to the bed where her father was sleeping peacefully, so she didn't waken him. It was a while before she fell asleep.

THE RINGING of the telephone wakened her the next morning. She groped blindly for the receiver as she tried to shake the sleep from her senses.

"Yes?" Her voice sounded as thick as her tongue felt.

"Wake up, sleepyhead," her father's cheerful voice admonished. "Rise and shine."

Glenna let her head fall back on the pillow while managing to keep the phone to her ear. "What time is it?" She frowned drowsily.

"Eight A.M."

"Why did you call me? Why didn't you just knock on the door?" She sat up in bed and rubbed her eyes, trying to wipe the sleep out of them.

"I'm downstairs, that's why. I've been up for a couple of hours, took an early morning stroll. I thought I might run into Coulson, but I understand he ordered breakfast in his room." The reference to Jett blinked Glenna's eyes open wide with the memory of last night. "Are you going to join me for breakfast or do I have to eat alone?"

"I'll be down, but dad...." Glenna hesitated. "Don't try to see Jett until I've had a chance to talk to you."

"Why?" There was a puzzled note in his voice.

"I'll explain it all when I come down. Just give me a few minutes to wash my face and get dressed."

In all it took Glenna a fast twenty minutes to

wash, put on fresh makeup, and don a pair of wheat-tan slacks with a matching knit top in narrow stripes of cream and tan. Her father was already seated at a table when she joined him in the restaurant for breakfast.

"What did you mean on the phone? Why do you need to talk to me?" her father queried almost before she had scotted her chair up to the table.

Briefly Glenna explained about Jett accompanying her on the walk last night, leaving out the intimate details of the kiss. "He suspects that you're setting him up for something," she concluded.

"He said that?" A troubled frown puckered his brow.

"To be precise, he said he knew he was being primed."

"Mmm." Orin Reynolds thought for a moment. "I don't want him to get the impression that I'm some kind of shyster, so I'll have to be more direct with him. Otherwise he won't believe that I want to make a legitimate business proposition."

"That's what I felt," she agreed.

"I had hoped to get on friendlier terms with him before making my proposal, but that's out," he sighed, then sent her a thin smile. "Thanks for the warning."

The waitress came to take their orders, but her arrival didn't affect their conversation. They had already finished their discussion. It was a quiet meal with her father lost in his own thoughts.

There wasn't any sign of Jett around the hotel that morning. They didn't see him until lunchtime when they were seated at a table in the restaurant. Glenna saw him enter the room and managed a whispered, "Dad," to draw her father's attention to the tall black-haired man approaching their table.

"Good afternoon." Jett's greeting encompassed both of them, a greeting that they echoed. Without any further preliminaries, he rested a hand on the back of Glenna's chair and leaned the other one on the table to face her at right angles. That caressing and intense look was in his eyes that made her feel she was someone special as he directed all of his attention to her. "Would you like to play a game of tennis this afternoon? I have a court reserved for two o'clock."

His closeness had a heady effect on her. She glanced at her father to escape the spell Jett was casting over her. Her father mistook the glance, believing that she was seeking his permission.

"Go ahead and enjoy yourself. I'll find something to keep me amused," he insisted.

"Two o'clock then." Jett repeated the time in confirmation of her decision.

"I'll be there." Glenna nodded.

As Jett straightened to leave her father spoke up. "There is a business matter I would like to discuss with you when you have time."

Jett eyed her father with a knowing half-smile. "I would be available at four-thirty, if that suits you."

"It's fine." There was a wealth of confidence in Orin Reynolds's expression, every bit equal to Jett's. "My suite or yours."

"Yours."

Glenna remembered, "I don't have a tennis racket."

"I'll get one for you," Jett promised and moved away with a waving flick of his hand. He walked over to join two men that Glenna recognized as having attended the dinner the previous night, obviously two of his guests.

"Well, all my cards will be spread on the table by five this afternoon," her father stated with a resigned sigh.

"What do you think he will do?" Glenna picked up her glass of ice water and sipped at it to cool the heat coursing through her veins, all the while keeping track of Jett's movements over the rim of her glass.

"That is one man I wouldn't begin to second-guess," her father declared and crumpled the linen cloth protecting his lap, depositing it on the tabletop. "If you are ready to leave, I am."

Glenna's answer was to push her chair back and stand up. After they had left the restaurant they returned to their suite of rooms so Glenna could change into her tennis clothes. She could hear her father prowling around in his adjoining room, alternately sitting and pacing. His tension become contagious. Everything they had rested on the outcome of his meeting with Jett this afternoon.

Wearing a white headband to keep the hair

out of her eyes, she arrived at the tennis courts. Jett was waiting for her. He gestured to a trio of rackets. "Take your pick."

She tried each of them before choosing the second one. Her nerves felt as taut as the racket strings, a combination of apprehension for their financial situation and the increasing havoc Jett was raising with her senses.

When they had taken the court Glenna agreed with his suggestion to loosen up with a few practice volleys. Usually she was an above-average player, but she was lacking concentration. In consequence she started out playing badly.

Halfway through the first set Glenna hadn't scored once. What was more damning to her pride was the knowledge that Jett was not trying to score. When she managed to get her serve in, he returned it and kept a slow volley going, never trying for a crosscourt or baseline. On her last serve she double-faulted to give him set point.

Angry with herself for playing so poorly, and with him for being so condescending, Glenna barely glanced at him when they switched ends. But he goaded her in passing.

"You'd better get your mind on the game. Your problem is you're not concentrating."

The criticism was a stinging prod. Glenna returned his first serve with a blistering crosscourt shot that caught him flat-footed. From that point on her game improved. Yet she was never equal to Jett. He would let her draw close, even win a game or two, but each time the match was in jeopardy, he'd slam home a shot that she couldn't return.

The strong competitive streak within Glenna refused to let her quit. Jett was controlling the game, running her legs off, but she kept battling until he won the match point. Perspiration ran in rivulets down her neck as she walked in defeat toward the net. Winded, she was gripping her side while he vaulted the net, barely out of breath.

"Congratulations." The handshake she offered him was limp, as exhausted as her voice.

"Tired?" There was a taunting smile in his tone.

Resentment flared wearily in her gray green eyes as she wiped her forehead with the back of her hand. Turning, she walked slowly off the court, aware that Jett fell in step with her.

"You could have annihilated me," she accused. "Wiped me off the court anytime you wanted. I don't like the idea that you were just toying with me, playing cat and mouse."

"It seemed more of a contest, didn't it?" he handed her a towel.

"I don't think you even worked up a sweat," Glenna complained, her voice partially muffled by the towel she used to wipe her face.

"I did," he assured her on a lazy note. "You are a pretty good player when you concentrate."

"No mouse likes to be patronized." She draped the towel around her neck, letting the ends hang down the front.

"I have never seen a mouse with chestnut hair before or a temper to match it," Jett chided with a wicked glint in his eye.

Her breath had returned to a more even rate. She lifted her head to look at him. "I'm not really a sore loser, although it might sound like that. It's just that...being allowed to come close is almost as bad as being allowed to win," she explained. "What satisfaction is there if you know someone *let* you do it?"

"You have a valid point." His hands caught the ends of her towel, pulling her closer to him. With each breath she inhaled his earthy male scent, heightened by perspiration and the heat of exertion. It did funny things* to her pulse. "But it wasn't my intention to appear patronizing. You are a fierce competitor. I felt you were entitled to some kind of reward for your efforts. You just wouldn't give up."

"I never quit." It was unthinkable.

Jett wiped her cheek with an end of her towel, managing to give the impression of a caress. "I realize that."

Then his hand was under her chin, lifting it so his mouth could claim her lips. Glenna tasted the salty flavor of him in the moist union of their lips as she swayed against the hard support of his length. She was still thirsting for more of his kisses when he slowly drew away from her clinging lips.

"I suppose you mentioned to your father what we discussed last night. Is that why he

265

asked to meet me this afternoon?'' Jett murmured.

Dammit! He was doing it again. Catching her off guard with her senses drugged by the potency of his kisses. Glenna straightened from him, containing her anger with an effort.

"Yes, I told him about your misguided suspicions," she admitted since there wasn't any point in lying. "I think he wants to meet you to correct the impression you were forming about him."

"What does he want to talk to me about?" Jett continued to watch her while he slipped his tennis racket into its protective carrying case.

"Dad could explain it better than I can." Glenna didn't try to convince him that she didn't know. "I told you before I'm not involved with any of his business affairs."

"Then it is about business?" He requested confirmation of the subject matter.

"Yes." It was a clipped response. She picked up the tennis racket she had used, holding it in an attitude of indecision. "What am I supposed to do with this?" Glenna made a subconscious attempt to divert the conversation.

Jett motioned to an attendant. "He'll return it." Glenna handed it to the young boy who jogged over. As soon as he'd left Jett asked, "Will you be at the meeting?"

"Probably. Why?" She tried to challenge him.

"I just wondered." With a hand resting on

the small of her back, he guided her away from the tennis courts.

Glenna was wary of such a noncommittal answer. "What did you wonder?"

His sidelong glance held her gaze for a moment. "If you were a shill."

"A shill," she repeated in growing indignation.

"A shill is a gambling term. It refers to a partner, a decoy used to dupe the victims into a game—usually a crooked game," he explained.

"I know what it means," Glenna retorted. "But I don't happen to be one."

"It's possible that your purpose could be to divert my attention. You are a very attractive diversion." His glance was swiftly assessing.

Glenna didn't trust herself to look at him, certain she would strike at him again. "But that isn't my purpose."

"So you said," he nodded.

"You really have a very suspicious mind," she stated in a low angry breath. "Does everybody have to have an angle, some ulterior motive?"

"They don't have to but they usually do." His delivery was smoothly offhand, but there was a wealth of cynicism in his words.

"Maybe it's because you do most of your business with underhanded people instead of honest ones like my father," Glenna suggested dryly.

"Get burned a few times, and you'll get leery of fire, too."

Her gaze slid to his face, noting the grimness of his mouth and the forbidding set of his jaw. Glenna realized that his toughness, his hardness came from harsh experience. It lessened her irritation.

"I don't have to be at the meeting," she pointed out. "If it would make you feel more secure, or less suspicious, I'll go for a swim or something. There isn't anything I can contribute to the discussion. And I certainly don't want you to regard me as a distraction. Neither would dad."

As they stopped in front of the elevators, Jett studied her for a long second before commenting on her suggestion. "I have no objection to your presence at the meeting with your father. If you want to attend, you can."

"If it's up to me, I'll be there." Because she knew her presence would provide moral support for her father, which was of greater importance than Jett's distrust.

The elevator doors slid soundlessly open as a bell chimed overhead. Glenna stepped to one side to let its passengers walk by her before entering the empty elevator ahead of Jett.

CHAPTER FIVE

THE MEETING was a nerve-racking experience for Glenna. She was curled in a chair off to one side, trying to be as unobtrusive as possible. Her father had begun the meeting by first establishing the profitability of the mine, producing studies and reports for Jett's examination. From there he had gone on to explain previous years' financial difficulties, then the inspection order for safety improvements and the long appeals in order to raise the money to comply with the required standards.

All the while Jett had listened, looked over the papers and reports, and studied the man doing the talking. And all the while his face had been devoid of expression. Never once had he glanced at Glenna since greeting her shortly after he had arrived. She shifted in her chair to ease a cramped leg, yet the movement didn't attract his attention.

"I think that gives you a fairly good idea of my present dilemma." Her father leaned back in his chair to study Jett and try to read his reaction. After an instant's pause he laid out his proposal. "And why I am anxious to form an association...a merger with your firm, to obtain the financial strength I need."

Jett glanced over a report in his hand before leaning forward to set it on the table atop others. "You have explained that your credit has been overextended because of recent economic reversals in the industry. While your operation can't be classified as lucrative, it appears to be stable. Lending institutions have made loans on less strength than what you've shown me. Their reason for refusing you can't be based on your indebtedness or lack of collateral. What was it?" There was something very casual and indifferent about the way Jett shook out a cigarette from its pack and lighted it.

"As you know, a single-mine owner is in a precarious position. He virtually has a one-man operation. If something happens to that one man, there is no operation. On the other hand—" her father shrugged "—your company is made up of a team of men. If something happens to one of them, you replace him, but the loss of one man does not jeopardize your company's existence."

"True," Jett agreed and waited for him to continue.

As Glenna studied her father she noticed the tightening of his mouth. She was well aware of the effort it took for her father to finish his explanation.

"In the last three years I've had two heart attacks. A year from now I may not be here. That's why I can't get a loan," he explained.

"If I'm gone, who would run the mine? Glenna certainly couldn't. Not because she's a woman. Her skills happen to be in another field. Without me there's no one to run the operation and make sure the debts are paid."

His statement prompted a question that Glenna unwittingly offered aloud. "What about Bruce?"

Tired gray eyes sent her a rueful look. "Bruce is a competent individual when he has someone to give him directions. He's a stopgap, capable of holding things together alone only over a short period of time," he explained to both her and Jett.

Her gaze was magnetically drawn to Jett. He was eyeing her with quiet contemplation, but she was struck by the emotionless set of his features. When his gaze broke contact with hers, it was to slide downward and linger on the soft outline of her lips. This betrayal of interest was the first he'd shown toward her. It was quickly gone as his attention reverted to her father.

"Without this merger I stand to lose a great deal," Orin said, which was an understatement. "But I'm not the only one who would suffer. The economy of our small community has barely recovered from the last shutdown. I don't know how many could survive if the mine is closed again for an extended period of time."

"I can appreciate what you are saying." Jett exhaled a stream of smoke and tapped his cigarette in an ashtray.

"Naturally I don't have to point out to you the tax advantages your company would enjoy by absorbing my operation. I wouldn't even make this proposition if there wasn't a way you could benefit from it," her father insisted, then paused as if suddenly realizing he had no more arguments to make. "I don't expect you to give me an answer right away. You need time to consider it."

"If I may, I'd like to take a copy of the reports you've shown me so I can go over them." He gestured toward the papers on the table.

"You can take those," her father offered.

"Between tonight and tomorrow I'll have a chance to study them." When Jett uncoiled his length to stand, it signaled an end to the meeting. Whatever followed was merely a formality. "I'll let you know tomorrow afternoon whether I think your proposal is something my company would wish to pursue."

"That sounds fair enough to me." Orin rose with difficulty to shake hands.

Glenna stood, too, as Jett picked up the stack of reports. Her gaze searched his face, but whatever opinion he had, he was keeping it strictly to himself. With a nodded farewell in her direction, he let her father escort him to the door.

When the door was closed behind him, her father turned back to the center of the room, glanced at Glenna, and sighed heavily. "We only have twenty-four more hours to wait before we have a decision. At least we won't be kept dangling for days."

272

"Excuse me, dad." She hurried to the door that Jett had just exited. "I'll be right back."

"Where are you going?" He blinked in confusion.

"I just want to have a word with him for a minute," Glenna rushed and disappeared into the hallway. She walked swiftly, the poise of maturity giving her an air of confidence. In the corridor ahead of her she saw him opening the door to his suite. "Jett." The firm ring of her voice requested him to wait for her. He paused on the threshold of his suite, an eyebrow slightly quirked in silent inquiry and speculation.

As soon as she reached him Jett entered his suite, sending an invitation over his shoulder for her, "Come in." From the doorway Glenna noticed a second person in the sitting room of Jett's suite. A conservative suit and tie covered his portly figure. His balding head made the man appear considerably older than she suspected he was. When he saw Glenna following Jett into the suite he stood up quickly, self-consciously smoothing his tie down the front of his protruding stomach and trying not to show his surprise.

"This is Don Sullivan," Jett introduced the man in an offhand manner. "He works for me in an organizational capacity. Don, meet Glenna Reynolds."

"How do you do, Mr. Sullivan," Glenna murmured as the man bobbed his head in her direction with faint embarrassment. She bit at

273

the inside of her lip, wondering how she was going to speak to Jett alone.

But he was already arranging it. "Would you mind stepping into the other room for a few minutes, Don?" It was an order, phrased as a question. Before the man could take a step, Jett was handing him the reports her father had let him take. "I want you to look these over, too, so we can discuss them later."

"I will." Again the man bobbed his head at Glenna as he moved his stocky frame toward an inner door.

When it was closed and they were alone Jett turned slowly to meet Glenna's steady look. "You wanted to speak to me?"

"My father told you the whole truth. He didn't leave anything out," she said evenly. "I wanted to be sure you knew that, considering how suspicious you have been."

"I ran a check on your father. The report came back before I met with him this afternoon," he stated. "So I was already familiar with his present situation."

"Then why didn't you let him know?" Glenna frowned.

"If your father is the businessman that I think he is, he has already guessed that I had him checked out. He would have done the same thing in my place." Jett picked up a sheaf of papers that Don Sullivan had been working on when they had come in, and glanced through them.

The implied compliment for her father eased

some of her tension. "Then you do believe he is honest."

"Your father mentioned two negative facts that I had no information about. . .and would probably have had difficulty obtaining. So, yes, I believe he gave me a fair picture." He replaced the loose papers on the table where he'd found them and allowed a faint smile to touch his mouth when he looked at Glenna. "Does that reassure you?"

"Yes." There was an inward sigh as that possible prejudice had been eliminated. A noise in the adjoining room reminded her of the man waiting for him. She took a step toward the hall door. "I won't keep you any longer."

"What? Aren't you going to add your voice to your father's appeal?" A gentle mockery gleamed in his dark eyes, taunting but not cruelly so.

"Would it do any good?" Glenna countered in light challenge.

"It might prove entertaining," he replied with a raking look that was deliberately suggestive. Then his expression sobered. "I will consider it as seriously as I would any business proposition."

Glenna didn't feel she could expect more than that. "Thank you," she murmured and left the room to return to her father's suite.

Despite the reassurance from Jett, the waiting for his decision was difficult, both for Glenna and her father. Throughout the evening she wavered between a certainty that Jett would agree and a cold fear that he would not.

She slept restlessly, waking with the first glint of dawn. After lying in bed for nearly an hour trying to go back to sleep, Glenna climbed out of bed and dressed in a pair of dark blue slacks and a cream white velour sweater. It was half-past five when she ventured into the corridor to take the elevator downstairs.

In the hotel lobby Glenna skirted the restaurant with its aroma of fresh-perked coffee in favor of the invigorating crispness of the early morning air, seeking its quiet serenity to soothe her troubled mind. She wandered through the dew-wet grounds with no particular destination in mind, yet aware her steps were taking her in the general direction of the stables.

For a while it seemed she had it all to herself, sharing the yellow morning only with the twittering birds in the trees, until she noticed a man strolling alongside an inn road. She recognized Jett immediately, her pulses quickening. Her meandering path intersected the road, and she turned onto it to walk toward him, neither hurrying her pace nor slowing it.

As she drew closer, she saw that he was dressed in his evening clothes—or had been. The tie was unknotted and hanging loosely around his neck, the top buttons of his white shirt unfastened. His suit jacket was slung over one shoulder, held by the hook of his finger, and his sharply creased slacks looked wrinkled. There was even a dusty film dulling the polished sheen of his black shoes.

"If you are just coming in, it must have been some party," Glenna remarked when Jett was within hearing. "What happened? Did you decide to go horseback riding at midnight and get thrown?"

"No, I haven't been riding. Only walking," he corrected dryly, both stopping when only two feet separated them. "You're an early bird this morning."

"I couldn't go back to sleep so I got up." Her gray green eyes inspected the weary lines in his face and the rumpled blackness of his thick hair. "Haven't you been to bed?"

"No. After dinner I went over some business with Don. It was around two A.M. before he left the suite. I went for a walk out in the hills to do some thinking, and stayed around to watch the sun come up." His features took on a faraway look when he partially glanced over his shoulder in the general direction he'd just come from.

Glenna leaned toward him, reading something in his expression that gripped her throat. "Have you decided about the merger?" she asked tightly.

His gaze glided to her face, moving over it for an instant, the line of his mouth slanting. "I'll give your father my answer this afternoon." He deftly avoided the question.

"Are you still considering it?" A breeze came whirling out of the trees to blow across her face, briefly lifting the chestnut hair away from her neck before it danced away.

Jett rested a heavy hand atop her shoulder. "There is a lot to consider, Glenna."

"I'm sure there is," she agreed on a subdued note, lowering her gaze to the front of his shirt. "It's just the waiting to find out that's so hard."

"All decisions are hard. Life is hard." His voice was gentle, but the grip of his hand applied pressure to her shoulder bone, drawing her half a step closer. He swung his jacket behind her in order to lock both his hands behind her neck. "It would have been easy if you had been the one to suggest a merger with me." The seductive pitch of his voice made it plain that he had something much more intimate in mind than a business liaison. "You present a very attractive package."

Glenna was conscious that he had bent his head toward her, but she didn't lift her gaze. If he was trying to divert her thoughts from her father, he was succeeding with his closeness. The flattery wasn't necessary.

"You didn't have to say that. I don't need to be sweet-talked out of asking questions about your decision. I can accept the fact that you haven't made up your mind," she told him.

"Glenna, I never say anything I don't mean." The firmness of his tone enforced his statement, compelling her to tip her head up to examine his face.

There were still signs of tiredness and lack of

sleep etched in his features, but the smoldering intensity of his eyes shallowed out her breathing. Jett eliminated the last few inches to claim her curving mouth while his hands slid down her back to enfold her in his arms.

Her senses erupted with a wonderful rawness that needed his embrace to soothe it. Everywhere her body came in contact with his muscled frame a wild current seemed to flow between them—a current that spread its tingling pleasure through the rest of her flesh. The ache of passion knotted her abdomen. Its sudden presence tempered the ardency of her response until she regained control of her senses to end the kiss.

She had always been cognizant of the sexual attraction Jett had aroused, but their previous kisses had not led her to expect this flaming leap into desire. It shook her. Glenna felt the weakness in her knees and didn't try to immediately move away from him. Her hands were spread across his shirt front. Beneath them she could feel the thudding of his heartbeat, its tempo disturbed like hers was.

"Your volatility isn't limited to your temper, is it?" Jett mused.

"I don't know what happened. I—" Glenna half turned, self-conscious and unnerved.

"Hey, I'm not complaining," he chuckled and caught at her hand, clasping it warmly within his fingers. "That looks like a comfortable tree. Why don't we sit down, rest a little before making the long walk back to the hotel?'' He led her toward a large tree on the lawn.

"The grass is wet," she pointed out, the green blades of grass glistening with the sheen of dew. Jett solved that problem by spreading his suit jacket on the grass. "It'll get grass stains on it."

"So? I'll send it to the cleaners." He lowered himself to the ground and pulled Glenna down beside him on the other half of his jacket. The trunk of the tree served as a backrest for him, but it wasn't wide enough for Glenna to lean against it, too. Instead Jett shifted her so she was resting diagonally across his chest, his arms overlapping around her waist. "Mmm." He nuzzled the curve of her neck. "Maybe I couldn't sleep last night because I was missing this," he suggested.

The stubble of his beard growth was pleasantly rough against her sensitive skin. It conveyed the rasping caress of a cat's tongue as he rubbed his chin and jaw along her neck. The hard support of his chest and arms, and the pressure of his hipbone began to embed themselves on her flesh. Glenna felt herself slipping again into that mindless oblivion of sensation. She changed her position to elude the mouth exploring the sensitive hollow behind her ear, turning sideways in his arms to rest a shoulder against his chest.

"Is something wrong?" Jett cupped a hand to her cheek, tipping her head so he could inspect her face.

"Not really." It seemed impossible that she had only known him for two days. The angled planes of his features seemed so very familiar to her. It was just that the pace of their relationship had just accelerated, and Glenna wanted to slow it down before it carried her away.

His hand idly left her face to reach down to lift her left hand. His gaze studied the bareness of her fingers, his thumb running over the tops of them. When he lifted his gaze there was interest, curiosity, and the banked flame of desire gleaming in his look.

"No rings," Jett observed. "Have there ever been any?"

"If you mean, have I ever been married? No," she replied with a slight shake of her head.

"Engaged?"

"No." The latent sexiness of his look was having a chaotic effect on her pulse.

"How old are you?" Jett continued with his questions.

"Twenty-four."

"No steady boyfriends?"

"None." At the skeptical lift of his eyebrow, Glenna qualified her answer. "Not unless you count Bruce."

"Bruce Hawkins. The man who manages the mine for your father?" His recognition of the name was instant. He asked only for her confirmation.

"Yes. Bruce and I have become close friends since my father had his first attack. Since dad has to restrict his activities, Bruce comes to the house a lot to discuss things with him," she explained.

"He's been like a brother to you then, another member of the family," he deduced.

"Something like that," Glenna agreed.

His hand continued to massage her fingers, rubbing them in a sensuous manner that aroused all sorts of tremors. "Do you think he regards you as a sister?"

She started to say yes, but when she met his knowing look she knew that wasn't true. After a pause she admitted, "I don't think so."

"Neither do I."

Jett released her hand to let his fingers seek the mass of hair at the back of her head. By the time Glenna realized his intention she had lost the will to resist. The searing possession of his mouth parted her lips to deepen the kiss with the intimacy of his exploring tongue. Hot flames shot through her veins, melting her bones and burning her flesh with a feverish heat.

Her hand slid under his arm to circle the back of his waist, her fingers spreading over the taut muscles of his spine. When he uncombed his fingers from her hair, he cradled her head on the flexed muscle of his upper arm. She let her fingers glide up the front of his shirt to slide inside his collar, discovering the exhilarating feel of his tanned throat beneath her hand and the wild tattoo of the vein in his neck.

Glenna shuddered with intense longing. The quiver continued when she felt the touch of his fingers pushing their way under her sweater to the bare skin over her rib cage. The breath she took became lodged somewhere, time standing still as he cupped a ripe breast in the circling cradle of his hand.

Through the spinning recesses of her mind a voice came to ask if what she felt was real. Or whether it was simply natural desire that had been suppressed too long and was now being uncovered by an expert. Her conscience rejected sexual involvement with the accompaniment of emotion.

Trembling, but with growing strength, Glenna began to strain away from his drugging kiss. At the first sign of resistance Jett began to seek control of his own passion, not attempting to overpower her.

When he lifted his head, both were breathing raggedly. Glenna sat up, shakily tucking a strand of auburn hair behind her ear. Silence stretched between them for several seconds. Then Jett rolled to his feet and held out a hand to pull her upright.

"Have you had breakfast?" he asked when she was standing.

"No. I wasn't very hungry." She watched him bend to scoop up his suit jacket. "I thought the fresh air might wake up my appetite."

"Are you hungry now?" His fingertips touched her elbow to start her in the direction of the inn.

"A little."

"For food?" His downward glance noted the very faint blush in her cheeks. "I guess I didn't have to say the obvious, did I?"

"No."

"Glenna."

Something in his voice raised her head. He was looking at her with an intensity that she found a little frightening.

"What?" she prompted when he didn't immediately speak.

A tiny frown appeared between his eyebrows as his gaze swung to the front. "Never mind. It wasn't important." He seemed suddenly very remote. Lifting a hand, he rubbed the side of his jaw. "I need a shave...and some sleep."

There didn't seem to be any comment for Glenna to make, so she fell into an uneasy silence. Jett made no attempt to break it during the walk back to the inn. Shortly after they had entered the lobby Glenna spied her father.

"There you are, Glenna." He hurried toward them. "I wondered where you were. Have you had breakfast?" A frown clouded his expression when he recognized Jett and took in his slightly disheveled appearance. "Good morning, Jett."

"Good morning, Orin," he replied and immediately excused himself. "I'll talk with both of you later today."

It was left to Glenna to explain, as Jett walked to the elevators, how she had come to meet him.

CHAPTER SIX

GLENNA GLANCED AT HER WATCH for the fifth time in the last five minutes. Irritated that so little time had passed she turned and retraced her path to the window overlooking the front grounds of the inn. It was the same view of trees and grass and driveway. She pivoted away to wander back toward the door of the suite.

"You are going to wear a hole in the carpet if you keep walking back and forth in the same place," her father complained, chiding her in a paternal fashion while he drummed his fingers on the armrest of his chair.

"You aren't exactly a picture of serenity," Glenna retorted dryly.

"No, I suppose I'm not," he admitted, releasing a long breath.

"Maybe I should call him," she suggested. "He might not realize we're waiting for him. There wasn't any specific time mentioned."

"Coulson knows we're waiting to hear from him," he assured her. "He'll be here...sooner or later."

But could her nerves stand the "later"? Glenna threaded her fingers together, squeezing them tightly while she tried to ignore the tension churning her stomach. Restlessly her gaze searched the room for some object to distract her attention from the endless waiting.

A sharp knock at the door snapped the fragile thread of her control. She whirled toward the sound, then paused to meet her father's glance. He drew in a deep breath and forced a grim smile on his mouth. Taking his lead, Glenna gathered together her composure before forcing herself to walk sedately to the door.

Turning the knob, she stepped to one side as she opened it to admit Jett. She struggled to behave normally when she met the blandness of his gaze. She even managed a smile of welcome.

"Sorry I kept you waiting. I was delayed or I would have been here sooner," Jett explained smoothly, pausing while Glenna closed the door behind him. "I received a long-distance phone call just as I was about to leave."

"It couldn't be helped." She accepted his apology while her gaze searched the impenetrable mask of his features. "You look rested. Did you get some sleep?" she asked conversationally as they walked the rest of the way into the room where her father was seated.

"A couple of hours."

Her alert gaze had already noted his smoothly shaven face and the starched crispness of his striped shirt and charcoal slacks. With him, Jett had the reports her father had given him the previous afternoon. Yet, more than the freshness of his appearance, Glenna noticed the coolness of his attitude. The pleasantness was all on the surface. A chill ran up her spine as she darted a look at her father.

When Jett walked over to set the reports on the table beside his chair her father said—quite calmly, "It's no, isn't it?"

Her gaze raced to Jett in a silent plea for her father to be wrong, but Jett didn't glance at her. He met the pair of gray eyes squarely, without a flicker of regret.

"No." It was a flat refusal.

Glenna nearly choked on the bitter taste of defeat, but she didn't make a sound. Her personal disappointment was fleeting. If the announcement was a crushing blow to her, it had to be much more severe for her father. It was his life's work that was being lost. Her heart swelled with pride at the stoic acceptance he was displaying over Jett's decision.

"Very well," he nodded. "It was worth a try."

"May I ask why you turned down his proposal?" Glenna felt her voice sounded quite calm, with only a trace of rawness in its tone.

"It's quite simple." The piercing blackness of his gaze was turned to her. "If my company is interested in acquiring your mine, it would be much more economical to let him go broke. A merger would mean assuming all of his debts and liabilities as well as his assets. Those debts are more than the mine is worth. Which wipes out the tax savings. Therefore the merger isn't to our advantage."

"I understand." Despite her outward composure, inside she was raging at his coldly logical reasoning that didn't take any human factor into account.

As if reading her mind his gaze narrowed. "Your father would be the only one who would really benefit from the merger. And Coulson Mining is not a charitable institution." He turned back to her father. "This was strictly a business matter. I had to make a business decision." It was a flat statement with no apology for the outcome.

"I understand perfectly," her father replied. "I didn't want you to regard it in any other manner."

There was a second's pause before Jett extended an arm to shake her father's hand. "I wish you luck, Orin."

"A gambler can always use some of that." A wan smile pulled at the corners of her father's mouth in a weak attempt at humor.

After he had released her father's hand, his gaze rested for a scant instant on Glenna. Then he crossed the room to the door and left without another word.

His departure released the paralysis that had gripped her limbs. Glenna moved to her father's chair, wanting to comfort him and wanting to be comforted herself. She reached out to tentatively rest a hand on his shoulder, worried by the lack of expression in his face. He patted her hand almost absently.

"We'll figure something out, daddy." Unconsciously she used the term "daddy" instead of dad. She hadn't called him that since she was a child.

"No, we've lost it. The mine, the house, everything," he declared on a hollow note, staring off into space. "If a merger wasn't profitable for Coulson, there isn't anyone else who can help us. I'm through. Finished."

"Don't say that, daddy." She knelt beside his chair, fighting the tears that were making the huge lump in her throat. "You are a Reynolds, remember? We never quit."

He didn't seem to hear her. She searched wildly through her mind for some alternative, some other way to save everything, but there was only blankness.

"I'm tired, Glenna," he said after several minutes. His eyes appeared empty when he looked at her. "I think I'll lie down for a while. Will you help me up?"

The request frightened her as nothing else had. He had always been too proud to ask for help, or to admit he needed it before. His pride was broken. Glenna felt she was picking up the pieces when she slipped an arm around him to help him out of the chair. She walked with him to his bed and spread the light coverlet over him.

"You'll feel better after you rest," she insisted in an effort to reassure herself. "Later on we'll call room service and order steak and champagne. We're going to go out in style, remember, dad?"

"I don't think I'll feel like eating tonight." He closed his eyes.

289

Glenna stared at him, then finally pulled up a chair beside his bed. He appeared to sleep. She remained near him, worried about his heart and wanting to be there if he became ill.

At seven o'clock she had a sandwich sent up for herself and a bowl of soup for her father. She was partially reassured when he wakened and voluntarily sat up to eat the soup. He continued to be withdrawn, unresponsive to her attempts at conversation, but the leadenness of depression had left his eyes. She turned on the television for a while until he announced that he wanted to go to bed. Leaving the connecting door ajar, Glenna returned to her own suite.

CHAPTER SEVEN

MECHANICALLY, Glenna changed out of her clothes into her turquoise green nightgown and matching satin robe. Too many things were running through her mind, leaving no room to think of sleep. She moved restlessly around the room, slipping in to check on her father half a dozen times.

Her head was pounding with the effort to find a solution. Two thoughts kept reoccurring in her mind. One was her father's insistence that Jett Coulson had been their only possible source of help. The second was the remark Jett had made to her early that morning about how easy his decision would have been if she had wanted a merger with him.

Pressing a hand to her forehead, Glenna tried to rationally think out her problem. Jett was attracted to her. That was an indisputable fact. He had made his decision on a purely business basis, but what if she appealed to him on a personal level? How much influence did she have? Could she persuade him to reconsider?

When the barrage of silent questions stopped, a calmness settled over her. She had to find out. For the sake of her father, she had to try. With a course of action chosen, Glenna moved to carry it out.

The hotel corridor was empty when she ventured into it. She walked swiftly to the door of Jett's suite and knocked lightly on it. Only at that second did she consider the possibility that he might not be alone—or that he might not even be there. The turning of the latch eliminated the last. When Jett opened the door a glance past him found no one else in the sitting room.

He stood in the opening, one hand holding the door and the other resting on the frame. Under the steadiness of his gaze, Glenna couldn't find her voice. Taking his time, he let his gaze travel over the draping fabric of her robe as it outlined the jutting curves of her breasts and hips. In a strictly defensive reaction to his visual assault, her hand moved to finger the satin ribbon that secured the front of her robe.

Without saying a word Jett opened the door wider and moved out of the way. Her hesitation was brief before she glided past him into the sitting room. She pivoted around to face him when she heard the click of the door latch. He was wearing the same pale gray striped shirt he'd had on this afternoon, but the sleeves were rolled up to expose his tanned forearms.

"It occurred to me that you might come to see me." Instead of walking to her, he went to a table strewn with papers that he'd obviously been working on, and half sat on the edge.

"Then you know why I'm here." Her voice came out husky.

There was a pack of cigarettes amid the stacks of papers. Jett removed one from the pack and lighted it. "You came to see if you couldn't persuade me to reconsider your father's proposal." He sounded so distant that Glenna unconsciously moved closer to him.

"Is it so much to ask, Jett?" she questioned. "My father has everything at stake. His whole life's work."

"A good gambler keeps an ace up his sleeve. I wondered if your father was going to play his ace of hearts." He studied her through the smoke screen of his burning cigarette.

"Ace of hearts? Are you referring to me?" Glenna frowned, confused by his attitude. "My father doesn't know I'm here."

"He didn't send you?" An eyebrow was arched in question.

"He's in his room, sleeping. He has no idea that I'm here. If he knew—" When she imagined her father's reaction, she averted her glance from Jett. "He wouldn't approve."

"Then this was all your idea," Jett concluded.

"Yes." She watched as he reached across the table for a half-filled ashtray. With one hip on the edge of the table and his other leg braced in front of him, he held the ashtray in the palm of his hand, the forearm resting on his thigh. She couldn't help noticing how his relaxed stance stretched the material of his slacks tautly across the hard columns of his legs.

"I don't think you understand how serious dad's situation is. It isn't just the mine he's going to lose, but his home, everything he's worked for all his life. In his condition, he can't start all over."

"I know he'll be lucky to end up with the clothes on his back." Jett took a drag of his cigarette, squinting at her through the smoke that swirled up to burn his eyes. "That's one of the things I learned when I ran a check on him. And I admired the way he underplayed how much he stood to lose, as if he had something tucked away while he was betting his last dollar. He's a proud man with a lot of class."

"You wouldn't say that if you had seen him after you left this afternoon." Glenna laced her fingers together in front of her, twisting them as she tried not to remember how he'd looked. "You broke him. I've never seen him like that—with no fight left in him—no pride. He's given up. When you left, he laid down as if he hoped he would fall asleep and die. I sat with him, trying to think of a way I could—" Her throat tightened, choking off the last of the sentence.

"That's when you got the idea to come here." His gruffness drew her glance. An agitated impatience dominated his action as he crushed his cigarette in the ashtray and set it aside.

"You were his last hope, Jett. There isn't anyone else in a position to help him." She took another step toward him, reaching out to touch his arm in an unconsciously beseeching gesture. "I accept that as a business move a merger with dad might not be that beneficial to you. But can't you reconsider his proposal on a personal level? Help him because he needs it?"

A muscle flexed in his jaw as his impenetrable gaze locked with hers. With an almost violent abruptness, he straightened from the table, moving so suddenly that one minute her hand was touching his arm and in the next there was only empty air.

"You don't know what you're asking, Glenna." He shook his head with an angry kind of weariness, his hand on his hips.

"He needs you," Glenna stood quietly in front of him. "Explain to me what I have to say or do to make you listen to me."

"What if I told you to take off your robe?" His glance flicked to the satin bow with raw challenge.

Slowly she raised a hand to untie the front bow. Her fingers trembled slightly as she pulled an end of the ribbon to unfasten it. When it was untied she eased the robe from her shoulders and let the shiny material slide down her arms. Catching it with one hand before it reached the floor, she reached out to lay it on the table atop his papers. Then boldly Glenna lifted her gaze to his face.

An inner warmth kept her from feeling the coolness of the air touching her exposed skin. The matching nightgown was styled like a slip. Turquoise green lace, the same shade as the satin material, trimmed the bodice. The clinging fabric revealed the rounded shape of her breasts, her nipples appearing as small buttons beneath the material. After tapering in at the waistline, the nightgown flared gently over her hips, ending just below her knees. The lace-trimmed hemline was broken where the gown was split up the side, almost to mid thigh.

Jett was making note of each detail before he finally returned her look. The black fires leaping in his eyes ignited an answering spark in the lower half of her body, aroused by the rapacious hunger in his gaze. Glenna swayed toward him. There was a slight tremor in his hands as he reached out to loosely grip the sides of her waist.

"How can I persuade you to change your mind, Jett?" Her voice was one step away from a whisper.

Her fingers were splayed across the front of his shoulders. Beneath the material of his shirt, she could feel the tautness of his muscles, as if he was holding all his instinct in check.

"This is an appeal to the lascivious side of my nature, isn't it?" he asked as his wandering gaze noted the uneven rise and fall of her breasts beneath the lace bodice of her nightgown. "You came here tonight to convince me to help by tempting me with your body. Are you prepared to carry it through?"

His bluntness seemed to cast a sordid light on her behavior. She lowered her gaze to the unbuttoned collar of his shirt as she struggled to defend her present action. "I love my father. I can't stand by while he's being destroyed without trying to save him. It doesn't matter what I have to do in order to accomplish that."

"Why did you think you could change my mind?" His breath fanned her temples, warm and tangy with tobacco smoke, while his hands inched her closer to him.

"You once said that I tempted you. I wasn't sure whether you meant it or if it was just a line you'd used many times before," Glenna admitted on a breathless note because his mouth was nuzzling her cheek and ear.

"You're not tempting," Jett murmured, working his way to the curve of her neck. "You're irresistible. You knew exactly what would happen when you knocked on my door."

"I hoped." She tipped her head to one side, giving him more access to the sensitive areas he sought and inviting him to continue the stimulating exploration.

From the base of her throat, he nibbled up the other side of her neck. A soft moan escaped her lips as they sought the satisfaction of his kiss. His mouth hardened on hers, spreading a hot and brilliant glow through her body. The pressure of his hands increased, threatening to crack her ribs as the intensity of his need engulfed him. His tongue probed apart her lips and teeth to unite with her tongue.

Her hands slid around his neck, her fingers seeking the thickness of his lustrous black hair. A fiery heat seemed to turn her bones to liquid as the crush of his hands fitted her to his length. The sleek material of her gown was a thin barrier, blocking out none of the sensations of his hard embrace. His caressing hands made restless forays over her shoulders, back and hips, relentless in their need to touch and possess every possible inch of her.

Slowly Jett dragged his mouth from hers while raising his head no more than a breath's reach from her lips. "You know I want to make love to you." His low husky voice was a rough caress. "I can feel the way you're vibrating. You knew this was going to happen when you came; that it would ultimately come to this moment."

"Yes." Her face remained uplifted, her eyes trained on the tantalizing nearness of his mouth, her lips parted in an aching invitation for his possession.

"And your sole reason is because of your father. Would you be here now, Glenna, if I was a fat old man?" Jett mused.

"I don't know," she admitted, because she had not been presented with that situation. Jett was a virile, exciting man who desired her, and who was in a position to help her father.

"Your loyalty to your father runs deep, but I'll never believe that you would have considered using sex as a bargaining tool if I hadn't aroused you." His mouth brushed her lips as he spoke the words, claiming them at the end of the sentence.

The tidal wave of passion that flooded through her veins made it impossible for Glenna to argue with his statement. His arms shifted to scoop her off the floor and hold her cradled against his chest.

The door to a bedroom was standing ajar. Jett kicked it the rest of the way open and carried her into the lightless room. Slowly lowering her feet to the floor, he stood her up beside the bed. His hands glided up her sides, pulling her gown with them and lifting it off her head. The room was all in shadows with only a glimmer of light shining in from the sitting room as he began unbuttoning his shirt. Glenna could barely see what he was doing. A wild anticipation licked along her veins, sending tremors over her skin.

"You are going to help my father, aren't you?" That was still the motive for her presence. It was where she got her strength. Discretion would have sent her from the room, long ago.

His arms clasped her shoulders to draw her naked body to the hair-roughened bareness of his chest. Despite the dimness, his mouth found her lips and locked sensually over them. His kiss gave Glenna her answer.

"No more talking," he murmured and leaving her standing beside the bed, he began to shed his clothing.

Everything was going to be all right, thanks to Jett. Her father was not going to lose his purpose in life, his will to live. Jett was giving it all back to him. Something wet trickled down her cheekbone. Tears that had been forbidden to fall for so long were now slipping out of her eyes. It seemed right, somehow, that they were being shed in happiness.

Her arms opened to Jett now undressed, gathering his muscled torso into her embrace. Her breast swelled as his hand took its weight in his palm. A muffled groan escaped his throat before his mouth claimed her yielding lips but then he dragged his mouth from hers and stiffening, lifted his head.

"Are you crying?" His puzzled question indicated that he had tasted the saltiness of her tears on her skin.

"Yes." She smiled while her hands glided over the steel smoothness of his shoulders. Glenna knew she had to explain. "I can't help it. I'm happy. You've made everything all right again. I can see dad's face when I tell him that you have changed your mind."

There was a long silence during which Jett remained perfectly still, looking at her in the darkness. Then, with a heavy sigh, he turned away from her. "I can't help your father, Glenna." An iron thread ran through his low statement.

It gripped her by the throat, numbing her with disbelief. "What?" It was barely a whisper.

"I can't help him," Jett repeated his statement more forcefully.

All she could see was the dark silhouette of his back. "You let me believe you were going to so you could make love to me," she accused in a voice that ached with his betrayal.

"Yes, I did," he muttered tersely. "And I wish to hell that I'd kept my damned mouth shut!"

"But I thought we made a bargain." Glenna saw him bend to pick up his pants. She heard the rustle of the material as he stepped into them and zipped them up.

"I never agreed to it," he reminded her. He tossed something at her in the darkness. It landed at her feet. "You'd better put that on."

The touch of her fingers recognized the material of her nightgown. When she looked up, Jett was vanishing through the doorway into the sitting room.

CHAPTER EIGHT

HER FINGERS CURLED into the material of the gown, its silken texture contrasting with the rawness of her nerves. A desperate kind of angry confusion pushed her into action as Glenna picked up the gown and slipped it over her head. She tugged its length down over her hips and hurried after Jett.

She paused in the doorway, her gaze sweeping the sitting room to find him. Shirtless, he was standing at the table, lighting a cigarette. Glenna seethed with the knowledge of how very close he had come to tricking her.

"Why did you do it?" Her voice shook on the hoarse demand.

His dark gaze sliced to her, slashing over the provocative nightgown that covered her shapely form. With a disregard for the order of the papers stacked on the tabletop, he snatched the robe she had laid on them and lobbed it across the room to her.

"You'd better put that on, too," he snapped.

She was forced to catch it as it swirled around her middle. Jett half turned away, tense muscles rippling and flexing along the back of his shoulders as he ran a hand over his rumpled black hair. Acting out of instinct, Glenna slipped her arms into the sleeves of the robe.

"Why?" she repeated her question with the insistence of hardness.

"My God, surely you can guess!" Jett retorted with a fury that was barely contained. "Let me run through the scene for you. A sexy redhead knocks on my door in the middle of the night, dressed in a clinging negligee. When I let her in, she asks for my help. And in return, she'll go to bed with me. Since I want to go to bed with her, I take advantage of the situation— the same as any man with a normal sex drive would do."

The anger of shame scalded her. "I trusted you, but it was all a deception." Glenna choked on a bitter laugh. "God, you must have been laughing at how gullible I was!"

"If that was true, we'd be in that bedroom right now making love!" The partially smoked cigarette was crushed in the ashtray and left to smolder. With long impatient strides Jett crossed the width of the room to a credenza and opened a door to take out a decanter of Scotch and a glass. "The deception worked, but unfortunately, I couldn't go through with it."

At the moment Glenna found no consolation in that fact as she watched him splash a jigger of Scotch in the glass and bolt it down. She was too filled with degradation because she had nearly sold herself for nothing. The loss of self-respect was shattering.

"Whatever gave me the ridiculous idea that

you would agree to help my father? I should have realized what kind of man you are when you admitted you knew he would be financially ruined if you turned him down this afternoon.'' Glenna had realized, but she had been too filled with her foolishly noble purpose to notice it at the time. ''You weren't interested in helping him—only yourself.''

''I *can't* help him!'' Jett angrily stressed the verb, slamming the glass down on the credenza.

''Ha!'' It was a scornful sound. ''You *won't* help him because it doesn't suit you to do so. You can't get any bigger than Coulson Mining. I'm not an expert, but even I know that!''

''Do you think your father is the only one in the industry who suffered financial problems during that long strike a year ago?'' he challenged. ''Multiply his problems a hundredfold and that's what I had. My company lost money then, too, because the overhead and management went on. My stock of coal supplies was exhausted because I had contracts to deliver coal. When that ran out I had to buy coal to make the shipments, which meant paying a higher price. My firm is recovering just as your father's would have if he hadn't ran afoul of the safety regulations. I can't absorb his losses without risking my company. I can't do that. It's his life versus hundreds. Can you understand that?''

His harshness, his roughness made Glenna see how impossible it had been from the outset— how hopeless. She burned over the way he had dangled them on a string, letting them think he might save them when he knew all along he couldn't.

"It was cruel to let us think you were considering dad's proposal," she accused.

"I did consider it...very seriously." Jett was gritting his teeth as if suppressing the urge to retaliate with matching anger.

"Do you expect me to believe that?" she taunted. "Why would you? You've already made it clear that it was impossible from the beginning."

"Why?" He repeated her question while he began taking ominous steps in her direction, his dark eyes blazing. "I can answer that in one word—you. It has to be obvious that I'm attracted to you, that I was from the moment I met you. When I found out how much trouble your father was in, I wanted to believe there was a way I could help because I cared about you. Why the hell do you think I stayed up all night, walking and thinking and scheming?"

"You knew this morning what the answer would be, didn't you? But you made us wait all day!" Glenna was near tears again, her eyes luminous with the gray green color of storm-tossed seas. "Why didn't you put us out of our misery? Why did you drag it out?"

"If I told you this morning, what would you have done?" he challenged coldly, coming to a stop in front of her. The intimidating breadth of his naked shoulders and chest towered before her eyes. "You'd be hating me—the way you are now. The name Coulson Mining means dollar signs to you. Even now after I've explained to you, you still believe I could have helped your father. I would end up getting blamed for your father's failure. So I stole this morning. And I would have taken tonight with you. I should have. You were more than willing."

He raked her with a look that reminded Glenna just how willing she had been. She was sickened by the way she had bartered herself, and subsequently embittered that he tread on her unsuspecting nature.

"You don't have to remind me of that," she protested huskily.

"You aren't going to give me credit for telling you the truth, are you?" he declared with disgust. "I didn't carry out the deception. I could have."

"I'm amazed that you didn't." Sarcasm crept into her voice as she blindly turned away. "I can't believe how incredibly naive I was. For my father's sake I was going to give myself to you, so certain that you would appreciate my gallant gesture. But I forgot I was dealing with a ruthless magnate instead of a gentleman."

"I can't prevent your father from losing what he has, but if you need anything, Glenna—" Jett began, ignoring her insulting words.

"I'll never come to you," she flared. "I never want to hear your name again."

Because she knew it would always remind her of the way she had opened herself to humiliation. She had lowered herself—cheapened her father's name—with her foolish tactics. She could never forgive Jett, because she couldn't forgive herself.

With hot tears filling her eyes she hurried toward the door. Jett called her name, but she didn't pause. Afraid he would pursue her, she rushed down the hallway to her suite, breathing in sobs. Tears were streaming down her cheeks when she slipped inside the room and closed the door.

"Glenna? Glenna, is that you?" Her father's voice called to her from the open door to the adjoining suite.

Quickly she swallowed the sobs in her throat and wiped hurriedly at hot moisture on her cheeks. "Yes." There was a thready sound to her voice. Footsteps approached the doorway. She sniffed back some tears and tried to sound calm. "Did you want me, dad?"

"Where have you been?" The forlorn question was echoed by his expression when he appeared in the opening. "I called several times but you weren't here."

Glenna was careful not to face him directly as she turned down the covers of her bed and took her time plumping the pillows. "I'm sorry. Did you need something?" Although she tried hard to conceal it, there was a definite waver in her voice.

"Where were you?" His attention sharpened at the way she avoided his question.

Hesitating, she realized she couldn't hide the truth from him. "I went to talk to Jett," she admitted thinly. "I thought I might persuade him to change his mind."

There was an awkward silence. "In your nightclothes?"

The accusal struck a raw nerve and lifted her hurt gaze to his paling face. The tiredness and defeat became mixed with dismay.

"Yes," Glenna whispered as she began to shake with the sobs she could no longer hold back. "I'm sorry, dad, but I just couldn't stand by while you lost everything." It seemed to take him a long time to cross the room to where she stood. Intense sadness gleamed in his eyes. Quietly he studied her wretched expression.

"What happened, baby?" he asked with grim concern.

"Nothing." She shook her head in a mute kind of pain and shuddered when his arms went around her to comfort her. "He insists that he isn't in a position to help you."

"Then he didn't—" Her father paused, not needing to finish the sentence.

"No." It was a rasped answer as Glenna began to cry softly. "I wanted to make things right for you. Instead I've hurt you more, haven't I?"

He gathered her into his arms and hugged her close. "This is all my fault," he murmured.

"No. You aren't to blame." She refused to let him take that burden as she rested a wet cheek against his flannel robe. "It was all my idea. I was so desperate that I didn't stop to think how embarrassing it might be to you. On top of losing everything you have worked all your life to build, now I've let you down."

"I'm afraid I let you down," he sighed heavily. "I had given up because I thought I had lost everything in life that mattered. But I still have you, Glenna. I should have remembered that."

She closed her eyes. "Can we leave first thing in the morning? I can't face Jett again."

"You were beginning to like him, weren't you?" He drew his head back to look at her.

"I could have, if he had been different." But that wasn't exactly the truth. "If circumstances had been different," she corrected.

He patted her gently. "You climb into bed. Maybe tomorrow morning things won't look as bleak as they do now." With an arm around her shoulder, he urged her toward the bed.

"Are you all right?" Self-consciously she wiped at the tears on her cheeks and lifted her head to study him.

"I will be," he promised, but he looked exceptionally tired when he smiled to reassure her.

After she was in bed he tucked the covers around her and bent stiffly to brush a kiss on her forehead. Before he left the room he turned off the light. Lying beneath the covers in the dark, Glenna thought about the episode with Jett and how much worse it could have been. He hadn't carried out the deception to its final conclusion. Her anger had been a face-saving device to salvage her pride. Knowing that did not improve Glenna's opinion of herself.

A HAND shook her awake. She groaned a protest, weighted by some sleepy depression that she didn't understand. But the hand on her shoulder was insistent that she should wake up. Finally she rolled onto her back and opened her eyes. Memory rushed back with the sunlight flooding the room. First, Jett's announcement that there would be no merger, then her father's despondency, followed by her disastrous attempt to appeal to Jett to reconsider. Pain sawed on her nerve ends.

"Good morning." Her father was standing beside her bed, smiling down at her.

Glenna blinked and tried to refocus. Her father looked so different from the man she had seen last night. He was dressed in a bright sport shirt and blue slacks. There was color in his freshly shaved cheeks and a twinkle in his eye.

"Come on. Get up," he coaxed. "It's a new day outside and I'm hungry for breakfast."

Confused, she pushed herself into a sitting position and stared at this cheerful replica of her father. Her expression drew a hearty chuckle from him. That only deepened her frown.

"What reason do you have to be so happy?" She shook her head in total bewilderment.

"Why are you so glum?" he grinned.

Her mouth opened, but all she was capable of doing was releasing a short incredulous breath. Her reasons were so obvious that there wasn't any need to list them. Helplessly she searched for some explanation for his attitude.

"How can you say that?" she said finally.

"Because I've just spent a night counting my blessings," he informed her.

"I know we have some, but... have you forgotten that we're losing the company, our home, everything?" It wasn't that she wanted him to become depressed again, but the change in his attitude was so drastic that Glenna was worried.

"And that's blessing number one," he stated with a brisk nod of his head.

"A blessing?" she echoed.

"Yes, because now we know it's a fact, so we can stop wondering and worrying whether we're going to find some way or someone to bail us out of our mess," Orin Reynolds explained as if his reasoning was perfectly logical.

"Dad, are you feeling all right?" Glenna eyed him warily.

"I'm fine. A good dose of optimism will cure what's ailing you, too. Hop out of bed and I'll give you your first injection over breakfast." He glanced at his watch. "I'll give you twenty minutes to get dressed and meet me downstairs at the restaurant."

As he moved toward the door Glenna protested, "But dad, I don't want to meet Jett again. He might be there—"

"That's blessing number two," he winked. "He's already checked out of the hotel and gone."

The vision of his beaming smile stayed with her after he had disappeared into the outer hallway. Driven by curiousity Glenna climbed out of bed. Her own low spirits had been overwhelmed by her father's ebullience. His sunny disposition was forcing her to venture out of the darkness whether she wanted to or not.

Exactly twenty minutes later she joined him in the restaurant. He'd already taken the liberty of ordering for her. She stared at his choices that were so indicative of his mood. First, a glass of orange juice—liquid sunshine—two eggs sunny-side up, a rasher of snapping-crisp bacon, and golden brown toast with orange marmalade.

"Dad, I'm not hungry enough to eat all this." Actually she wasn't hungry at all.

"You'd better eat it," he shrugged good-naturedly. "After all, we can't be sure where our next meal is coming from."

"And you're smiling about that," Glenna accused, quickly swallowing the sip of orange juice she'd taken. "I don't understand because last night—"

"Last night I was selfishly looking at all I was losing instead of what I was gaining," her father interrupted.

"What are you gaining?" She couldn't see where there was anything. "We are going to lose our home."

"We're going to lose a *house*," he corrected with gentle patience. "It's just walls, ceilings and windows. It's too big for us and costs too much to heat. What do we need all those rooms for? And look at how many things we've accumulated over the years. We can sell two-thirds of the furniture and still have enough left

312

over to furnish a small house. What we do sell, we can call them antiques and make a handy sum.''

''But—''

''I know what you're going to say,'' her father interrupted again with a knowing smile. ''What about all the memories? Happy memories are stored in your heart, not in a house. They are something you can never lose.''

''And what about the mine?'' Unconsciously Glenna found herself eating the breakfast her father had ordered.

''Ah, yes, the mine. What a responsibility—what a burden has been lifted from my shoulders,'' Orin Reynolds sighed in contentment. ''No more worrying about payrolls, insurance, unions, contracts, taxes, regulations, deliveries, and the hundred and one other things that are part of running a business.''

''But what will you do?'' she frowned.

''Do you know what I remembered last night?'' he asked rhetorically. ''Do you know I never wanted to run the mine? But it was the family business, so when it came my time I took over for my father.''

Glenna never knew that. She had never even suspected it. ''What did you want to do?''

He paused for a minute, considering her question. A sudden gleam sparkled in his gray eyes, dancing and mischievous. Chuckling laughter flowed, its contagious amusement making Glenna smile.

''I remember when I was a teenager I always

wanted to make moonshine." He laughed louder. "Maybe that's what I should do. Take what little money we get from selling the furniture and buy a patch of ground back in the hills and brew up some moonshine."

"Dad, you can't be serious!" She was amused, astonished, prepared to believe almost anything after the revelations of the last few minutes.

"Why not?" His expression continued to be split by a wide grin. "I've heard that there's still money to be made in it. If any revenuers come around, we can dress you up in a Daisy Mae outfit and you can try a little of your friendly persuasion on them. You might improve with practice."

Her cheeks burned at his teasing reference to her attempts last night to get Jett to change his mind. She hastily lowered her gaze to her place setting.

"How can you joke about that?" she murmured tautly.

"You've got to learn to laugh about it, Glenna." His voice was softly insistent, gentle in its understanding. "What else can you do? Are you going to hide your eyes every time you think about it?"

All the logic in the world didn't make it any easier for Glenna to bear the knowledge of what she'd done. It would be a long time before she could laugh about it.

"I admit," he continued, "that when you first told me, I was outraged...shocked. Then I was flattered that you cared so much for me to go to him. Flattered, and a little proud. I guess there are some people who wouldn't understand that. They would say that the best of intentions wouldn't excuse a wrong. But I don't think that is what's making you hang your head. Do you want to know what I think it is?"

He waited until Glenna asked, "What?"

"It's because you were beginning to like Jett Coulson. When he didn't accept your offer and its conditions, you felt that you had cheapened yourself in his eyes. You're afraid that if he'd look at you now he wouldn't see a lady of strong principles, but a woman who's an easy make. Am I right?"

His accuracy strangled her voice, forcing her to nod in admission. There was a fine mist of tears in her gray eyes, enhancing their greenish cast. Her father reached over to crook a finger under her chin and lift it.

"You hold your head up," he ordered with a smiling wink. "If he's so dumb that he doesn't see what you're made of, then he isn't worth your tears."

She smiled, a little tightly, but the warmth and adoration shining in her eyes wasn't forced. "How do you do it?" There was a thread of amazement in her emotionally trembling voice. "I was feeling so terrible this morning. I still hurt, but—" There was an expressive shake of her head as she paused.

"That's what fathers are for." He leaned back in his chair, a touch of smugness in his

look. "To bandage up their daughters' wounded hearts and make them feel better. Clean up
your plate," he admonished with paternal insistence. "We have to get packed and make the
drive back. There's a lot of things that need to
be done, plans to be made. Instead of sitting
back waiting for things to happen it's time we
started making them happen."

"You make it all sound like an adventure,"
Glenna murmured wryly.

"It's going to be."

It was difficult not to believe him. Glenna
hadn't seen her father this carefree and light-
hearted since her mother was alive. Perhaps the
mine and all its problems had been too much of
a burden for him. She knew it had taken its toll
on his health. Without the pressure and stress of
the business, he was like a new man. His mood
was infectious.

CHAPTER NINE

IT WAS LATE in the afternoon before they finally arrived home. The housekeeper, Hannah Burns, had evidently been watching for their return, because she was out of the front door before Glenna turned off the car motor. She came puffing down the steps to help with the luggage.

"It's about time you got here," the woman rushed the minute they were out of the car. "Don't keep me in suspense. What happened? Did you see that man Coulson?"

Her father glanced across the top of the car at Glenna. "Whatever happened to 'Welcome home?' I'd even settle for a plain 'Hello.'"

"Hello and welcome home. Now tell me what happened," the housekeeper demanded. "Was he there? Did you talk to him?"

"Yes, he was there, and yes, we talked to him." He nodded his head with each answer. "But he turned us down flat."

Hannah stared at him. Glenna could appreciate the housekeeper's confusion. How could a man look so cheerful when he had just announced—for all intents and purposes—that he was going broke?

"You're pulling my leg," she accused.

Her father assumed an expression of shocked innocence. "I haven't even laid a hand on you, Hannah. How can you say that?"

"Orin Reynolds, you know precisely what I mean," the housekeeper scolded him impatiently and turned to Glenna. She was having trouble hiding a smile as she unlocked the trunk to remove their luggage. "You tell me what happened, Glenna."

"Dad told you the truth, Hannah." There was an instant's hesitation before she added, "Mr. Coulson wasn't interested in dad's proposal."

"Would I lie about something like that, Hannah?" her father chided.

"Well, I certainly didn't expect you to be smiling about it," the woman retorted. "Don't you realize that you're going to be losing the roof over your head? Where are you going to get the money to put food on the table? Providing, of course, that you still have a table. And—"

Picking up one of the lighter suitcases, her father clamped a hand on the housekeeper's shoulder in action that indicated he was considering joining forces with her. "Hannah, you are an excellent cook. You wouldn't happen to have a recipe for a good sour mash?"

The plump woman had taken one step toward the house. She stopped abruptly at his question, her mouth opening in silent shock. Glenna wouldn't have been surprised if she had dropped one of the suitcases in her hands.

"What's the matter with this man?" She turned roundly on Glenna for an explanation. "Has he taken leave of his senses?"

"It's a long story, Hannah," Glenna laughed. "I'm sure dad will tell you all about it."

The housekeeper eyed him sternly before starting again for the house. "It'd better be good. Otherwise I'm calling a doctor. You could be having some side effects from that medicine you're taking," she grumbled.

As they reached the front door a car turned into the driveway. "It's Bruce." Glenna recognized the wagon.

She and her father waited on the stoop while the housekeeper went on inside. Bruce stopped the car beside the red Porsche and smiled a greeting as he climbed out.

"It looks like I timed it just right," he remarked noting the luggage they were carrying. "How did it go?"

"It didn't." Her father held the door open for Glenna to precede him into the house.

"I was afraid of that," Bruce replied with an I-told-you-so look and followed them into the house. "What are you going to do now?"

Setting the luggage inside the door, her father took the question seriously and didn't tease him the way he had Hannah. "Since we can no longer postpone the inevitable, we might as well start planning for it and make it as painless as possible." He led the way into the study.

"How?" Bruce raised an eyebrow and

glanced at Glenna as if expecting a protest from her, but she had been over all this with her father during the drive home.

"We can begin the necessary legal proceedings to turn the company assets over to its mortgage holders and debtors. Tomorrow I'm going to contact a real-estate company and put the house on the market." His gaze swept the room in a mental assessment of its contents. "We have a lot of furniture, household goods and miscellaneous items. We need to decide what we're going to keep so we can start selling the rest and get the best price that we can."

"But where will you go?" Bruce appeared a little dumbfounded by Orin's calmness.

"That's another thing." Her father stopped beside his desk and absently picked up a wood-carved decoy that served as a paperweight. "We need to look for a smaller place to live, maybe closer to town, although we might find a cheaper place if we stay in the country."

"What will you do without the income from the mine?" Because Bruce was well aware that a man of Orin's age with a history of heart trouble would have a difficult, if not impossible time finding work.

Glenna offered her solution to that. "Tomorrow I'm going to start making job applications. I should still be able to keep submitting free-lance articles and supplement my income with writing."

"I used to be pretty good at woodworking." Her father studied the handmade decoy in his hand. "When you were younger, Glenna, I used to mess around in the workshop a lot. Remember the dollhouse I made for you and all the doll furniture?"

"There were lights in the room that you could turn on and off, operated by batteries," she recalled.

"That was enjoyable, building that." He smiled reminiscently. "It would be good therapy, too. Maybe I could set up a little shop. I have all the tools."

"Why'd you ever stop doing that?" Glenna wondered aloud.

"I don't know." He considered the question. "The business began taking more of my time, more paperwork, more problems. Then your mother died and...you know the rest."

"Personally I think the workshop is an excellent idea," she concluded. "What about you, Bruce?"

"Sure," he agreed with a trace of vagueness. "It sounds good."

"Is something bothering you?" her father questioned at the bewildered look on Bruce's face.

"No." There was a slightly dazed shake of his head. "I was just wondering how you came up with all these plans when you only talked to Coulson this weekend."

That drew a smile from her father. "Once you stop concentrating on keeping your head above water, it's easy to decide to swim to shore."

"I guess that's true," Bruce conceded.

"How were things at the mine while we've been gone? Did anything happen that I should know about?" It was an inquiry that was reluctantly made. Glenna could tell her father was asking because he was aware that it was still his responsibility for a while longer.

There was definitely relief in his face when Bruce shook his head. "No, it's just been routine."

"Good." He nodded and began turning the decoy in his hand, inspecting it absently. Coming to a decision, he set the wooden duck down. "I think I'll walk out to the garage and see what kind of shape my tools are in." He was halfway across the room before it occurred to him that he was deserting his guest. "You will be staying for dinner, won't you, Bruce?"

"I'd like that, thank you, if you think there's enough to go around," Bruce accepted.

"With Hannah cooking there always is." Her father continued to the foyer. "I won't be long."

Alone in the parlor-turned-study with Bruce, Glenna wandered to the fireplace. In the last few minutes she had caught herself making unfavorable comparisons between Bruce and the more dynamic Jett. One puzzle had been solved. At last she understood why she hadn't been inclined to let her relationship with Bruce develop into a more serious one. Despite all his good qualities, and Bruce had his share, there was a vital ingredient missing from his physical

322

chemistry. Without it there was no volatile combustion.

The knowledge convinced Glenna that her relationship with Bruce would always be a casual one, but that didn't mean she didn't care about him, or wasn't concerned about his future. She turned to look at him.

"What are you going to do, Bruce, when the mine does shut down?" He had become such a part of her life in the past three years it was difficult for Glenna to picture a time when he wouldn't be around. "Have you given any thought to it?" she asked, since he had always been convinced it was unavoidable.

"I've managed to put a little money aside. I thought I might take a couple of months off, enjoy a long vacation for a change," he smiled lazily. "I can give you and your father a hand settling into a new place, and help him set up his workshop if that's what he finally decides to do. That way I can take my time and look for a really good job instead of taking the first one that comes along."

"Will you put in your application at other mining companies?" If he accepted a position away from this immediate area, Glenna knew they would inevitably drift apart. Sooner or later, she supposed, that had to happen.

"Naturally." He moved to stand beside her and lean a hand on the fireplace mantle. "That's where my expertise and experience are."

"But is it what you want?" It had been something her father had been forced into doing. "Do you like it?"

"Like it?" Bruce repeated with a shake of his head, an ardent glow firing his eyes. "I love it."

"Doesn't it ever bother you to go down that shaft?" Glenna was curious.

"I feel at home there. In a strange way I feel safe as though I was in the womb of the earth. It's something I can't really explain," he shrugged finally. "I wouldn't want to do anything else. What made you ask that?"

"I guess because I never knew until this morning that dad never wanted to run the mine. He's been in the business all these years, but it's never been what he wanted. Yet he's struggled and fought all this time to keep it in operation." She felt it spoke highly of his dedication and sense of responsibility. "It's ironic, isn't it, that out of something bad there is good. Dad is finally free of the mine."

"It's hard to believe he's the same person I saw last week. He's a changed man," Bruce commented. "I was afraid he might take it hard. But you're right, he seems relieved and happier than I've seen him."

"I know. It's wonderful."

"You've changed, too, Glenna." His gaze narrowed slightly, as if puzzling over the difference.

"Me?" She stiffened a little, sensitive to his scrutiny, not certain what his probing gaze might discover.

"Yes. I don't know quite what it is, but you

don't seem the same. It's as if you had grown up overnight. Which is crazy," he mocked at his own statement, "because you were an adult before. You look more like a woman now."

She moved away from the fireplace to escape his astute study of her. "I'll bet you've simply forgotten what I look like in the four days since you've seen me," Glenna chided him, trying to joke her way out of the situation. "You just don't want to admit it."

Bruce laughed his denial. "I'm not likely to forget what you look like." Pushing away from the fireplace, he leisurely followed her. "I know what it is." The difference dawned on him slowly. "You look vulnerable now. Before you always seemed so confident and self-assured, capable of tackling anything."

"That's silly." Her laugh of protest was brittle.

"No, it isn't. All of this has hit you harder than it has your father," he reasoned. "That's why you look lost, and a little afraid, isn't it?"

"No—" Then Glenna realized he was offering her a logical excuse. She checked her denial to hug her arms around her waist in an unconscious gesture of self-protection. "Maybe it has," she lied.

His hands gripped her shoulders to turn her around. "You know I'll help in any way I can. You don't have to face this thing alone. I'll be with you."

When he bent to kiss her Glenna turned her head aside and his mouth encountered the coolness of her cheek instead. "Don't, Bruce." Her voice was flat as his caresses left her cold. There was no need to experiment to see how his kiss would compare with Jett's. It couldn't. Glenna stood rigid within his hold, not fighting him as she stared to the side.

"What have I done, Glenna?" He was irritated and bewildered by her rejection. "Anytime I get close to you anymore you pull away from me."

"It isn't you. It's me," she replied because it wasn't fair to let him wonder if he had done something to upset her.

Sighing heavily he let his arms drop to his side. "Do you want me to leave? I don't have to stay to dinner."

Glenna lifted her head to look at him. "I'd like your company tonight, Bruce." She tried to tactfully make him understand her view of their relationship.

"My company but not my kisses." He read between the lines.

"I'm sorry, but yes," she admitted her meaning. Her expresssion remained composed, gentle but firm.

"I guess we've got that clear." His mouth tightened grimly as he turned away and walked to an armchair. "Why don't you tell me about your weekend, then?"

"There isn't much to tell." Glenna wished he'd chosen a less disturbing topic—like the weather. "The Greenbrier is a fabulous place, but it wasn't exactly a pleasure trip."

"What was Coulson like?" His choice of subject went from bad to worse.

"Just about what you would expect—although he's difficult to describe." Which he wasn't. Black hair and eyes, hard compelling features, with a latent sexuality about him that awakened hers. "He's intelligent and self-assured. He isn't one to suffer fools gladly." She remembered that he had walked in the woods and watched the sunrise. "He has an appreciation for the serenity and beauty of nature."

"How was he to deal with?"

A wry smile broke around the edges of her mouth as she remembered his afternoon meeting with her father. "Jett is...." Glenna paused, realizing how easily his name had slipped from her, but there was no way to hide it. "A better poker player than my father."

"Jett. You were on a first-name basis with him?" Bruce raised an eyebrow.

"We saw him socially, as well. I called him Jett. He called dad Orin." Glenna shrugged and tried to make it appear an insignificant item. "There's nothing special about that."

"He's a bachelor, isn't he? Good-looking as I recall." His gaze searched her face.

"Yes." She knew she wasn't doing a very good job of appearing indifferent, but just thinking of Jett made her remember things that made her blood run warm.

"I suppose he flirted with you," he accused, jealousy simmering in his eyes.

"What does it matter?" Glenna had to take a stand somewhere or Bruce would continue to ask personal questions that she'd rather not answer. "It isn't any of your business, Bruce."

Taking a deep breath, he released it in a long sigh. "Things are changing too fast for me to keep up with."

The awkward moment following his comment was filled by the sound of footsteps in the foyer. Glenna recognized her father's tread and glanced toward the study door.

"Hannah sent me to tell you dinner is ready," he announced from the doorway. "The condemned are going to eat a hearty meal tonight. I came in through the kitchen and I think she was under the impression the local boy scout troupe was coming to dinner tonight. I hope you brought your appetite with you, Bruce."

The sandy-haired man was slow to respond. Glenna was relieved when she saw him fix a smile on his face. "When Hannah is cooking I always bring my appetite, Orin." Standing, he waited politely for Glenna to pass and followed her to the dining room where the table was set.

"What kind of shape were your tools in, dad?" She sat in her customary chair on her father's right while Bruce took the one opposite her.

"They are dirty and need oiling, but they are in good shape considering how long it's been since they were used last," he declared with a touch of complacency. "I'm going to enjoy puttering around out there again."

"Make sure you don't get overtired," she cautioned.

"I won't," he promised as the housekeeper entered the dining room carrying a green salad and four wooden bowls on a tray. Her father shifted closer to Glenna so he wouldn't be in Hannah's way as she lowered it to the table. "Glenna, do you remember where we stored your dollhouse? Was it in the attic or that back bedroom?"

"That does it!" Hannah dropped the tray on the table and whirled away. "I'm calling the doctor."

"Why?" Glenna was the first to recover. "Hannah, what's wrong?"

The housekeeper paused near the kitchen door to impatiently explain. "First he comes with a lot of crazy talk about making moonshine. Now he's asking about dollhouses. He's going through his second childhood. That's what it is."

Laughter began slowly, then gathered force. Finally Orin managed to catch his breath and explained his plans to the housekeeper.

CHAPTER TEN

THE RADIO was turned on full blast, which was the only way Hannah could hear it above the vacuum cleaner. The racket was getting on Glenna's nerves. "Be patient," she told herself. Hannah was almost finished cleaning the living room.

Stretching, Glenna ran the long-handled dust mop around the top of the walls where the cobwebs invariably gathered. A faded blue bandanna was tied around her head to protect her auburn hair from the dust. A plaid shirt and brushed-denim jeans made up the rest of her work clothes.

It seemed strange to see the study empty of furniture and the fireplace mantle bare. The last load of their belongings was stacked in the foyer, waiting for her father to return with Bruce and one of his friends to take it to their new and smaller home.

Everything else had been sold. The larger items had been sold individually through advertisements in the paper. Others had been included in a garage sale. The items that were left had been taken to an auction and sold.

So she and Hannah were busy cleaning so the

new owners of the house could move in this coming weekend. And Hannah liked to listen to the radio while she cleaned. Between the radio and vacuum cleaner, Glenna could barely hear herself think.

"Glory be! Glenna!" Hannah shouted from the living room. "Come in here!"

The strident summons sent Glenna racing to the living room, certain some disaster had occurred. From the doorway everything appeared all right. The housekeeper was over by the window with the vacuum cleaner and the portable radio was blaring on the floor near Glenna's feet.

"What is it?" Glenna shouted. Hannah answered her. At least Glenna saw her mouth moving and heard pieces of words above the din of the radio and the vacuum cleaner, but not enough for it to make sense. Losing her patience she demanded, "Will you turn something off? I can't hear you."

As she reached down to switch off the radio, the housekeeper turned off the vacuum cleaner. The sudden silence was heavenly to Glenna. She could even hear herself sigh.

"There's a helicopter out there in that cleared patch of field by the driveway," Hannah announced and motioned for Glenna to come to the window and see.

"A helicopter?" She took a step toward the window.

"It's mine." A man's voice spoke behind her. Not any man's voice, but Jett's.

Glenna pivoted to find him standing inside the opened front door. A pair of mirror-dark sunglasses hid his eyes from her, but there was no mistaking him. The sleeves of his white shirt were rolled up the length of the cuffs and he was wearing dark slacks. His coal-black hair was windblown into a careless order.

After the initial shock was over, the blood rushed through her veins. Two months had not dimmed her memory of him nor lessened the impact he made on her. The longing to erase that one night when she had lost his respect gnawed at her like a cancer.

"I knocked, but with all the noise no one heard me," he explained.

"I'm sorry." Glenna found her voice, thin though it was. "But as you can see, we were busy cleaning." She loosened her grip on the dust mop. It moved slightly as if to illustrate her explanation.

Hannah came forward to draw attention to her presence, which had been virtually ignored by both Glenna and Jett. She stopped beside Glenna to study the man the helicopter had brought.

"Hannah, this is Jett Coulson...of Coulson Mining." She added the last in case the housekeeper didn't immediately make the connection. "Hannah Burns is...has been...our housekeeper for years."

After today it would be the past tense. Hannah was starting a new job as a restaurant cook, which Glenna's father thought was appropriate since she was inclined to cook for large numbers.

The introduction was acknowledged by twin nods. Hannah was plainly curious, eyeing him warily while she tried to decide what he wanted. The mirrored sunglasses made Jett's reaction even more unreadable.

"Was your helicopter forced down?" What a cruel twist fate had made if he had reentered her life by accident.

"No. We landed quite safely," he replied in lazy assurance.

"Why are you here?" Glenna felt herself becoming nervous, crazy little quivers running over her skin.

"I came to see you." It was a simple statement.

But Glenna made it quite complicated because she didn't know if it was "you" in the singular or the plural. "My father should be back shortly."

"I said—" Jett paused to take off his sunglasses and slide them in the pocket of his shirt, turning his dark eyes fully on her "—that I came to see you."

She caught her breath, not certain what he meant by that, or why. Her poise was holding, but it was becoming brittle. She lifted her chin a little higher, needing the pride that she had cast aside the night she'd gone to him.

"What is it you want?" she asked smoothly.

"I want to talk to *you*." The emphasis implied he wanted a private discussion alone with her.

Glenna darted a glance at the housekeeper who had unwittingly provided her with the moral support of her presence. No one but her father knew of that night. If that's what Jett wished to discuss, she had no choice but to send Hannah away.

"Why don't you finish packing those boxes in the kitchen, Hannah?" she asked, knowing full well there was nothing in the kitchen to be packed. Before Hannah could remind her of that, she silenced her with a look.

With a sniff of disapproval Hannah turned on her heel and stalked to the kitchen. Her gaze wavered when she tried to meet Jett's again. His was moving over her, making Glenna conscious of her appearance. Her hand reached up to remove the bandanna from her head. She combed her fingers through the weight of her hair, raking the rich chestnut curls as she turned aside.

"You said you wanted to talk to me," she reminded him.

"Coulson Mining has negotiated a contract to operate the Reynolds Mine. I wanted to tell you before you heard it from some other source."

"Congratulations. You got the mine after all!" Glenna hadn't said it with bitterness, but the connotation was there just the same.

"I hoped you wouldn't resent it." The grimness of resignation laced his voice, drawing her glance to the quiet study of his eyes.

"I can't see that it matters how I feel about it." She lifted her shoulders in an uncaring shrug.

"It matters," Jett said with calm insistence. "This contract is business."

"I never thought for a minute that it was anything else," Glenna replied. "You explained quite clearly two months ago that it would be more economical for you to obtain the mine after dad lost it. This management agreement certainly proves it."

His hand caught her arm, holding her but not turning her. "After all this time, don't you understand yet?" There was an urgency to his low demand. Heat spread from his hand through her system, scorching nerves that had not fully healed from the last time. "I did what I had to do, Glenna."

Without making it look too obvious that she needed to escape his touch, she extricated her arm from beneath his hand. "The best thing that happened to us was when you turned down my father's proposal for a merger. We don't hold your decision against you, Jett.'

"Don't you?" His tone was skeptical.

"That's difficult to believe, isn't it?" She faced him, summoning all her pride and composure. From somewhere Glenna found a faint smile. "You should see my father now that he's free from the burden of the mine. He'll be here shortly. We've sold this house to move into a smaller place."

He glanced around the room, emptied of furniture and all signs of habitation. There was a rigid line to his jaw. "You said you would lose your home."

"It's too big, and the upkeep was too high, anyway." She repeated her father's statement concerning the loss.

"What are you going to do?" His gaze was back to her, boring and intense.

"I have a job at a printing company. Naturally I'll keep on writing in my spare time." The last thing Glenna wanted was his pity so she was quick to paint an attractive picture of their new life. "Dad is going to have a workshop where he can make toys—dollhouses, rocking horses and the like."

"You don't appear to have a problem in the world," Jett observed dryly.

"We have problems, but we're managing very well," Glenna replied. "The situation didn't turn out to be the disaster we thought it would be."

"So you no longer need or want my help?" It was a challenging statement that Glenna mentally shied from because she needed and wanted a lot of things from him, but his help wasn't one of them.

"As I told you, we're getting along just fine." Which she had been up to this moment.

"What if I said your father could have his same position at the mine again, with fewer responsibilities?" He leaned a hand against the inner door frame, his dark head tipped to one side.

"I don't think he'd be interested, but you'd have to ask him." Her tension was building under the strain of his nearness. She could feel the threads of control threatening to snap. "I'm sure he would appreciate the gesture, though."

"It isn't a gesture. It's a serious offer." His reply was curt although his expression remained steadily impassive. "It wasn't his lack of skill or competence as a manager that shut down the mine, but a series of outside influences that were beyond his control. He knows the miners, the working conditions, and the potential of the mine. We both can benefit from his experience and knowledge."

"I know you never do anything out of the goodness of your heart." Irritation crept into her reply because Jett always seemed to gain something from whatever he did.

"Don't I?"

The mask dropped from his features, but the flaring anger was merely an offshoot of the smoldering intensity of his gaze. Glenna started to turn away from its desirous message. His hands snaked out to stop her and force her to face him.

"Have you forgotten that I let you go when I could have made love to you?" Jett demanded. "Don't you remember that night? You were willing. I could have taken you but I didn't because I couldn't let you go on believing that I would help your father in return for the pleasure of your body...a body that I wanted so desperately." His voice had dropped to a hoarse whisper. "If that wasn't the right thing to do—the good thing—what was? Was I wrong to let you go?"

"No." With her head turned away from him, she stared sightlessly at a bare corner of the room. The blood was thundering in her ears and her hands rested lightly against his middle, ready to stiffen if he tried to pull her closer. "I don't want to talk about that night. I want to forget it."

"I haven't been able to forget it any more than you have." His hand tunneled under her hair and lifted aside its weight to expose the curve of her neck. He bent his head to run his mouth along it, reexploring old territory with familiar ease. "I have dreams about it at night," Jett murmured with his lips moving against her skin and his breath caressing sensitive areas.

Glenna closed her eyes to try to shut out the wild sensations licking through her veins, but it only started her head spinning. She tried to interfere with his nuzzling by turning her head into him and lifting a shoulder to deny him access to her neck. The effectiveness of her action was negated when Jett transferred his attention to the edge of her cheekbone near her temple.

"In my dreams my mind became filled with the perfume of your body." Jett continued talking against her skin, leaving male-rough kisses to punctuate his sentences. "I could feel the roundness of your breasts in my hands and hear the sweet seduction of your voice whispering in my ear. I'd wake up hungry for the taste of your lips."

"Don't." Her breath was coming in tiny gasps of tormented pleasure.

His hands were sliding down her shoulders and spine, applying pressure to bring her closer. Her forearms remained stiff in resistance, but her elbows started bending, forcing her hands up the muscled flatness of his stomach to the rock-ribbed wall of his chest.

"Why did you have to come here?" Glenna protested weakly.

"I stayed away as long as I could." Jett dragged his mouth over her lips, his warm breath mingling intimately with hers. "I wanted to give you time to get over the hurt. You don't know how I dreaded telling you and Orin that I was powerless to help. I didn't want to be the one to put that forsaken look in your eyes."

His strong teeth took gentle love bites of her lips, separating them. She was defenseless against this form of attack. Her fingers curled into the material of his shirt, clinging to it to avoid clinging to him.

"When I turned the merger down, I still had hope that I could keep you out of it. I thought if I made it clear that it was strictly business that I could later persuade you to keep on seeing me," he continued while his hands impelled her hips to rest against the powerful columns of his thighs, turning her bones to water. "Then you came to my room late that night."

"Please, I don't want to remember." She tried to elude his mouth, but it followed her.

"I knew that as soon as you realized your attempt to change my mind was hopeless, you would be sickened by what you were doing." His accurate assessment of her reaction drew a gasp from her throat. "And I knew you wouldn't want to face me after that. That's when I decided that if I was going to lose you, I was going to have that evening to remember...until I realized how much you would hate me for it. I couldn't risk that no matter how much I wanted you. I haven't stopped wanting you, Glenna."

She was helplessly confused by his uncanny perception of her behavior. Drawing her head back, she tried to wade through her dazed senses to study him.

"But how could you know that was how I felt?" This was what she didn't understand.

"You can't successfully run a company the size of mine without knowing what motivates people," Jett explained, letting the short distance remain between them while the compelling possession of his gaze roamed over her face. "I had a chance to find out a little bit about you as a person before that night. I wasn't wrong in my conclusion, was I?"

"No," Glenna admitted with aching relief.

It required no encouragement to persuade her to meet him halfway. His demanding kiss exorcised the guilt from her conscience and replaced it with self-respect. With her worth restored, she could meet him on common ground again. There was no longer any need to hide her face from him. Jett wouldn't have permitted it if she had tried, and Glenna didn't try. There was too much wondrous rapture to be found in his kiss.

"I want to keep on seeing you." His voice was muffled against her throat.

"I want to see you, too," she whispered, because she didn't ever want to stop seeing him. The certainty of that knowledge left her a little giddy.

Jett lifted his head and ran a hand over her cheek before tangling his fingers in the thick mane of her hair. "Where are you moving? How far is it from here?"

The trembling roughness of his voice and the implied possession of his touch convinced Glenna that Jett was equally disturbed by her nearness. It gave her a fleeting sensation of power.

"The new house is only a few miles away," she told him.

The velvet blackness of his gaze became shadowed by a raw regret. "Do you know how impossible it is for me to commute back and forth between here and Huntington even with a helicopter at my disposal? My schedule fills a sixteen-hour day. I would barely arrive here before it was time to leave."

"I know." Glenna felt his frustration ripping through her, leaving behind an awareness of how precious each moment was.

"Move to the city," he urged. "At least there we can spend more time together and I won't be wasting so much traveling time to and from. You don't need to worry about work. I have some connections at one of the newspapers. I can arrange for you to be hired as a reporter.''

"It isn't that easy," She shook her head in a reluctant protest. "We've signed a year's lease on the house. Besides, dad wants to live in the country. I can't walk off and leave him, not in his condition. Don't ask me to do something like that, Jett.''

"I'm not going to be content to see you only a couple of times a month, Glenna," he warned. "It's been too long now.''

Glenna agreed wholeheartedly with the last, but she was plagued by a sense of lost time. "Why didn't you come sooner? You should have told me how you felt before now instead of letting me imagine what you were thinking," she protested.

"You wouldn't have believed me. You were too caught up in your own self-guilt to listen," Jett replied wisely.

"It's been such an agonizing two months," she admitted and traced the outline of his cheek with her fingertips. "If it hadn't been for Bruce and dad, I think I would have crawled in a hole and buried myself.''

A muscle flexed along his jaw, tightening its line with grimness. His attention shifted to a lock of curling auburn hair, the hardness of regret darkening his eyes. Glenna swayed toward him, needing the reassurance of his kiss that everything was all right now.

The slamming of the front door stopped her while the sound of her father's voice reversed her direction out of Jett's arms. "Fred is backing the pickup truck to the door so we can load these boxes, Bruce. Did you ask Glenna about that helicopter outside?"

As she turned toward the doorway to the foyer, she saw Bruce frozen within its framework. His very stillness indicated that he had been standing there for several seconds, if not several minutes. Glenna could tell by the numbed look of disbelief in his face that he had seen and heard enough to know what had been going on prior to his arrival. The atmosphere in the room became electric when his gaze met Jett's in silent confrontation.

Her father's appearance on the scene kept it from becoming volatile. Glenna was standing freely beside Jett when her father paused in the doorway. The instant he saw Jett a broad smile spread across his face.

"Jett!" He greeted him with obvious delight and came striding across the room, a picture of health. "What brings you here? I saw the helicopter outside, but I didn't get a good look at the insignia."

"You're definitely looking better, Orin," Jett shook hands with him.

"Thank you, Jett. I'm feeling better, too," her father stated with a decisive nod, then turned to invite the third man to participate in the conversation. "Bruce, come here. I want you to meet Jett Coulson. Bruce Hawkins was my engineer and manager at the mine," he explained to Jett.

Bruce walked stiff-legged across the room like a challenger about to do battle. "I've heard a great deal about you, Mr. Coulson." He measured him with a firm handshake.

"Orin has mentioned to me what an asset you were to him," Jett returned as he sized the sandy-haired man up with a sweeping look. Neither made a reference to Glenna. Yet, when the introduction was over, Bruce assumed a protective position at her side.

In the interim her father ran a quick eye over Glenna. Astutely he noted the glowing flush in her cheeks and the kiss-swollen softness of her lips despite the slightly uncomfortable atmosphere that prevailed.

"What brings you here, Jett?" her father questioned with a smile of benign interest. "Is this a social call or business?"

"A little of both," Jett admitted, sending a glance at Glenna to indicate the social side of his visit. "I stopped by to let you know we've negotiated a contract to manage your mine."

"My ex-mine," her father corrected without bitterness. "Congratulations. I'm glad to hear it's going to be in competent hands. When will you be reopening it?"

"Soon. Naturally we'll have to make the necessary changes to pass the safety inspection before we can go into production. But first I want to find myself a good man to put in charge." Jett took a cigarette from his pack and lighted it, studying her father over the flame. "You immediately came to mind. Would you be interested?"

"Oh, no, you don't!" her father laughed. "I just got that elephant off my back."

"I would like you to seriously consider it," Jett persisted. "The responsibilities would be considerably fewer this time around. You have all the qualifications and experience I'm looking for, plus a knowledge of this particular mine's characteristics."

"I'm flattered that you should offer me the position, but I'm not interested," her father refused as Glenna had guessed he would. "But if that's what you're looking for, Bruce fits the description. He may be a little shy on the experience side, but I'd recommend him. I happen to know he's looking for a position that would keep him in this same general area. Isn't that right, Bruce?"

Before he answered Bruce slid a look at Glenna. The glance confirmed she was the reason he didn't want to move away. It was a message no one in the group missed, including Jett. Glenna felt the penetrating study of his gaze. At this point she couldn't reassure Jett that her relationship with Bruce was still very platonic, on her part.

"That's true, sir," Bruce replied to her father's question.

"Would you be interested in the job?" Jett inquired in that brisk yet smooth business tone Glenna knew so well.

"I might be." Bruce didn't reject it. "It would depend on the terms of employment."

"Come by the mine office tomorrow morning at ten and ask for Dan Stockard. I'll tell him to expect you," Jett stated.

"I'll be there," Bruce nodded, committing himself to no more than a job interview.

A knock at the front door interrupted the conversation. "I'll answer it," her father volunteered. "It's probably Fred checking to see if we're ready to load the boxes."

But it was the copter pilot instead. "Sorry, Mr. Coulson," he apologized for his intrusion. "But we're already going to be ten minutes late for your next meeting. I thought I should remind you."

Impatience rippled through Jett's expression before he moved toward the foyer. "I'm ready to leave." He paused to let his gaze encompass the three of them. "Goodbye." But he looked directly at Glenna when he said, "I'll see you."

"Take care," she murmured and was warmed by the silent promise of his words and the brief flash of his smile.

As Jett left by the front door his departure carried her to the doorway opening to the foyer. Glenna was only half-aware that Bruce followed her until her side vision noticed him standing by her elbow. Self-consciously she turned her head to meet his look.

"It was more than just a mild flirtation that weekend, wasn't it?" His question didn't expect an answer, and the faint rise of color in her cheeks was the only one he needed. He moved past Glenna to the door where Jett had just exited the house. "I'll see if Fred is ready to load this stuff," he mumbled.

When the door closed behind him, her father raised an eyebrow and sent her a wry smile. "It sounds like Bruce walked in on a private moment."

"You could say that," Glenna agreed and listened to the sound of the helicopter taking off.

"In that case would it be fair to assume that you and Jett have straightened out your problems?" The knowing glint in his eyes twinkled at her.

"I think we have," she admitted, then eyed him suspiciously. "But why did you make that remark to Jett about Bruce?"

"You mean about Bruce wanting to find a job in the area? It's true," he shrugged.

"Yes, but you implied it was because he wanted to be near me. You know very well that Bruce and I are just friends," she reminded him. "But you deliberately planted a different idea in Jett's mind."

"I can't help the conclusion he reached," her father asserted his innocence with a beaming smile. "Besides, it won't hurt Jett to wonder whether he might have a little competition."

"Dad," she sighed and shook her head.

A voice echoed through the empty rooms of the house. "Can I come out of the kitchen now?" Hannah called with terse impatience.

"Hannah. I forgot her," Glenna realized with a laughing gasp. The statement immediately demanded an explanation, which Glenna made. Her father found it all very amusing, but the housekeeper's sense of humor didn't match his when she arrived on the scene.

BY THE END OF THE WEEK Glenna still hadn't completely settled into their new house. Except for the day they had actually moved she had worked the rest of the week, which left the bulk of the unpacking to be done in the evenings.

After the Friday evening meal she was in the kitchen unpacking the boxes containing the good china and crystal that had been among their family's possessions for generations. They had been among the few things they had not sold.

Glenna was on her knees unwrapping the tissue from the dinner plates when someone knocked at the back screen door. A lingering sunset silhouetted the figure outside, but she recognized him at a glance.

"Come in, Bruce," she called without getting up.

"I saw Orin out at the workshop. He's like a kid with a new toy," he remarked as he entered the kitchen.

"He spends nearly all his time out there," she agreed.

"Do you want some help with this?" Bruce knelt down beside her.

"Sure." Glenna handed him a plate with its tissue-paper covering.

Bruce unwrapped it and added it to the stack on the counter, announcing almost casually, "I start work Monday morning at the mine." Outside of that one remark he'd made when Jett had left, Bruce hadn't referred to him since.

Glenna sat back on her heels to look at him. "They offered you the position of manager."

"Yes."

"And you accepted it?"

"Yes."

"Why?" That question was too blunt. She quickly tempered it with an explanation. "I thought you were going to take a couple months off before starting another job."

"I discovered I had too much idle time on my hands with no way to pass it. Plus, the offer was a good one." He concentrated on his task, not looking up as he named his reasons. "And I liked the idea of going back to your father's mine. I feel as though I left a job half done and I need to finish it. Are you sorry I accepted it?"

"No." Glenna shook her head, auburn hair swaying at the movement. "As long as you didn't take it for the wrong reason." Which was to stay near her.

"I don't think I did."

With the last of the dinner plates out of the box, Glenna stood up and positioned the step stool in front of the cupboard. Climbing it, she opened the door to the top shelf where the china was being stored.

"Would you hand me the plates, Bruce?" She half turned to take the plates he passed up to her a few at a time. The phone rang when he gave her the last. "Will you answer it? It's probably for dad."

"Sure." Bruce walked to the extension phone on the wall. "Reynolds residence, this is Bruce Hawkins. Yes, just a moment." As she climbed down the step stool, he extended the receiver toward her. "It's for you. Jett Coulson."

Her heart flipped over, and her hand was unsteady as she reached for the phone. "Hello?" Glenna had been half expecting to hear from him before the weekend, but now that the moment had arrived, she was disturbed by it.

"Hello. I guess I don't need to ask whether you have company." There was a thin thread of grimness in his tone.

"No." She couldn't elaborate, not with Bruce able to overhear her side of the conversation. He was kneeling beside the box on the kitchen floor, unpacking the china sauce dishes.

"Did I interrupt anything?" His question was slightly challenging.

"No. I was unpacking the last of the boxes, trying to get the last of our things put away," Glenna explained. The suspicion of jealousy in his voice was a little gratifying even if it was unjustified. At this point it was a difficult thing to let him know.

"Did Hawkins tell you he's going to work for my company?"

"Yes."

"You aren't very talkative," Jett accused. "What's wrong? Is he listening?"

"Yes." She wound her fingers in the coil of the telephone cord.

"In that case I might as well come straight to the point," he sighed with a trace of disgust. "I can't get away this weekend to see you."

"Oh." That one small word was filled with disappointment.

"I have no doubt that Hawkins will do his best to keep you entertained," he inserted dryly and continued without giving Glenna a chance to comment. "I should be able to adjust my schedule to have an afternoon and evening free one day next week. I should know by Monday afternoon whether it will be Wednesday or Thursday. I'll call you then."

"Don't forget I work until four-thirty," she reminded him.

"I'll pick you up after work."

"All right."

"I'll talk to you Monday. Hopefully there won't be anyone listening then and you'll be more communicative." It was a clipped statement that betrayed his impatience. "Goodbye, Glenna."

"Goodbye, Jett." She waited until she heard the disconnecting click on his end of the line before she hung up the receiver. When she turned, Bruce was quietly studying her.

"Are you in love with him, Glenna?" he asked.

She hesitated, then rubbed her arms, remembering how it felt when Jett touched her. "Yes, I think so," she admitted on a warmly confident note.

"Is he in love with you?" was Bruce's next question.

That required a more cautious answer. "I don't know. I'm not sure." Glenna bit at her lower lip, positive that it couldn't all be one-sided. "I think so."

Bruce straightened and walked to the step stool. "Where do you want these sauce dishes? On the same shelf with the plates?" The subject was changed, not to be raised again by him.

CHAPTER ELEVEN

ON MONDAY, Glenna left the printing office early to make some deliveries for the company on her way home. Although she knew most of the customers where she stopped, she didn't stay to chat. Jett had said he would call her today. She wanted no delays that might make her miss the phone call.

That was the reason for the gleam in her gray green eyes and the smile that hovered on her lips. Even the mountain air seemed electric with anticipation as she turned into the driveway. She wasn't quite used to the small home where she lived, but it was the last thought in her mind when she stopped the car.

The slamming of her car door coincided with a ringing of the telephone in the house. Certain it was Jett, Glenna raced for the front door only to hear the telephone cut off in mid ring as her father answered it. Still she hurried into the house, breathless yet radiant.

"Is that—" She never completed the question, silenced by the sharply raised hand of her father and the stern white look in his expression.

Glenna only heard him make one response to

the caller on the phone before he hung up, and that was a clipped, "I'll be there immediately."

"What is it? What's wrong?" She read all sorts of dire things in his expression. "Has something happened?"

He measured her with an even look as he moved into action, taking her arm and steering her back toward the front door. "There's been a cave-in at the mine. That was Bidwell on the phone." He opened the door and ushered her outside.

"Bidwell." Glenna remembered he had been one of the foremen on the shifts. Evidently he'd been rehired. A single line creased her forehead as she dug the car keys out of her purse again. "Why did he call instead of Bruce? Was anybody hurt?"

"They think there are six men trapped." He left her and walked around to the passenger's side of the car while Glenna slid behind the wheel.

"Oh, no." His statement stopped the hand that started to insert the key in the ignition. On the heels of her alarm came another more frightening thought. "Bruce?"

"He's one of the men believed trapped." It was a simple statement not designed to spare her.

Its bluntness caught at her breath, squeezing her lungs until she wanted to cry out. Her rounded eyes sought her father. Neither had to say the things that were silently understood. Bruce could be trapped or buried under a rubble of rock. He could have escaped harm or be seriously injured. He could be with the others or isolated from them. Yet her father's calm strength reached out to invisibly steady her, and prevent any panic from letting her imagination run riot.

"Was there an explosion?" Her hand trembled as she succeeded in inserting the key in the ignition. "Fire?"

"No fire." He relieved one of her fears. "Bidwell was outside the entrance and said he felt the ground vibrate, then heard the rumbling inside the mine and saw the coal dust belch from the opening."

Glenna started the car and reversed out of the driveway, picturing the scene in her mind and feeling the terrible dread that must have swept through the workers on top. She blocked it out because she knew it would give rise to panic. She concentrated on her driving, suddenly impatient with the twisting mountain roads that denied speed.

"When did it happen?" she broke the chilling silence that had descended on the car.

"About twenty minutes or so before Bidwell called me," her father answered. "He notified the main office first, then called me."

Even though her father had no more to do with the mine, Glenna understood the reasoning. This was a close-knit community. In a time of crisis everybody helped. When miners were trapped, every mining man in the area volunteered his services. With her father's intimate knowledge of the mine and experience, he was an obvious choice to be notified in the event of an emergency.

Time was the enemy. It ticked away as Glenna drove as fast as she dared. She wondered if the word had reached Jett. Surely it had by now. Bruce, and the men trapped with him, had to know that every available resource was being galvanized to effect their rescue. If they were still alive. A chill went through her bones, making her shudder.

On the last mile to the mine Glenna encountered other traffic headed for the same destination. News of the cave-in had traveled fast through the West Virginia hills. Others were already arriving on the scene when she turned the car into the parking lot.

Leaving the car parked alongside others, Glenna hurried with her father toward the fence gate. There was already a hubbub of milling people outside the mine buildings and entrance. They were an assortment of miners, families, and townspeople.

A small wiry man separated himself from the group to meet her father. Glenna recognized him as Carl Bidwell, the foreman who had called her father with news of the accident.

"Am I ever glad to see you, Mr. Reynolds," he declared.

The man's face was pale and etched with lines of stress and worry. Glenna knew her face showed the same brittle tension marked with latent fear as the faces of all those around her.

Her gaze sought the mine entrance, but the steadily growing crowd of people blocked it from her view. Bruce was somewhere inside that mountain. Glenna clung to the belief that he was still alive. He had to be.

"Has anything developed since you called me?" her father questioned. "Have you made contact with any of those inside?"

The negative shake of Bidwell's head was in answer to both questions. As others in the milling crowd recognized Orin Reynolds they pressed forward, besieging him with questions he hadn't had a chance to ask for himself.

The chopping whir of a helicopter interrupted the conversation, drowning out the voices as it approached. All eyes turned to it. Glenna recognized the Coulson Mining insignia on its side. Coming in low over the heads of the crowd, it whipped up a wind that swirled dust clouds through the air. Turning her head aside, Glenna shielded her eyes from the blowing particles of dirt with her hand and tried to keep the dark copper length of her hair from blowing in her face.

It landed on a helicopter pad within the fenced area around the mine, kicking up more dust to obscure the vision of those on the ground. Three men in business suits emerged from the chopper and crouched low to avoid the whirling blades as they hurried toward the crowd. The minute they were clear, the helicopter lifted off.

With a profound sense of relief, Glenna recognized Jett as one of the three men. Just the sight of his sun-bronzed craggy features gave her strength. Once free of the overhead threat of the chopper blades, he straightened his tall frame and let long strides carry him to the knotted group of onlookers. A hand reached up to absently restore some order to the untamed thickness of his black hair.

The concentration of concern had darkened his eyes to an ebony pitch. Glenna felt the penetration of his gaze the instant he singled her out from the crowd. He altered his course slightly to approach her, but it was to her father that he spoke.

"I'm glad you're here, Orin." He grasped her father's hand, the edges of his mouth lifting in a grim semblance of a smile.

"Bidwell phoned me," her father replied.

"We can use your help," Jett stated.

"I'll help any way I can. Even if you hadn't asked, I would have been here. Like the others—" her father's glance encompassed the crowd of people gathered at the site "—waiting to lend a hand if needed."

"What's the status?" Jett made a search of the encircling ring of people. "Where is Hawkins?"

Someone on the outer edge answered, "He was in the mine when it collapsed."

Jett's gaze swerved sharply to Glenna, revealing his ignorance until that moment of the fact that Bruce was one of the missing men. His piercing look seemed to question while it reached out to comfort. Tears sprang into her eyes and her chin began quivering. Desperately she wanted to have his arms around her and ward off the chill of uncertainty with his warmth. But it was impossible and improper in this mob of people.

Something flickered across his expression, a raw frustration mixed with a savage kind of anger. Then a poker mask covered his features and his gaze was withdrawn from her. This was the time for cold clear thinking—not emotions.

"Let's go to the office." At his clipped statement the milling crowd separated to form a corridor through which Jett walked toward the mine buildings. Bidwell, the two men from the helicopter, Glenna and her father followed him. Jett continued issuing directives as he walked. "I want to see a diagram of the mine. I want to know the location of the collapse and the approximate location of the men inside when it happened."

Glenna swallowed the lump in her throat and blinked away all the tears but one that trembled on the edge of her lashes. It she brushed away. Her father's arm was around her shoulders, silently offering her support and comfort as they followed Jett and the others into the building.

"How many men were inside? Eight?" Jett shot the question at Bidwell.

"We thought it was eight, but we accounted for two men. It looks like there are only six inside, sir,'' the wiry man replied, intimidated by the presence of the head of the firm.

Jett paused in an outer office. "Do you have their names?''

"Yes, sir.''

"Have all their families been notified?''

"All except two, sir. We haven't been able to reach them yet.''

Until that moment when Jett swung around to face her, Glenna hadn't believed he knew she had followed him inside. His eyes made an impersonal inspection of her. "Are you all right?'' he asked flatly.

She knew he was really asking if she was in control of herself. "Yes,'' she assured him.

"Would you get the names of the two men from Bidwell and take the responsibility of making certain their families are notified?'' It was an unpleasant task he was offering her, but it showed his belief in her ability to handle it.

"I will.'' Glenna quietly assumed the role he had given her.

While Jett, her father, and the other two men went to the inner office, Bidwell remained behind to give her the names before joining them. Both families knew Glenna through her father. It took her the better part of an hour before she was able to locate both of them and break the news to them with a woman's compassion.

Even when that job was done a sense of responsibility remained with her, a desire to do something that might in some small way help.

She emptied the morning black dregs from the large coffee urn and made fresh coffee. That would be needed and more before all this was over.

All the while there was a hum of activity around her. Directives came from the private office where Jett had set up his headquarters. And reports flowed back in. The crowd outside grew larger with friends and relatives of the trapped men as well as the multitude of volunteers. Naturally the press arrived, first newspaper reporters and later on television crews.

Cleve Ross, one of the men who had arrived with Jett, emerged from the privacy of the inner office to issue a statement to the news media. It dealt in specifics, pinpointing the location of the cave-in on a diagram and the possible location of the men inside when it happened. Although the extent of the collapse wasn't known, the statement held out hope that the men were behind the wall of rock and dirt. The report actually contained little that Glenna hadn't already known.

Afterward she and two office workers volunteered to answer the incessantly ringing telephones and respond to the endless inquiries regarding the fate of the trapped miners. It kept Glenna occupied, even if it didn't allow her thoughts to stray from the worry over Bruce and his companions.

By half-past seven Glenna had stopped paying attention to who came and went through the door to the yard. As she replaced the telephone receiver on its cradle she heard the griping tone of a familiar voice behind her and turned in the swivel chair to recognize the plump figure of their former housekeeper, Hannah Burns.

"I can't stand here holding this forever," she was complaining, a large foil-mounded baking sheet in her hands. "Someone will have to clear a table to set this on."

Directly behind her there were two high-school-aged girls carrying similar pans, and a boy holding a large commercial coffee urn. A shirt-sleeved man was hurrying to clear space on a long worktable.

"Hannah." Glenna ignored the ring of the phone to rise quickly to cross the room. "What are you doing here?"

"I knew you and your father would be here," the woman replied with a brief glance. "I figured nobody would be thinking about their stomachs at a time like this. So I took it upon myself to do it for them. I brought some cold sandwiches, salads, and chips. A couple of the grocers donated the food and these young people volunteered to help fix it."

She set the baking sheet down and folded back the aluminum foil to reveal the stacks of sandwiches, then motioned the two girls to set their trays beside hers. The boy found a place for the coffee urn beside the one Glenna had fixed.

"Go get the rest of the things from the car,"

Hannah ordered and her trio of helpers set off to obey.

"You're right, Hannah," Glenna admitted. "No one has thought about eating. I'm glad you did."

The practicality of the woman had a steadying influence on Glenna. Her mere presence offered support, and the comfort of someone who had weathered many a crisis with Glenna before.

"We certainly aren't going to feed the entire mob of gawkers out there, but the men's families and the workers are going to need some nourishment before this is over. People always have more hope when hunger isn't gnawing at them," Hannah philosophized.

The remark made Glenna aware that the hollow feeling inside might be filled by some food. The three teenagers returned with sacks of chips, paper plates and cups, as well as huge bowls of potato salad. Glenna helped them arrange the assortment of food into a buffet. When word spread there was food in the building, there was an influx of hungry people with the alternating shifts of rescue workers always having priority at the table.

A security man who had worked for her father and been rehired by Coulson approached Glenna. She knew the man only as Red, although his hair had long ago thinned and turned gray.

"Miss Reynolds," he addressed her respectfully, removing his cap. A deeply etched worry shadowed his pale eyes. "There's a Mrs. Cummins out there with two small children. Her husband is one of the men in the mine. I tried to get her to come in and eat, but she refused. She just sits out there with the little ones huddled around her, starin' at the entrance to the mine. Maybe if you spoke to her, she'd listen."

"I'll see," she promised.

Leaving the security guard she paused to tell Hannah where she would be in case she was needed and went outside in search of the woman. Local sheriff's deputies had joined the company's security force to cordon off the area around the mine entrance and separate the sightseers from those directly associated with the situation.

Glenna had no difficulty spotting the woman the guard had described. She was standing away from the others, a four-year-old pressing close to her legs, a two-year-old in her arms, and her protruding figure indicated a baby on the way. Twilight was pulling a dark curtain over the mountainscape but floodlights made the fenced yard around the mine and its buildings bright as day. Glenna crossed the lighted space to the woman and her children.

As she drew closer she heard the four-year-old boy whimpering, "I want to go home, mommy. I'm hungry."

"No. We can't go 'til daddy comes," the woman replied as if repeating it by rote, her attention not straying from the mine.

"Mrs. Cummins." Glenna saw the ashen

strain on the woman's face as she half turned in answer to her name, reluctantly letting her gaze waver. "I am Glenna Reynolds."

The surname immediately drew a response. "Have you heard something?" the woman rushed. Glenna was shocked to realize the woman was no older than herself, but worry had aged her with haggard lines. "Tom? Is he—"

"I'm sorry. There hasn't been any news," Glenna explained quickly to check the outpouring of wasted questions. "It might be a while before we know anything. We have sandwiches and hot coffee inside. Why don't you come in and have something to eat? You'll feel better.'

"No." The woman had already lost interest in her. "I'm not hungry."

"Maybe you aren't, but you have to think of the children and the baby you're carrying," Glenna insisted, but the woman indifferently shook her head.

The little boy tugged at his mother's skirts and repeated, "I'm hungry." He didn't understand what was going on, or the silence of all the others in the crowd that was broken only by the murmur of hushed voices.

"If you won't come in," Glenna persisted, "would it be all right if I brought out some sandwiches for the little ones?" The woman hesitated, then nodded an absent agreement. But Glenna wasn't satisfied. She hated leaving the woman alone like this. "Is there someone I could call to wait with you? Family or friends?"

"No." The woman shook her head and protectively hugged the little girl tighter in her arms, a hand reaching out to touch the little boy at her side in silent reassurance. "All our kin is in Kentucky. Tom...." Her voice broke slightly. "Tom just got enough money saved to send for us last week."

"I see," Glenna murmured inadequately. "I'll bring some food for the children, and a hot cup of coffee for you."

Her remark didn't receive a response and Glenna turned away. As she started to recross the yard another woman called to her. It was the wife of one of the miners who had escaped the collapse.

"Miss Reynolds, is Mrs. Cummins all right?" she questioned anxiously. "The poor thing doesn't know a soul here."

"She's frightened." *As we all are,* Glenna thought as she allowed herself a moment to fear for Bruce. "I'm going to bring out something for them to eat. Would you stay with her until I come back? It has to be difficult being so alone."

"Of course, I will." The older woman agreed quickly to the suggestion.

When Glenna reentered the building she went straight to the buffet table of food and fixed two plates for the children. She added more than they could eat in hopes their mother would eat what was left.

Walking to the coffee urn she noticed Jett standing not far from it, deep in conversation with two other men. His suit jacket and tie were gone and his sleeves were rolled short of his elbows. Lines of sober concern were cut into his features, his dark eyes narrowed with concentration. Glenna wished she could go to him, touch him and ease some of the burden he carried, but it was just as impossible now as it had been that afternoon.

She filled a paper cup with hot coffee, unaware that Jett glanced at her, his gaze reaching out for her. She juggled the plates until she could carry them and the cup, too, then returned outside.

When she approached with the food Mrs. Cummins sat the small children cross-legged on the ground. They acted starved, hardly waiting to be given the plates before snatching the sandwich halves to begin eating. Glenna offered the cup of coffee to Mrs. Cummins.

"No. I don't want anything," she refused irritably.

Mrs. Digby, the miner's wife who had been standing silently by, pursed her lips in temper. "Miss Reynolds was thoughtful enough to bring you the coffee. The least you can do is thank her."

"I'm sorry. All I can think about is Tom," the woman began in a frightened kind of explanation.

"All you can think about is yourself," Mrs. Digby criticized.

"Please," Glenna didn't think Mrs. Digby was handling the situation properly.

But the miner's wife paid no attention to her. "Do you think you're the only one whose man is in there? Miss Reynolds has a man in there—Bruce Hawkins—and you don't see her standing around feeling sorry for herself. She's trying to help. You have two little babies here and look who is making sure they have something to eat."

When Glenna saw that the woman's words had shocked Mrs. Cummins into an awareness of her children, she understood the woman's tactics. When soft words failed, a figurative slap in the face usually worked. It was now.

"Is it true?" Mrs. Cummins searched Glenna's face, seeing someone else's plight other than just her own. "Is your man really in there, too?"

"Yes." It was a small deceit. After all, she did truly care about Bruce even if "her man" was too strong a description. "He is." There was no harm in a white lie.

"I'm sorry. I didn't know." She reached for the coffee Glenna had brought. "Thank you... for everything."

"It's all right." When she handed her the cup, she noticed a fourth long shadow intruding on the ones they cast. She turned to see Jett standing to one side, and pivoted to take a step toward him. A question leaped into her eyes as she scanned the impenetrable mask of his features, but a brief shake of his head told her there was no news.

"I came out for some fresh air," he said in explanation of his presence.

Taking a cigarette from his shirt pocket, he bent his head to the flame of his lighter. Glenna took the last few steps to be closer to him. She found it difficult to talk; all her thoughts were overshadowed by the knowledge that men were trapped in the mountain beneath them. It almost seemed wrong that her pulse should quicken because she was near him.

"The accident happened when they were installing an air duct to make it safer to work in the mine," she murmured. "There's a certain irony in that."

She knew instantly that she had chosen the wrong subject. She could almost see Jett shut her the rest of the way out. If he had sought her out, as she suspected, it had been to escape talk of the accident and the rescue efforts.

"Jett." She didn't know how to reach him so she turned away instead. "Hannah may need me. I'd better go in."

He said nothing when she walked away.

CHAPTER TWELVE

TWENTY MINUTES LATER Jett entered the building and went directly to the private office, never glancing Glenna's way. She squared her shoulders and helped the plump housekeeper rearrange the buffet table into a snack counter. A few stragglers came in to eat some of the remaining sandwiches.

At half-past ten her father came out of the private office and stopped to pass on the message, "Jett wants some coffee. Take him a sandwich, too," he added. "He hasn't eaten anything."

"I will," she said as he continued on his way to the washrooms.

With a cup of coffee balanced on the sturdy paper plate, she knocked on the inner office door. There was a curt response, granting her permission to enter. Jett barely glanced up when she entered, seated at his desk and bent over an array of papers and diagrams.

"I brought you some coffee and something to eat," Glenna said and set it down on a small cleared space on the desk top. She discovered there was no one else in the room as he reached for the coffee, but showed no interest in the sandwich. "You need something. Dad said you haven't eaten."

Her voice seemed to make no impression on him, his concentration not wavering from the papers he was studying. Jett took a sip of the coffee and set it back down to lean an elbow on the desk and rub a hand across his mouth and chin.

"That's where they've got to be if they are alive," he declared aloud, his jaw hardening. A wave of grim exasperation broke over him. "Dammit, right in the bowels of the mountain!"

"Bruce called it a womb," Glenna remembered, this time claiming Jett's attention. She was drawn to the window that overlooked the mine yard, its dusty panes creating a haze. "He said he felt safe inside it, safe and protected. I know he isn't afraid, and that helps me."

The squeak of the swivel chair told her Jett had risen. "I promise you it won't be his tomb, Glenna." He came to stand beside her by the window. "I'll get him out of there."

She lifted her gaze to him, a smile touching her mouth. "I know you will." She knew it as surely as she knew her own name. Some powerful force seemed to flow between them in that moment—until Jett shut it off by looking out the window. Disappointed, yet knowing this was not the appropriate time to press a personal issue, she glanced at his desk and the untouched sandwich. "Is there anything I can get you? Anything you want, Jett?"

His head turned to slide her a hard and hungry glance. "I want you, Glenna." He reached out to possessively take her hand and draw her toward him. His gaze ran roughly over her face. "I want what *you* can give me. What *only* you can give me."

She didn't know what he meant, but when his mouth moved hungrily onto hers, she gave him the only thing she possessed—all of her love. It flowed from the wild singing of her heart, a searing rapture that knew no end.

Yet there was something desperate in his need, something raw and aching that a single kiss couldn't satisfy. His hands were all over her—stroking, feeling, caressing yet never able to get their fill of her. Through it all her senses clamored with the desires he aroused. They quivered through her every nerve end like concentric circles in a pond, each ripple as perfect and delightful as the first.

A knock on the door she had left ajar brought the embrace to an abrupt end. Before the shutters fell to block out his expression, Glenna saw the glitter of wildness in his eyes and was shaken by the force of it.

His broad shoulders and back blocked her from the view of the interloper. Jett turned his head to the side, but didn't turn around to see who it was.

"What is it?" he snapped over his shoulder.

"There's a phone call on line two...about that equipment—you wanted to know whether it was available or not," was the answer.

Glenna heard the sigh rip through him, heavy and long. The grip of his fingers loosened on her arms, gradually letting her go altogether. "All right. I'll take it." He left her to walk to the desk and pick up the phone, punching the second button for the incoming call. "Yes."

Their moment of privacy was gone. The present situation had reclaimed its priority. Glenna slipped quietly out of the room, inwardly radiant with the emotions Jett had aroused yet confused by his attitude.

The embrace seemed to have left her with a keener perception because she immediately noticed the tiredness in her father's face, something that had escaped her notice only moments before. He was on his way into the office so it was natural for their paths to meet as she was coming out.

"Are you all right, dad?" Her concern was instant.

"I'm fine," he insisted, but on a weary note.

"Don't overdo it," Glenna warned. "Get some rest. Isn't it enough that I have to keep wondering about Bruce? Don't make me start worrying about you, too."

"Glenna is right." Jett's voice came from a few feet behind her. He had the coffee cup she had brought him in his hand. "Sack out on the couch, Orin, and get some rest. I'll wake you if anything develops. I want that ambulance outside used for the men in the mine, not you."

Her father glanced at the green vinyl couch in

the outer office. "Maybe I'll lie down for a little while," he conceded to his tiredness.

"The equipment?" Glenna referred to the phone call he'd taken before she left.

"It's on its way." He left the office, walking past her. "The coffee is cold." Jett walked to the long table and poured a fresh cup from the urn. Someone came in and immediately sought out Jett to make a report. Within a few minutes he was surrounded by people. Glenna walked to a desk to take up a post answering the telephones.

Around midnight the activity slackened. The strain and the late hour began to take their toll on Glenna. She found a straight-backed chair in a quiet corner and settled onto it, resting her head against the wall. It wasn't long before she dozed off. She had a wonderful dream. Jett was carrying her in his arms again, and putting her in his bed, lightly kissing her.

The first gray light of dawn wakened her, but her senses were slow to leave behind the dream. The aromatic scent of Jett's after-shave and the pungent blend of tobacco mixed to make the smell that belonged uniquely to him. With her eyes closed she could feel the rich fabric of his suit jacket against her cheek, the texture of it and the scent of him surrounding her. It was several seconds before she realized she was lying down, not seated in the chair propped against the wall.

Glenna opened her eyes slowly. She was on the couch in the private office. His suit jacket

374

was folded to make a pillow for her head. It hadn't been a dream. Jett had carried her in here and laid her down, slipping off her shoes and leaving the sensation of a soft kiss to linger on her lips.

"Good morning." Jett was standing beside his desk, leaning on it while several others, her father among them, studied papers spread in front of them. Jett was half turned to watch her, but the others only glanced her way. His face was haggard and drawn from no sleep, a dark stubble of beard shadowing the lean hollows of his cheeks, but a slow smile spread across his mouth. A warm reckless gleam was in his ebony eyes, catching at her heart.

"Better have some coffee," he advised.

"Yes," she murmured and sat up, wiping the sleep from her face. He sent him a secret smile left over from her dream. She sobered quickly as she remembered the reason they were all gathered in this place. "Is there any news?"

The special look was erased from his expression, replaced with a cool aloofness. "No. Nothing." Jett turned his back on her, focussing his attention on the quiet discussion of the other men.

Sighing over the loss of that brief intimacy Glenna rose and went to the washroom in the outer area to freshen up. No one had made fresh coffee since late last night, so she put on a fresh pot. By the time it had finished Hannah arrived. This time she brought pans of homemade sweet rolls, still warm from the oven.

Whether it was the aroma of hot rolls or freshly perked coffee, or simply the starting of a new day, a crowd of people invaded the building. Workers, families, and members of the news media arrived to learn the progress that had been made during the night, if any.

Before the rolls and coffee were gone, Glenna fixed a large tray to carry to the men closeted in the inner office. Her appearance broke up the discussion under way, especially when they saw what she brought.

While she was passing out the coffee and rolls, one of Jett's advisers said, "The reporters are going to want a press conference, an update on our progress. We won't be able to put them off for long."

"Schedule it for seven o'clock." Jett rubbed a hand over his beard and glanced around the room. "Does anybody have a razor?"

A razor was found as well as a clean shirt. The outer office was transformed into a make-shift conference room, complete with television lights and microphone stands. Glenna sat back in a corner of the large room where she was out of the way of the proceedings.

Promptly at seven Jett came out of the office accompanied by three other men. The first was in work-stained clothes, the man physically superintending the rescue efforts. The other two were the key advisers Jett had brought with him. These three read the prepared statements and fielded the questions from the reporters while Jett remained in the background.

At the very last a reporter put a question directly to him. "Mr. Coulson, would you explain why you are personally directing this rescue? Don't you have any qualified people working for you who could handle the operation?"

Jett moved to the microphones, but before he responded to the question, Glenna saw his gaze seek her out in the far corner of the room. "The three men with me are very highly qualified and extremely capable. They have answered your technical and, sometimes, very pointed questions for the past twenty minutes. I believe that proves their ability."

"But you didn't answer my question," the reporter reminded him.

"No, I didn't answer it," Jett agreed with a taunting half-smile. "Because if I was in Huntington, you would ask why I was there when six men are trapped in one of my mines." His barbed retort brought a moment of silence to the room. He glanced around it and announced, "That's all the questions for now."

Jett and the other three men shouldered their way through the crush of reporters trying to have one last question answered before they disappeared into the private office, but their clamoring voices were ignored. It was a full quarter of an hour before the bulk of the news media gathered their gear and left.

An hour later things had returned to normal—at least as normal as they had been the night before, with telephones endlessly ringing and people forever coming in and out of the building. Glenna wasn't sure the exact minute the atmosphere changed, but it started as a thin thread of excitement flowing in from outside.

Everyone seemed to notice at the same moment that the voices of the waiting people seemed louder with a certain cheerfulness in the sound. The building buzzed with questions. From a window someone saw the rescue operation's superintendent crossing the yard to the building. The word instantly flashed that he was smiling. It brought everyone to their feet and the men out of the inner office.

Unconsciously Glenna gravitated to Jett's side, afraid to anticipate the news yet silently doing so. When the door opened to the man, a white smile was showing in his coal-dusted face.

"They're alive," he announced. "The second unit punched into an unblocked air shaft and made contact."

Cheers went up around her, but Glenna dug her fingers into Jett's forearm, needing his strength and support. "How many?" she asked the all-important question.

"Six. All six of them!" he confirmed. "Hawkins said there was one broken leg, but the only other injuries were minor bruises."

She went weak with relief and turned into Jett, hugging her arms around his waist and burying her head against his chest. "Thank God. Thank God," was all she could whisper. She felt the answering tightness of his arms around her and the pressure of his cheek against

378

her hair. Then his hands slid to her shoulders to push her from him. She looked up, beaming with the good news. "They're alive," Glenna repeated under his probing gaze.

His hands moved to pull her arms from around him and hold her hands in front of him, but when Jett spoke it was to quiet everyone. "Let's save the celebration until we have them out of there." A sobered chorus of agreement followed his suggestion. "When will that be, Frank?" he asked the man.

"Hell, we'll make it by noon!" the man declared on a decisive note of optimism.

"Don't take any chances," Jett cautioned. "Do it safely."

"Yes, sir."

"There's still work to do." Jett broke up the party, sending them back to their individual duties. Glenna received a brief glance before he let her go to return to his office with his select group.

With the uncertainty removed, the atmosphere in the building was much lighter. People talked louder, joked, and found more reasons to laugh. The high spirits were infectious.

Most of the four hours passed swiftly, then dragged at the last when it started to stretch into five. As the moment of final success drew closer everyone was outside waiting for the moment when the rescued miners emerged. Jett was one of the last to come out, but he didn't join Glenna standing with her father on the fringe of the anxious families.

379

Two ambulance attendants waited close to the mine entrance with a stretcher for the one injured miner with the broken leg. It was one of them with a closer view who raised the shout, "They're coming!"

As expected the injured man was first, carried in the saddle of two men's arms. Glenna stretched on tiptoe for a glimpse of Bruce, wanting to see for herself that he was safe and unharmed. He was one of the last to come out.

With all the other families hurrying forward to greet their menfolk, it seemed the natural thing for Glenna to do the same. A wide but tired smile spread across Bruce's face when he saw her approach. He dragged off the hard miner's hat and narrowed his eyes against the bright sunlight.

Laughing and crying at the same time, Glenna ignored his coal-blackened clothes to hug him, not caring that the dust on his cheeks rubbed off onto hers. There were so many voices, she couldn't hear hers or his above the others. When Bruce kissed her, she kissed him back. But when his mouth hardened to demand passion, she stiffened in resistance and drew away. A troubled light entered her eyes, making them more gray than green. Bruce probed her expression, his smile fading.

"I'm glad you're safe, Bruce. I—"

"You don't have to say anything." He shook his head to check her explanation and loosened the arms that held her. "It's all right." His gaze drifted beyond her to scan the crowd, stopping once on a target. Then he took her hand, turning her around. "Come on."

He laced his fingers with hers so she was walking beside him. It was several steps before she realized he had a specific destination, and that destination was Jett. She felt the piercing stab of Jett's gaze knife into her, but he turned away before they reached him.

"Coulson!" Bruce called out to stop him.

Glenna was stunned by the harsh and savage light that glittered in Jett's sidelong glance. "I got him out for you, Glenna." His voice was a low angry sound. "Don't ask for more than that."

She was shaken by the suppressed violence that rumbled through his voice. His features were set in rock-hard lines, but there was no mask to conceal the bitter rage under their expressionless surface.

Jett's reaction only made Bruce smile with a wry twist of his mouth. He took Glenna's hand and extended it to Jett. "I believe she belongs to you," Bruce said as calmly as if he was returning lost property.

There was a puzzled flash in Jett's expression. After a second's hesitation, he reached out to claim her hand. His frowning gaze sharply locked with hers to probe deeply into the recesses of her soul. Neither seemed to notice when Bruce moved away.

"Is it true what he said?" There was an uncertain quality in his voice that Glenna had never heard before. "Do you belong to me?"

The smile that broke on her face was one of vague disbelief. "I've always belonged to you... since that night I came to your room... probably even before that," she admitted.

His fingers tightened on her hand, nearly crushing the delicate bones. "Last night I heard you admit to those women that Hawkins was your man."

"I agreed because it made Mrs. Cummins feel less alone in her fears," Glenna explained earnestly. "And I did care about Bruce, but as a good friend. I already told you that. Surely you didn't believe I had changed my mind."

"It happens," Jett said, towering closer. "When a woman has taken a man for granted a long time, she can suddenly realize how much he means to her when he's in danger."

"It didn't happen," she assured him.

"It could have. Hawkins was there when you needed him. I wasn't. He helped you through the rough times when I couldn't." His fingertips stroked her cheek in a caress that bordered on reverence. "When I saw how worried you were about him, I was determined to get him out of that mine. I couldn't let you down again, even if it meant you wanted him instead of me."

"It's you I love, Jett." Glenna swayed toward him.

Violent tremors ran through him as he gathered her into the crush of his arms and began smothering her face with rough kisses. In that moment she was convinced of the depth of his feelings for her and a wild joy raced through her blood.

"Marry me, Glenna. I don't want to lose you." The words came in a raw whisper from his throat. "Never let me lose you again."

"Never," she breathed into his descending mouth.

Harlequin Celebrates

Thirty-Five Years of Excellence

...and our commitment to excellence continues. Indulge in the pleasure of superb romance reading by choosing the most popular love stories in the world.

Harlequin Presents

Exciting romance novels for the woman of today— a rare blend of passion and dramatic realism.

Harlequin Romance™

Tender, captivating stories that sweep to faraway places and delight with the magic of love.

HARLEQUIN SUPERROMANCE™

Longer, more absorbing love stories for the connoisseur of romantic fiction.

Harlequin Temptation™

Sensual and romantic stories about choices, dilemmas, resolutions, and above all, the fulfillment of love.

Harlequin American Romance™

Contemporary romances— uniquely North American in flavor and appeal.